FIC   Myers, Tamara.
MYERS   The wife

D0113476
...upe Public Library

DOCTOR'S WIFE

NOV 0 2 2009

Den of Antiquity Mysteries by Tamar Myers

POISON IVORY
DEATH OF A RUG LORD
THE CANE MUTINY
MONET TALKS
STATUE OF LIMITATIONS
TILES AND TRIBULATIONS
SPLENDOR IN THE GLASS
NIGHTMARE IN SHINING ARMOR
A PENNY URNED
ESTATE OF MIND
BAROQUE AND DESPERATE
SO FAUX, SO GOOD
THE MING AND I
GILT BY ASSOCIATION
LARCENY AND OLD LACE

Don't miss the next book by your favorite author.
Sign up now for AuthorTracker by visiting
www.AuthorTracker.com.

FIC
MYERS

THE WITCH
DOCTOR'S WIFE

Tamar Myers

AVON 904480

An Imprint of HarperCollins*Publishers*

Fairhope Public Library
501 Fairhope Ave.
Fairhope, AL 36532

This book is a work of fiction. The characters, incidents, and dialogue are drawn from the author's imagination and are not to be construed as real. Any resemblance to actual events or persons, living or dead, is entirely coincidental.

THE WITCH DOCTOR'S WIFE. Copyright © 2009 by Tamar Myers. All rights reserved. Printed in the United States of America. No part of this book may be used or reproduced in any manner whatsoever without written permission except in the case of brief quotations embodied in critical articles and reviews. For information address HarperCollins Publishers, 10 East 53rd Street, New York, NY 10022.

HarperCollins books may be purchased for educational, business, or sales promotional use. For information please write: Special Markets Department, HarperCollins Publishers, 10 East 53rd Street, New York, NY 10022.

FIRST AVON PAPERBACK EDITION PUBLISHED 2009.

Designed by Rhea Braunstein

Library of Congress Cataloging-in-Publication Data
Myers, Tamar.
   The witch doctor's wife / Tamar Myers. — 1st Avon paperback ed.
      p. cm.
   ISBN 978-0-06-172783-2
   1. Congo (Democratic Republic)—Fiction. I. Title.
   PS3563.Y475W58 2009
   813´.54—dc22
   2009012887

09 10 11 12 13 OV/RRD 10 9 8 7 6 5 4 3 2 1

This book is for Kabemba and Mishumbi, wherever they are. They were Bashilele tribesmen, brothers born of "sister wives," and students at my parents' mission school. My parents hired them to protect me from snakes, and other dangers, whenever I "explored" the pristine forest deep within the canyon in front of our house. Kabemba and Mishumbi became more than my bodyguards; they became my friends. They taught me many Bashilele customs, entertained me with Bashilele folktales, and how to survive in the wilderness: which of the jungle leaves were edible, how to make snares to catch small animals, how to trap birds, and even how to make a simple shelter.

Many years later, during a tribal war, my parents came to my bedroom one night and my father said, "I think that Mommy and I might be killed tonight. But there is a secret alcove up there" —he pointed above the door—"which will fit you. If we are attacked, you climb in there, and we'll push boxes in after you to hide you. If you survive, follow the Kasai River all the way down to Angola."

Although our neighbors were burned out of their house that night, for some reason we were not attacked. But had we been, and had I survived long enough to reach the forest, I could have used the skills that Mishumbi and Kabemba taught me. I will never forget them.

ACKNOWLEDGEMENTS

I am, as always, indebted to my husband for his support and comfort. Thank you. And sincere thanks go to my editor at Avon, Tessa Woodward, for her many wonderful suggestions, and to my copy editor, Ellen S. Leach. The same thing goes for my agent, Nancy Yost. The book would not be the same without these fine ladies.

The tragic savanna fire scene in this book is based on a true incident. When I was five years old, my best friends, Ndombe and Kahinga, ages five and seven respectively, were caught inside a circle of fire intentionally set by hunters. As with the character Geete, my friend Ndombe did not survive. May he rest in peace.

PROLOGUE

The dominant female danced along the edge of the manioc field, impatiently awaiting the arrival of her pack. Her sudden appearance had scared away the jackals whose yips had filled the air since sunset. Although her jaws could crush the bones of a buffalo, she dared not attack an adult human by herself. Something in her primitive brain told her that a human, although unarmed by fangs or claws, was a beast to be feared. A tasty beast, nonetheless.

In only a day or two the female would give birth to her second litter. Already she'd co-opted the burrow of an aardvark in which to have her cubs. But for now, despite her distended belly and swollen teats, she was ravenous. If her pack did not arrive soon, she would have no choice but to move on, in search of some less dangerous prey.

The human was aware of the hyena's presence; the disappearance of the jackals had been the clue. At first the human thought a leopard was responsible for the silence. But then the hyena, apparently unable to restrain her excitement, burst into the hideous laughter that characterized her species.

The human dug faster, strong fingers raking the damp soil. A leopard might have been scared off by a show of strength—false bravado in this case—but a pack of spotted hyenas would tear a person limb from limb, and then laugh about it afterward. The human knew that the pack would announce itself by whooping, from perhaps a kilometer away, and when it did, a life-or-death decision must be made.

But just as the first faint sound of the advancing pack reached the human's ears, digging fingers touched something cool and hard. A moment later the priceless object glinted in the light of the rising moon.

CHAPTER ONE

The Belgian Congo was the name applied to a vast area of Central Africa between the years 1908 and 1960, when it was a colony of Belgium. Later the name was changed to Zaire, and eventually to Congo. Approximately eighty times the size of Belgium, this former colony covers as much territory as the eastern third of the United States. The land stretches from a narrow outlet along the Atlantic Ocean in the east to snow-covered peaks bordering the Western Rift Valley. The interior portion forms a shallow bowl that contains one of the world's largest tropical rain forests.

It's nothing to worry about," the stewardess said, but her eyes told another story. She groped for the jump seat. "The captain has it all under control."

The passenger in 3B knew the truth. She'd seen the left propeller chop through the branches of a eucalyptus tree like a butcher knife through lettuce. She'd watched, unbelieving, as the engine seized and the blade quit turning.

And now a second jolt, not much harder than one might expect from a roller coaster. But this one from the belly of the plane. Maybe the landing gear. Maybe not.

What was that streaming behind the wounded wing? The

stewardess saw it too. She closed her eyes and made the sign of the cross.

The large man seated at the rear began shouting the rosary. A child cursed: vile, sexual language it had no business knowing. Or perhaps that was the woman directly behind her. Someone was crying. Possibly more than one. The rank smell of urine filled the air.

The passenger in 3B couldn't tear her gaze from the window. Was that patch of dirt the landing strip? It couldn't be. It was way too short—and there were pigs on it. Pigs!

Now a jeep. Out of nowhere. The driver was firing a gun with one hand. At the plane? At the pigs? It was too late. There was nothing to do but watch yourself die.

Only at the impact did the passenger in 3B look away, and then involuntarily, as her head slammed into the seat in front of her.

The plane roared over the village for a second time, its left wing slicing the top off a eucalyptus tree. Children screamed, goats bleated, and chickens scattered in all directions like feathers in a whirlwind, yet the witch doctor and his two wives barely gave the aircraft a second glance.

"And now they cut our trees. When will the Belgians tire of scaring us?" First Wife said, and returned to the book she was reading.

Second Wife grunted. After a full day's work in the field, she'd managed to prepare the evening meal single-handedly, despite having a toddler clinging to her wrap cloth and a baby strapped to her back. Who had time to be afraid?

Husband, who'd been relaxing in the family's only chair, a sling-back covered with rattan, sat up wearily. "They will never stop. Only when we get our independence, when we fly our own planes, will this foolish behavior end."

The engine noise abated. The plane was finally headed for the dirt landing strip across the river. This was the third day that the pilot had circled the village, and it was common knowledge that the harassment was a warning to the people of the village that they must not revolt like the people up north. There would be grave consequences if they did.

Second Wife clapped her hands and called the children—her children—to supper. Tonight they would get a special treat. In addition to the mush, cassava greens, and palm-oil gravy, there were grubs. Wonderful, fat, juicy grubs. Second Wife had taken special care to cook them just the way Husband preferred: fried crisp on the outside, but not cooked so long that they lost their creamy inner texture.

First Wife had purchased the grubs that morning in the market from a woodcutter, who'd found them in a rotten log, deep in the forest. Good for First Wife. It was good that she did something worthwhile with her time. Perhaps one day—

Second Wife's hands flew to her mouth. The ground was shaking as it had once during an earthquake.

Husband swung to his feet. "Second Wife, what is it?"

"Husband, do you not feel it?"

"Feel what?"

"The earth moves."

"I feel nothing," First Wife said, but she rose slowly from the stool and laid her book on it.

"There," said Second Wife. "And there."

Husband's brow wrinkled. "I too feel nothing," he said, but his words were drowned out by the explosion.

CHAPTER TWO

The Congo River is second only to the Amazon in the amount of water that it discharges into an ocean. So powerful is the Congo River that, after its juncture with the Atlantic, it continues to flow underwater for another hundred miles, carving out a canyon in the ocean floor that is four thousand feet deep in places. It has been estimated that the Congo River and its tributaries have the potential of supplying the world with one sixth of its energy needs, although there has been very little hydraulic development.

Police captain Pierre Jardin was waiting inside Belle Vue's one-room terminal when he heard the plane begin to circle for the second time. Damn that heartless bastard. This was the third day in a row the jerk was pulling that stunt.

The day before yesterday Jardin had issued the pilot a stern warning. Yesterday Jardin had been out of town when the plane landed, but he'd heard about it just the same. Well, today the miscreant pilot was going to be in for a surprise; he was going to be only the second white ever to be locked up in Belle Vue's tiny jail. The officials at Sabena Airlines were going to be so pissed at their employee that they'd undoubtedly sack him.

And where the hell was Monsieur Ngulube, the terminal

manager? He was supposed to run the pigs off the runway fifteen minutes prior to a scheduled landing. And since, on average, there were only six flights in and out a week, it was his job to fill in the holes the pigs made.

The pigs. They belonged to everyone, and to no one. Captain Jardin had warned the villagers countless times to keep their livestock off the dirt landing strip, but he may as well have been talking to the pigs themselves. But when he shot a pig—an old arthritic boar—the people nearly rioted. Twenty-seven men stepped forward then, clamoring for payment, and the sums they demanded were absurd.

After much palavering, the captain drove to nearby villages, returning with twenty-seven piglets. The claimants were delighted, but suddenly fifty-two more people claimed ownership of the boar. The captain, at wit's end, threatened to call in the army and have the soldiers shoot every damn pig on the runway. He was bluffing, of course, but the people believed him and backed down. The pigs, however, stayed put.

Now they dotted the runway like raisins in a bread pudding. Meanwhile the plane was coming in fast, and it sounded odd. Damn that Ngulube! There was only one thing to do. Captain Jardin sprinted outside to his jeep, and giving it full throttle, raced along the runway, firing his handgun over the pigs in an attempt to scare them off. A modern swineherd on a life-saving mission.

But instead of dashing off into the elephant grass on either side of the strip, the beasts merely milled about in confusion. Not that it mattered much, because Captain Pierre Jardin was too late. The shadow of the right wing passed over his head at the same time the wheels first hit the ground.

Then Pierre Jardin, the man, watched in horror as the plane bounced over the backs of the pigs, never maintaining that precious contact with the ground. All too soon the strip ended, and the hapless plane lunged into the savanna scrub, mowing down head-high grasses and acacia saplings. The screeching of metal being shorn was only barely audible above the squeals of wounded and frightened pigs. Finally the plane stopped, its nose buried deep in a thicket of mature acacias.

When he reached the plane, Pierre discovered to his astonishment that every one of the thirteen passengers, plus the crew, was off the plane. The pilot had a broken arm, a laceration across his temple, and no doubt a bad concussion. Given the damage to the plane, it was a wonder he was even alive.

Even the copilot was relatively unscathed. Of course there were bumps and bruises, a little blood, and some vomiting, but all and all the occupants of Sabena Flight 111 were more terrified than they were wounded. The challenge now was to get them away from the plane before it exploded.

Amanda Brown didn't deserve to be in Africa; she deserved to be in hell. And that's exactly where she was.

Her journey had begun in South Carolina, from there by ship to Belgium, where she'd spent six months studying French and Tshiluba, a major Congolese language. Finally, after a series of plane rides, she found herself suspended over Eden.

It was amazing how fast one could travel in 1958. That morning she'd begun her day in Leopoldville, the capitol of the Belgian Congo. Her prayers had been answered and she had been assigned a window seat: seat 3B. She'd watched, spellbound, as the small commercial plane climbed steeply over the limestone backbone of the Crystal Mountains and then leveled off over a sea of broccoli tops. Yes, broccoli tops. That's exactly how she planned to describe the closely packed canopy of the vast equatorial rain forest below.

The jungle stretched forever, unbroken except for the muddy red of an occasional river, or the glint of sunlight reflected from the ink-black waters of mysterious lakes whose shores appeared uninhabited. Only after several hours did the trees finally yield to rolling grasslands, although forests still reigned in the deepest valleys and along the water courses.

It was all gorgeous, unbelievably beautiful, like nothing she'd seen in a Tarzan movie. Suddenly she saw a village of thatched huts. People were running for cover, like ants streaming back into their mounds. Lord have mercy! Ahead loomed a tree—at eye level! They were never going to miss it.

Had she only been dreaming? She felt like she was waking from a nap with a terrible headache. But that's how she always felt if she napped too long. No, this was different. People were screaming. The large black man from the rear of the plane was pulling her from her seat. She tried to protest, but her screams were soundless. She pummeled him with her fists, but he picked her up anyway and carried her off the plane.

She could see now that the plane had crashed. People shouted at her, telling her to run because a wing was on fire. There was going to be an explosion. She attempted to run, but her legs wouldn't cooperate. Her heart pounded so hard she could scarcely breathe. Where was the man who'd helped her? Why was no one turning around to lend a hand? Were people really that selfish, or was this just how it was in her own personal Hell?

Amanda closed her eyes. It would be easier not to see death coming. Perhaps she could will her spirit to leave her body before the onslaught of pain. But first, she would pray one last time . . .

Strong hands picked her off the ground as if she were a child. A doll even. Her heart pounding even harder, she opened her eyes.

"The airplane has crashed," Husband said.

"Truly?" First Wife knew instinctively that this was the case, but she felt it her wifely duty to question some of Husband's assertions. He was, after all, a witch doctor of some renown. He had a reputation to maintain. More and more villagers were demanding empirical evidence for his pronouncements, thanks to the corruptive influence of the Western colonialists. It behooved Husband to think carefully, and not jump to conclusions.

"*Eyo*," Husband said in the affirmative. "And now the airplane burns. I read something similar in a book my employer loaned me. It is all because this airplane hit a tree."

They were speaking loudly, because many voices in the village had been raised. Even now Mukuetu, their nearest neighbor, appeared panting at the edge of their compound.

"Neighbor," he said, with fear in his voice, "did you hear the bomb?"

"*Eyo*, I heard something."

"It was the airplane," First Wife said. "Did you not see the airplane hit the tree?"

"I am not blind, sister," he said. "But it did not fall from the sky."

"Nevertheless, it is so." Husband smiled, for he could never be angry at First Wife, even when she usurped what was his to tell.

"Where did this happen?"

"I should imagine at the airstrip, for this plane was wounded like a bird, and could not land properly." He had better be right this time.

"Shall we go see?"

"Most definitely."

"I will go too," Second Wife said.

First Wife started. "Then who will take care of the children?"

"You will," Second Wife said.

"I want to come as well," Oldest Boy said.

"So do I," Oldest Girl said.

"Very well," Husband said, "we will all go except for Baby Boy, whom we will leave with you." He scooped up the child and hurriedly, but tenderly, placed him in First Wife's arms.

There were no telephones in the village, but there were drums. Within minutes everyone knew what the explosion meant. Also within minutes the entire population of the village, except for those incapable of covering that great a distance, headed for the airport. Most of the people ran.

Poor First Wife was not among them.

The passenger in seat 8C intended to slip away unnoticed after the plane landed—well, as unnoticed as a seven-foot Nigerian in orange robes can manage. Although he stood out physically, he was not an anomaly by any means. Nigerian businessmen were a common sight in the Congo, and because they represented wealth, they were welcome. After all, anyone who could afford an airline ticket from the capital city of Leopoldville to a backwater place like Belle Vue was somebody. Just as long he minded his own business, he'd be left alone. That was the plan.

The crash changed everything. As a human being—as a man—he had no choice but to rescue the young woman from the plane. He didn't think twice about it. But once the deed was done, so to speak, he realized he'd set himself up as a hero, as someone to be sought out and thanked. Perhaps questions would be asked, questions that he preferred not to answer.

The Nigerian didn't consciously make a decision. When the others ran one way from the plane, he ran in the opposite direction—if indeed the word *running* could be applied to his rate of progress. Their escape route took them out into the open airstrip; his took him into the bush, into an almost impenetrable wall of elephant grass punctuated by thorny acacia trees.

When the plane exploded he was still so close that the force it generated knocked him flat on his face. He covered the back of his neck with his hands as burning debris rained from the sky. But within seconds he was on his feet again, pushing through the razor-sharp grass with balled fists. The savanna was alight with dozens of small fires. They crackled into existence and then roared into life, fueled by the brittle grass, the result of three months without a single rain. The Nigerian gasped for air as the flames sucked the oxygen out of his lungs.

Somewhere close was a river; he'd seen it from the plane. A spectacular waterfall as well. It had to be downhill. It was the same direction in which the flames were racing. If he could get to it first, he'd risk the crocodiles and snakes and hippos, whatever dangers lurked in the water.

His biggest impediment, besides lack of oxygen, was his clothes. His flowing robes caught on thorns, and with so many fires raging and sparks flying everywhere, it was only a matter of time before they ignited. Without a second's hesitation the Nigerian pulled his robes off over his head, inadvertently removing his hat as well. Clad only in a loose white undergarment that protected his privates, he ran for his life.

CHAPTER THREE

The Belgian Congo was home to two hundred tribes, each with its own language or dialect, and different customs. The majority of the people were Bantu (meaning "people") who settled the region from the north and west during the 10th to 14th centuries, and shared some physical and linguistic traits. The rain forest, however, was home to the Pygmies, who were, perhaps, the earliest inhabitants of the area.

Amanda Brown awoke with a killer headache. All through the night she'd awakened from nightmares, reliving those last moments on the plane or, worse yet, the certain knowledge that the exploding fuselage would kill her. Of course, as with any dream, sometimes they were bizarre and bore little similarity to the chain of events. Eventually, however, it became difficult to sort fact from fiction.

Each time she'd awakened, a kind, handsome man appeared just as she thrashed her way into consciousness. He told her repeatedly that she was safe, then sat by the cot on which she lay until she'd drifted back to sleep. He'd told her his name a million times, and it was simple enough—Paul—no, Peter—that's right, *Pierre*! French for "Peter."

But where was he now? She sat up on the narrow cot and

swung her feet over the edge, bringing them to rest on a cool cement floor. The darkened room was vaguely familiar from the night before. She looked down and was relieved to see that she was still dressed in yesterday's clothes, including her bobby sox.

"Pierre," she called softly.

She called several times, and after receiving no answer, padded to the door. With each step her head throbbed. Amanda breathed a sigh of relief when she discovered that an open door directly across the hall led to a bathroom. There was a mirror above the sink and she took the time to examine the lump on her forehead, wash the rest of her face, and run her fingers through her short brown hair. A bob, they called that style. It was old-fashioned and not particularly attractive, but was supposed to be suited to the intense African heat.

Feeling much refreshed but still headachy, she wandered down the hall toward the strongest source of light. The room was empty, save for chairs and books—acres of books—but French doors opened onto a patio. At a small, round table sat a man drinking coffee. It was Pierre.

He smiled and stood. *"Bonjour, mademoiselle."*

"Bonjour, monsieur."

"How are you this morning?" His accent was barely noticeable.

"I feel like I got hit on the head with a—uh—an airplane."

Pierre laughed. "Here," he said, handing her a white paper packet. "The doctor said to take these for a headache. Start with one, because two might make you sleepy. You may not wish to be sleepy on your first day in the bush."

The doctor was right about that. Outside, in the cool sunshine, the air was suddenly magical. She took the pill with a glass of freshly squeezed orange juice, even though she'd already begun to feel much better. She looked around. The patio was completely encircled by orange trees, but the world just beyond promised adventure. And redemption.

"*Mademoiselle—*"

"Please call me Amanda."

"Ah, what a beautiful name. Amanda, the doctor had to drive the pilot to the hospital in Luluaburg. He will be back late this afternoon, but we are in communication by shortwave radio. So, if there is a problem, a need to see him before then, I am to let him know. In the meantime, I am to keep a close watch on you."

"The poor pilot! How bad is it? Was anybody else hurt?"

"It is a broken arm that needs special attention, but do not feel too sorry for the pilot. Because of him, all of you might have died. After he receives the necessary treatment, he will be put in jail in Luluaburg. As for the rest of the passengers—well, your bump on the head seems to have been the worst of the injuries."

"Thank God!"

"Amanda, now that you are fully awake, please allow me to introduce myself properly." He bowed slightly at the waist and extended his hand. "I am Captain Pierre Jardin of His Majesty's Colonial Police. My jurisdiction is the town of Belle Vue, where we are now, and the workers' village across the river."

Amanda couldn't help but smile. Pierre was tall, deeply tanned, with curly blond hair and dancing blue eyes. But it was his courtly manner, and the khaki uniform, with its baggy, wide-legged shorts and epaulettes, that made her think of British officers she'd seen in movies. He even had his own version of bobby sox, although his came up to his knees. But of course Pierre was Belgian, and the king he referred to was King Baudouin.

"I am Amanda Brown," she said, "from Rock Hill, South Carolina. I'm here to run the missionary guesthouse."

"Yes, I know, I've been expecting you. Please, to sit."

"*Really?* You've been expecting me?"

"You are the replacement for Monsieur and Madame Single-ton, am I correct?"

"Yes, but how did you know?"

"They are friends of mine. Besides that, Belle Vue is a very small town, and everyone knows the—how shall I say this—business of everyone else. Do you understand?"

"Like Rock Hill."

"But very much smaller, I think. We are less than two hundred Europeans, and the Singletons are the only Americans. At any rate, they regret that they were unable to meet you here at the plane yesterday and will, in fact, be stuck—if that is the word—in Kikwit for some time."

"For how long?"

The handsome captain gave her a Gallic shrug. "Perhaps two weeks, maybe three. You see, Amanda, we are almost at the end of our dry season, and river levels are very low. The Loange River, which they must cross, has no bridge. Only a ferry. At the moment the water is too shallow and the ferry cannot cross."

"Can't they drive across?"

"I'm afraid that it's impossible. A vehicle would get stuck in the soft bottom. And also, there are still places where the water is too deep. The Singletons must either wait for the rains, or else wait until the state constructs a new ferry landing in a place where the water is deep all the way across."

Amanda felt a moment of panic. Her official reason for being in the Belgian Congo was to run the missionary guesthouse. George and Catherine Singleton were supposed to train her for a month before they retired to the States. How could she possibly do the job without any training? And she couldn't very well just shut it down.

From what she'd been told, the guesthouse was very important to long-term missionaries. Isolated on mission stations deep within the bush, and without electricity and running water, the average missionary went weeks without seeing any new white faces, and even years between visits to a real store. That's why Protestant missionaries vied for the available rooms (Catholic missionaries, of course, were not welcome).

A visit to Belle Vue meant a chance to shop in a small department store stocked with merchandise flown in from Brussels, as well as a grocery store that sold meat and fresh vegetables. For visiting whites there was even the opportunity to swim and play tennis at the mine-owned Club Mediterranean. And for those who craved a little more decadence, the clubhouse served real Coca Cola and freshly churned ice cream. It also served beer and a variety of hard liquors, but, with the exception of a few Presbyterians, any missionaries caught indulging in the latter were soon sent packing back to America.

She couldn't resist a smile. "Hmm."

"Perhaps you would wish to share your joke?"

"I was just thinking that if I can't handle the job—running the guesthouse, I mean—I could always go to the club and have a drink."

Pierre laughed heartily. "Ah, like Madam Wheeler, yes?"

"You know about her?"

"It was my misfortune to drive her back to the guesthouse on more than one occasion. But you should not worry. The Singletons left detailed instructions in case there was just such a problem. You see, in the Congo we have many unexpected interruptions. And there is also a well-trained housekeeper who will be of much help."

"Oh good. I look forward to meeting her. I have never met an honest-to-goodness African. Of course I have only been in the country two days."

"Ah, yes. But this housekeeper, I am afraid, is a man."

"A man?"

"Most housekeepers here are men. The women are too busy

raising their children and working in the fields. Fieldwork, *that* is women's work."

Amanda bristled. She was a modern woman, born in 1938, for heaven's sake. Thanks to Rosie the Riveter and the other women who had stepped up to the plate during the war, her sex had proved they were capable of succeeding quite well in the workplace.

"I hope these are not your personal views, Pierre."

He grinned. "No, Amanda. And if they were—well, I am not such a foolish man, I think. Ah, now before I forget: I sent the Singletons a telegraph last night, informing them of the unfortunate circumstances of your arrival. They have already replied." He patted his pockets, but not finding it there, took a deep breath and plunged in. "Mrs. Singleton was quite distressed to learn that all your luggage was lost in the explosion. She has instructed me to tell you that you may borrow her clothing until you have a chance to make, or purchase, some of your own. She said that from the description of you that the missionary board sent her, you appear to be the same size. I am inclined to agree."

Amanda gasped. It had not yet sunk in that her luggage had been destroyed along with the plane. In the bathroom she'd thought briefly about her toothbrush and comb, but had consigned their existence to someplace unspecific—someplace other than in the charred wreckage.

"Don't worry, Amanda. I will take care of you. May I suggest I begin by giving you breakfast?"

The Nigerian had not slept a wink. Adrenaline had gotten him to the river—albeit covered with cuts and abrasions—but now the river was keeping him prisoner. In the light cast by the hungry fires, he'd managed to climb down the sheer rock wall of the gorge. His trajectory had landed him just downriver from the falls. As a consequence he'd spent the night drenched with spray, trying to huddle in the protection of a narrow overhang.

He'd been prevented from moving farther away from the catchment pool by the presence of an enormous crocodile. Without the light from the fires, which were reflected in the reptile's eyes, the Nigerian might well have walked right into its jaws. The beast appeared to be at least twenty feet long and was stretched across a sandy beach, just on the other side of a pile of boulders.

In the morning the crocodile was still there. Although the Nigerian had spent all of his adult life in Lagos, on the "bulge" of Africa, he'd been born and raised in crocodile country. He knew that crocodiles shied away from turbulence, much preferring calm water. This behemoth was pushing those boundaries to the extreme.

No doubt it was the imminent prospect of being the first to feed on animals—and humans—unlucky enough to be swept over the falls that brought it so close to the escarpment. The Nigerian realized that although the roiling waters of the catchment pool, and the pile of boulders between him and sandy beach, would keep him safe from predation, he was virtually trapped. And since crocodiles can survive weeks without eating, this could well mean death by starvation. Still, there was always a chance the beast would lose interest.

In the meantime the bright white undergarment he wore around his loins could be easily spotted from above. Without the slightest hesitation the Nigerian removed his last article of clothing and stuffed it deep within a rock fissure. Then he crammed his seven-foot frame back under the ledge where he'd spent the night. One must do what needed to be done.

CHAPTER FOUR

With more than 6 million speakers, Tshiluba is one of the official languages of the Congo. It belongs to the Bantu family, a group of languages throughout most of Central and Southern Africa. Tshiluba words always end in vowels, and since there are no guttural sounds, it is a very melodic language. As in other Bantu languages, word plurals are created by changing prefixes. Thus the word *muntu* ("person") becomes *bantu* ("people") in the plural.

Amanda was in love. Despite the stressfulness of her arrival in Belle Vue, Africa had managed to capture her heart. And just as a lover might be introduced to her senses—first through sight, then sound, followed by touch, and finally scent—so did Africa reveal herself to the young American.

On the flight down from Leopoldville she'd seen a huge chunk of Africa, and this morning during breakfast she heard the call of a francolin. The bird had barely been audible above the roar of the falls, which unfortunately could not be seen from the captain's patio. But when Amanda slipped past the orange trees and looked over the garden wall, there was a mother and her four striped chicks.

Upon returning to breakfast she discovered that someone had placed a single blossom next to her place. Instinctively she picked it up and inhaled its fragrance. The petals themselves were as soft as Chinese silk, but the scent—it was the most intoxicating thing she'd ever smelled.

"Frangipani," Pierre said. "*Plumeria* in Latin. It's originally from Southeast Asia, but it does very well here."

"It's wonderful! It's like—well, I don't know. Maybe like a cross between gardenias and water lilies."

"They were my mother's favorite flowers."

"I wonder if I could grow these back home."

"Probably not; they're very frost sensitive. But this is your home—for now—yes?"

"Yes, for now."

He laid his napkin on the table. "Come, I'll drive you to the guesthouse. You can plant as many frangipani trees as you want there."

Amanda soon went on sensory overload. Pierre kept up a running monologue all the way to the guesthouse. That was great, but at the same time there was so much to see that she was torn between listening to his explanations and paying close attention to what was outside her window. When they reached the river, the window won.

Never in all her born days had Amanda seen such a dramatic sight. The Kasai River, which was impressive by itself, suddenly dropped several hundred feet into a narrow gorge, only to boil out at the other end. Adding to the thrill was the fact that the bridge, which connected the two halves of Belle Vue, the white and black, was built almost directly over the falls. Surely there was nothing else like it in the world.

Amanda saw Pierre pointing and leaned in closer. "What did you say?"

"I said, 'Let's get out.'"

She was happy to comply. She was even happier when he took her hand, telling her that mist from the falls sometimes made the bridge slippery.

"Amanda," he said, "do you see the black hillside above the gorge?"

"Yes."

"That's from your plane. Fortunately the wind was blowing towards the river, and not away from it."

"The explosion did that?"

"In a way, yes. The dry-season grass caught on fire. Now look to the left; see how that house barely escaped the flames?"

She saw what he meant; a sprawling house, with an even larger, meandering patio, perched high above the gorge. The fire line came with a few hundred feet.

"Who lives there?"

"A Portuguese couple—Cezar and Branca Nunez. You will undoubtedly meet them. He runs the store."

She then looked at the opposite hillside. The dead elephant grass was tan, as she supposed it should be at this time of the year. But it stopped abruptly along the edge of the precipice, where another house clung, like a barn swallow, to the black granite cliff.

"Whose house is that?"

"That is yours."

"*Mine?*"

He laughed. "Didn't the Singletons tell you the guesthouse had a view?"

"A view, yes, but—"

She laughed with him. Had she known Africa was going to be like this, she would have pushed to come earlier. But then with a pang she remembered why she'd really come, and it had nothing to do with any of this.

* * *

Captain Pierre Jardin did not have a key to the guesthouse, but it was unlocked. He opened the door with a flourish, as if he was very much at home there.

"You'll be quite safe here, and there is no need to worry about stealing."

"I'd really feely better if I could lock it—especially at night."

"Do you lock your doors in America?"

"No. Not unless we're going on long trips."

"Perhaps the housekeeper has a key."

Amanda nodded, suddenly distracted by the details of the decor. In essence the house was a much larger version of Pierre's house: same concrete floors brought to life with scatter rugs; same handmade wooden chairs with woven backs and seats, made comfortable with brightly colored cushions; same tribal masks and artwork on the walls. Were all colonial houses decorated like this?

"Mademoiselle Brown," Pierre said, breaking through her reverie, "this is your housekeeper, Protruding Navel."

Amanda jumped. She hadn't seen the man enter the room. She also hadn't heard right. It sounded like Pierre had introduced the man as "Protruding Navel."

Quickly she proffered her hand, but he didn't reciprocate. "*Muoyo webe*," she said, speaking her very first Tshiluba words to an African. Although she'd spent six months in Brussels studying this major trade language, along with French, her instructors had been Belgian.

The housekeeper bowed, but almost imperceptibly. "*Bonjour, mademoiselle.*"

Amanda was deeply disappointed. She had so looked forward to her first conversation in an African language. She'd worked hard and finished the course at the top of her class.

"Do you speak Tshiluba?" she asked.

"Of course," he said, speaking French. "I am an educated man; I speak four languages."

Pierre put his hand gently on Amanda's shoulder, while giving the housekeeper a somewhat disapproving look. "Protruding Navel is not a Muluba, so Tshiluba is not his native tongue."

"Monsieur, as you well know, I am a Bena Lulua. We also speak Tshiluba."

"Then you will speak it to Mademoiselle Brown, won't you?"

"If you insist, Monsieur Captain."

"I do." Pierre cleared his throat. "Well, I think I'll leave you two to get better acquainted."

As the door closed behind him, Amanda felt panic setting in. Perhaps the Singletons couldn't help their delay, but if only they knew what a lurch they'd left her in. She tried to smile.

"*Tatu* Protruding Navel, do you have any questions?"

"You should not address me as 'father,' mademoiselle. I am your servant."

"Should I say *muambi*?"

"That is even worse. Nor should you call me *mukelenge*. To address me with such respect will fill my foolish native head with too much pride. How then will I remember my station in life?"

Amanda was too shocked to respond.

"Tell me, *mamu*, what does this name—Brown—mean?" At least he'd switched from French.

"This color," she said, and tapped the wooden arm of a chair. Unfortunately there was no precise word for brown in his language; *kunze* meant red, yellow, brown, and even purple. Context was everything.

"Why is your name Brown, *mamu*, when you are not?"

"Well—I don't know. It was my father's name, and his father's before him."

"Were they brown?"

"No."

"Than it is a silly custom."

"Tell me about your name," she said, trying to remain pleasant.

Without taking his eyes off Amanda, the housekeeper calmly rolled up his shirt. And there it was—a navel the size of a loblolly pinecone!

"When my mother was with child, she looked upon two white people—a man and a woman—who were bathing in the river. She saw them, but they did not see her. Of course, the evil spirits who resided in the white people saw everything. Mamu Brown, it is a fact that evil spirits do not like water. When the woman plunged beneath the water, the spirit within her fled and entered my mother. It is because of this that I have been cursed with this protruding navel."

"You are occupied by the evil spirit of a white woman?"

"Tsch! *Mamu*, do you mock me?"

"No, of course not. Why do you ask?"

"Because only an idiot, or a missionary, would refrain from visiting a witch doctor to have the evil spirit removed."

"But I thought they hated water. Why not just go and bath in the river?"

He recoiled in surprise. "The other *mamu* does not challenge what I say. It is a pity that she must return to the land of her ancestors."

"On that we are agreed. Protruding Navel"—she forced herself to use the awful name—"would you care to sit down? We could have a cup of tea together. Or whatever else is in the house."

Surprise turned to disdain. "*Mamu!* Do you not respect me?"

"But, of course. I merely meant that we could talk, get to know each other better—like the captain said."

"You have deeply offended me, *mamu*. I am not the common sort of servant who is too ignorant to know his place; I am a *housekeeper*, a man of distinction. I run the household and supervise the other servants. Only a common table boy, one untrained in the art of dealing with the white man, could possible entertain such a suggestion."

Fairhope Public Library

"I am sorry, Protruding Navel. It was not my intent to insult you."

"Aiyee! And now you do so again."

"What do you mean?"

"You apologize to me, an African, and for what? Have you committed such a grave offense against me that you must seek forgiveness from your God? Have you run over my pigs or insulted my wife?"

"No."

"Then do not apologize, *mamu*. It is not fitting for someone of your superior position."

Amanda swallowed her words of anger. "Go get me a cup of tea," she ordered.

"Yes, *mamu*."

The Nigerian crouched like an animal all day, unable to move lest he catch the attention of the people above as they gaped down at the falls. Meanwhile the monstrous crocodile remained at its post. Being a cold-blooded animal, it had to regulate its body temperature by immersing itself in water in order to cool down, followed by periods of lying in the sun to warm up again. But all told it never moved more then ten meters from the spot where the Nigerian first spotted it. Perhaps it was guarding a nest of eggs, or perhaps, as the Nigerian was truly beginning to believe, the giant reptile was patiently waiting for a delicious West African feast.

At least now the sun was setting and swallows were darting about in search of their meal of mosquitoes. Soon the Nigerian would be able to stretch and get a drink of water. And even eat something!

Earlier that afternoon a large fish had fared badly going over the falls. It flopped about on the rocks, trying to get back into the river, but instead it became stuck in a fissure at the water's edge.

Although the Nigerian had never eaten raw fish, he was hungry enough to eat almost anything.

Then, after he'd satisfied his basic needs, there was something he needed to investigate before it grew totally dark. During the day something had caught his eye; something that might make all this suffering worthwhile.

CHAPTER FIVE

Although some tribes were closely related to their neighbors and shared many traditions, most tribes had very distinct ethnic identities and followed their own customs. Neighboring tribes often built different style houses, wore their hair in different styles, and even advertised their tribal affiliation with their dental patterns. For instance, traditional Bashilele lived in rectangular houses, knocked out their two front teeth, and wore their hair in a closely cropped natural style. Traditional Bapende, on the other hand, lived in round houses, filed their teeth to points, and sculpted their hair into pointed mounds by adding clay.

First Wife, whose given name was Cripple, sat up on the sleeping mat and rubbed her left leg, which was almost two inches shorter than the right. It was something she did every morning to alleviate the pain, and it was as natural as yawning. It was still dark out and Second Wife's bothersome children were sleeping. Husband was sleeping as well.

But Second Wife could be heard outside, huffing as she blew on glowing embers to bring them back to life. Once the fire was started, Second Wife, using a broom made of palm fibers, would sweep the sitting area in front of the hut. When everything was tidy, she would balance a pot of cornmeal and water on three blackened rocks, and stir the bubbling mixture until it was thick and about to scorch. After that she would use two sticks to remove the pot from the flames before stirring into the porridge enough manioc flour to make it stiff enough to form a ball. It was the manioc flour which gave the *bidia*—sometimes known as *fufu*—its distinctive taste. Second Wife was famous for the texture of her *bidia*, which some said was as smooth as the surface of the banana leaves upon which it was served.

Good for Second Wife. She was the one who did the bulk of the fieldwork, chopped the wood, and had borne seven perfectly formed children. Praise be dumped on Second Wife, not only because she deserved it, but because Husband would never love her as much as he loved Cripple. Never mind that Second Wife perpetually reminded Cripple that it was she, and not Cripple, who had given Husband all the things that were expected of a normal wife. And as for the perfectly formed, bothersome children, praise be dumped on their heads too, for it was not their fault that Second Wife had set a bad example for them. In their defense, they called Cripple *baba*—mother—as was the custom, and never made fun of her in Husband's presence.

Having rubbed the stiffness from her shorter leg, Cripple stood and adjusted her brightly colored wrap cloth. At night she covered herself with it like a sheet, but during the day she wore the long cloth wrapped securely around her waist. A matching blouse, sewn by the village tailor, and a coordinating headscarf, purchased from the Portuguese store, completed her outfit.

"Where are you going, Cripple?" Husband asked, startling her.

"Today I am getting a job," Cripple said.

Husband laughed softly. "They do not accept women workers in the diamond mine. You know that."

"I am not going to the mine. I will be working for the new *mamu*."

"The young white woman? The American?"

"Yes."

Husband, whose name was really Their Death, sat up with interest. "You have spoken to this woman?"

"No."

"Then she has asked about you, yes?"

"No."

"Then what is this nonsense about a job?"

"It is not nonsense, Husband. I have figured it all out. As soon as the old Americans return to the land of their births, their housekeeper—he with the vile temper—will surely quit. There is no doubt that this horrible man will refuse to take orders from a woman alone. And even if this does not come to pass, the new *mamu* will want a woman's presence. Why should I not be the one to fill that position?"

"Why not, indeed," Husband said. He thought for a moment. "But who will chop her firewood, and sweep her floors?"

"Husband, everyone says that the Americans are very rich, almost as rich as the Belgians. There are already many boys to do the chores. I will be replacing only the housekeeper. It will be me who gives the orders. Am I not good at giving orders, Husband?"

"Truly, you are. But Cripple, you do not know the ways of the white people. Trust me, their ways are very complicated, and frankly, do not make a lot of sense. They eat three times a day, not two, because their food is insubstantial. They must drink only water that has been boiled, and they cannot tolerate even one small chili in their food. Did you know that they sit on a chair to relieve themselves?"

Cripple giggled. "Husband, you joke."

"No, I speak the truth."

Husband knew of which he spoke. He worked for the post office, in the Belgian city across the river. Although he had graduated from the sixth form at the Catholic mission school and spoke passable French, he did not work inside the post office, but outside. Monsieur Dupree, an exuberant Belgian of the Walloon tribe, did the actual handling of the mail. Meanwhile Husband kept the grounds in order. Once a week during the growing season he hacked at the grass with a scythe, and all year long he kept the stones along the path freshly whitewashed. He also whitewashed the trunks of the two mango trees that shaded the small brick building. Oh yes, every now and then he was called inside to kill a snake. But the task that Husband enjoyed the most was that he got to raise the Belgian flag every morning and lower it again at the day's end. "Each day I imagine that this is the last day the Belgian flag will fly over our country," Husband once told her, "and each evening I pretend that it is coming down to stay."

"Cripple," Husband said, "do you want me to walk with you to the foreigner's house?"

Cripple was surprised by the offer. How unlike a man to offer such a thing, even a man as kind as Husband. She took her time to answer, savoring the look she imagined Second Wife would have on her face if she knew what Husband had just proposed.

"No," Cripple said. "You will be late for work. Besides, if you come with me, maybe the white woman will catch your eye, and then there will be a Third Wife."

At that Husband laughed so hard he woke up the bothersome children.

CHAPTER SIX

In the Belgian Congo of the 1950s, most Africans survived on diets that were abysmally low in protein. Tribes that still hunted were marginally better off than tribes that were primarily agrarian. Chickens and Muscovy ducks were kept by both cultures, but snakes and other varmints took their toll on the number of fowl, which meant they were usually reserved for celebrations. Goats and pigs were owned by the wealthy, but as with the former, were not eaten on a daily basis. Grasshoppers, caterpillars, and grubs were welcome additions to one's diet, especially for women and children, who were usually excluded from eating the best cuts of meat under any circumstance.

Smoke and dust painted the African skies in sepia tones, as the great dry season came to an end. In a week or two, before the rains came, the women of the workers' village still had much to do in the manioc fields. Although weeds and brush had made little progress infiltrating the plots, what little there was had to be carefully chopped out, so that when the harvest days arrived, there would be no place for snakes to hide. Harvesting required all of one's attention.

The green mamba, known locally as *nyoka wa ntoka*, is one of the deadliest animals on the planet. It is also exceptionally aggressive, even for a reptile. The number-one cause of death amongst the villagers was infant mortality, the second was snakebite, and the victims were primarily women. When a green mamba released its full load of venom, the victim had approximately three minutes to settle her affairs with whichever god she prayed to.

Second Wife had taken her two youngest daughters, who were not yet in school like their older sister and brothers, and her infant son with her to the fields. They were joined by a dozen or so other women and their children, each family with its own little plot of manioc bushes to cultivate. Normally, Second Wife kept the baby strapped securely to her back with a strip of cloth, but fearing that the action of her short-handled hoe might cause a snake to strike, she left the children in the shade of an acacia tree at the edge of the forest. It was too early in the day for mammalian predators to attack humans. Besides, there was safety in numbers, even if only from a statistical standpoint.

More dangerous than predators were the heavy seedpods of a massive baobab tree not thirty meters away. These pods were the size of ten fists, each with a shell as hard as wood. Just last year, at another nearby field, a baby girl had been killed when struck on the head by a falling pod. Such trees were tolerated in the landscape because the pods contained edible pulp and seeds. Did this not prove that to everything there was both a good and a bad side? Only Cripple was the exception; Second Wife could think of nothing to merit her sister wife's existence.

Ten children in all were stashed beneath the low, spreading limbs of the more benign acacia. To occupy the little mouths and hands, one of the wealthier mothers had chopped a length of sugar cane into manageable pieces and distributed them to each child, even the babies.

As the women chopped, bent at the waist, the sun toiled to break through the haze, never quite making it. The children, for the most part, behaved themselves. For much of the time they were kept amused by giant flying locusts, the size of sparrows, that were sent into the air by the advancing hoes. Every now and then a locust would land within reach of the children, who eagerly pounced upon it. A locust that size was more protein than many of them had eaten in a month. The lucky child had the privilege of devouring the insect; crunchy head and thorax, tickling legs, squishy belly, everything but the wings, which were generously distributed to the others to play with.

With all this commotion, it was inevitable that Second Wife's infant son, known for the time being as Baby Boy, would be knocked over, perhaps even trampled by little bare feet. And indeed, it did happen. But the boy, still not a year old, appeared not to mind. And why should he? He was perfectly happy, playing with the large, shiny stone he had found lying half-buried at the base of the acacia tree.

Husband walked Cripple down the hill as far as the lane that led toward the missionary guesthouse. He didn't think Cripple would get the job as housekeeper, but if she did, that was all right with him. They could always use the money.

Everyone Husband knew wanted more money. Even Monsieur Dupree, his Belgian boss, wanted more money. But it wasn't always this way, not according to the old-timers. Once there had been a time when everything one needed was either hunted, cultivated, or made by hand. If there was a shortage, then one either did without or found an honest means of acquiring the necessity. In those days stealing was unknown.

Of course the old-timers spoke only of conditions within their own tribes. Stealing from another's tribe was not—well, it was not really stealing. The concept of stealing came with the Belgians, along with money. To raid other tribes for food, wives, or slaves was merely survival. Those days were in the long ago, and could never be reprised, so they were best forgotten.

Today there was money. And there were things one did not need but nonetheless regarded as necessary. Did one *need* brightly colored cotton cloth, when cloth could be made from the fibers of palm leaves? Never mind that palm cloth was more durable than cotton. Did one *need* a lantern that burned kerosene, when the forest still contained plenty of wood? Never mind that kerosene was dangerous, and many people had been scarred by the mishandling of it. Did one *need* the white man's medicine, when traditional cures prescribed by witch doctors were just as effective, if not more so? Never mind that many hereditary healers and diviners, like Husband, now had to support themselves with outside jobs.

True, from time to time villagers would approach Husband, seeking to acquire a protective amulet or some healing potion—even the occasional curse was requested—but few thought to bring with them a hindquarter of antelope as payment, or some sharp arrowheads, or at the very least a stalk of bananas.

Thus it was that Husband, whose personal name was Their Death, had been forced to seek income from the Belgians, whose very arrival had precipitated the decline of his profession. Now, Cripple would work for the white man as well—*if* she got the job.

Amanda Brown stayed in her room far longer than she suspected was appropriate for her as mistress of the guesthouse. Just because there were no guests to deal with didn't give her license to lollygag about like a lazy teenager. A teenager—that's exactly how she'd been acting, and thanks to the roar of the falls, she even slept like an adolescent. If it was up to her, she'd continue sleeping for the next several weeks, at least until the Singletons returned from their trip.

It wasn't even the plane crash, or losing all her possessions, that was getting her down; it was that man—Extended Bellybutton, or whatever his name was. Why did there always have to be a fly in the ointment? A cross to bear? This should have been one of the most exciting days of her life, and could have been, despite the fact that Mrs. Singleton was two sizes larger than Amanda, and her clothing had not been updated since the Dark Ages.

Well, at least it had been fun—sort of—to speak Tshiluba with him. Although he hadn't let on, he had to have been surprised. After all, surely not everyone could speak a native language that expertly upon just arriving in the country.

Amanda had excelled in language school. Her primary instructor, a Belgian nun who had been born in the Congo, had said that Amanda's ability to mimic accents was unparalleled, in her experience. Her grammar was flawless as well, and she'd learned twice the number of vocabulary words required to pass the course. This effusive praise did not surprise Amanda; it was not in her nature to do less than extraordinary work.

The only daughter of two physicians, Amanda's high marks throughout her school years, and her wide range of interests, had insured her a position at any top university that accepted women. When she announced to her parents that God had called her to spend her life bettering the people of Africa, her parents' keen disappointment was almost unbearable. Both agnostics, they tried to persuade Amanda that the best way to "better" anyone was to do so within the framework of academia. *American* academia.

But Amanda, who had been converted while still in high school as a result of visiting a classmate's church, could not be dissuaded. To her, bettering meant not only improving the living standards of those around her, but also ensuring that those people had the opportunity to accept Jesus Christ as their savior, and thus secure for themselves a place in heaven.

And now this. Amanda stared morosely at the raging water in front of her. Yes, the view of the falls was dramatic—in the States it might even be a million-dollar view—but sightseeing wasn't the reason she'd come to Africa. Well, at least she was on the African side of the river, and not the Belgian. Rising sharply behind the guesthouse was a large hill, and atop it was the native village. Later on, if she could slip past the housekeeper, she would take a hike up there.

A soft rap on the door made Amanda feel both guilty and annoyed. "Yes?" she called.

"*Mamu*, I must speak with you."

"Very well."

She didn't dawdle, but neither did she hurry to cinch tight Mrs. Singleton's robe, and smooth the hair from her face with Mrs. Singleton's hog-bristle brush. Yet, when she opened the door, there was nobody there.

"Protruding Navel," she shouted down the corridor.

He slowly materialized from around the corner, grinning from ear to ear. "Yes, *mamu*?"

"Why didn't you wait until I opened the door?"

"*Mamu*, my time also is valuable. Would you have *me* waste it doing nothing?"

"Protruding Navel, what is it you wish to speak with me about?"

"There is a woman here to see you, *mamu*."

"A white woman?"

"No. Shall I send her away?"

"What does she want?"

He shrugged. "That is for you to ask her. But at any rate, she is waiting for you at the front door, instead of the back. They are a pushy people, those Baluba."

"*What* did you say?"

"Only the truth, *mamu*. Can you deny that the Baluba are a pushy people?"

Amanda had heard that the Baluba were a motivated people, which is not the same as pushy. Besides, she hadn't met all the

Baluba, had she? Just as she refused to harbor thoughts of racial superiority back in her home state of South Carolina, Amanda would not tolerate ethnic remarks such as this.

"What is your tribal affiliation again, Protruding Navel?"

"My people are the Lulua. I am a Bena Lulua."

"I am quite sure," she said, choosing her words carefully, "that the Baluba have their own generalizations about the Lulua. But in this house, Protruding Navel, we will either speak kindly of others, or not at all."

"Then there will be much silence, *mamu*."

CHAPTER SEVEN

The author spent her formative years (ages 2–12) living with the Bashilele tribe. At that time the boys in late adolescence practiced headhunting as a rite of passage. The skulls, once cleaned, were used for drinking palm wine, and an ear of the victim was worn on a thong around the waist as a sign of manhood. The Bashilele were extremely territorial, and in general the victims were outsiders passing through, although occasionally raiding parties were formed.

Amanda had been warned about Africans who appear at the door uninvited. The instructor of her orientation course, a *white* missionary, had said that these people wanted one of two things: to sell you something or to ask for a favor, and *favor* was a euphemism for money. If they are selling, and you have use for their merchandise, then by all means, buy it. But stay clear of favors of any kind. One favor begets two, which begets a million. And whatever you do, don't stare at them; they'll think you're giving them the evil eye. But don't break eye contact with them first, either. In order to gain their respect, you need to show them who's boss. In this case, however, the small, frail handicapped woman standing on the verandah made Amanda feel protective, not domineering.

"*Mamu*," Cripple said, "you do not look very well."

"I'm fine," Amanda said. "What is it you want?"

"I have come to work for you."

"What did you say?"

"I am to be your new housekeeper."

"I don't understand. I already have a housekeeper. Did Mamu Singleton send you?" Please God, please let it be so.

Cripple shook her head. "I am here because news of your arrival has spread to the village. The white *mamu* will need someone to look after her, and it cannot be Protruding Navel. He has a vile temper and is very prejudiced against others not of his tribe."

Amanda couldn't help but smile. "Please, tell me your name."

"Cripple."

"*Kah!* I cannot call you that."

"Why not? It is my name."

"Yes, but it is . . . well, you can't help being that way—crippled, I mean—can you? It would not be polite for me to call you that. Don't you have a Christian name?"

"*Mamu*, I am not a Christian."

The calmness with which the African woman confessed her soul's peril stunned Amanda. Perhaps she hadn't understood the woman.

"Are you a Catholic?" she asked. It was sad, but true, that in the Belgian Congo the Protestant missionaries and the Roman Catholic priests were adversaries. If only the Catholics would stop worshipping Mary and be truly born again, then they could work together to save souls.

Cripple didn't even flinch. "No, I am not a Catholic. I am what you call a heathen."

Amanda was stunned. "A *heathen*?"

"I am aware, *mamu*, that this is a bad word to you. Perhaps *traditional* might be more acceptable."

Amanda smiled, despite the seriousness of the moment. "And your family? What are they?"

"They are mostly heathens as well, *mamu*. I would be quite worried if they were not. After all, my husband is a witch doctor."

"Why I declare!" Amanda said, slipping into English.

"*Mamu?*"

"Never mind. Help me understand this, please. You, and your family, worship all kinds of spirits?"

"*Eyo*. But my sister wife is somewhat of a Christian, so she worships mainly the spirit you call *Yehowa*. And what does the *mamu* worship?"

"I worship the true God, *Yehowa*."

"Is he not also a spirit?"

"*Baba*," Amanda said, and paused to collect her thoughts. Although the word translates as "mother," and is used to show respect, it is applied only to Africans. Even this distinction between races made Amanda uncomfortable. "Look, I am very sorry, but I cannot employ a heathen—even if I were looking for someone to hire, which I am not."

"Then you do not wish to save my soul?"

"Of course I do."

"Then what better solution is there? I will work for you, and you will tell me about your invisible God."

"Yes, but you see, we already have a housekeeper."

"Like I said, *mamu*, Protruding Navel has a violent temper. Even those of his own tribe attest to that. I have heard that he beats his wife. Perhaps he will beat you."

"Me? That's foolishness."

"Why? Because you are white?"

"I find that I like you, *baba*, even though you're a heathen. You don't spare your words, which is refreshing. But even if I agree to give you work, what will I call you? I can't agree to Cripple."

"It is my name." The African's dark eyes flashed. "My mother gave birth to three others before I was born. Each was a cripple, and each died while still an infant. When I was growing in my mother's belly, she asked the witch doctor for special medicine to ward off the evil spirits and to make sure that I was born healthy. The witch doctor gave her a brew to drink, and told her that I should be named Cripple in advance of my birth. The spirits, he said, would be confused, thinking that they had already done their job, and would leave me alone." Cripple refrained from adding that this same witch doctor, the man whom she called Husband, had contracted her into marriage when she was fourteen.

"Yes, but—"

"But I am still a cripple?"

"Yes, something like that."

"Ah, but you see, *mamu*, I am not as badly crippled as the others were, and among all my mother's children, I alone have survived. Believe me, it would have been much worse, had I not been called Cripple. This name is my protection."

Amanda shook her head, clucking softly to herself. She liked the feisty woman, but hiring a heathen for a housekeeper would surely be the talk of the mission field. Besides, Protruding Navel would be outraged by having to train her as his replacement—

"When can you start?"

"I am here now, *mamu*, am I not?"

"You will have to be trained."

"I did not expect less."

"And it will be Protruding Navel who will do most of the training."

"So be it."

Amanda smiled. "Good. By the way, do you speak French?"

"Rarely. Sometimes at the market I encounter vendors from other provinces who don't speak our local languages, nor I theirs. Then, and only then, do I speak French. After all, it's the language of our oppressors."

It took Amanda a second or two to realize that Cripple had just answered her in perfect French. Truth be told, her accent was even better than Amanda's.

"Where did you learn to speak like that?"

"When I was a girl, *mamu*," Cripple said, still in French, "I wasn't allowed to attend school. So I sat every day outside my brother's classroom and listened to his teachers lecture."

"Do you know math as well?"

"Only through the sixth form. That's as far the mission school went in those days."

"What about English?" she asked.

Cripple shook her head. "I wouldn't mind learning it, if *mamu* is willing to teach. But frankly, it sounds like just so much gibberish to me. Monkey talk, some in the village call it."

Amanda tried in vain to keep a straight face. "Well, now that you are hired," she said, switching back to Tshiluba, "you will want to know what to call me. In language school I was given the name Mamu Hurry Up, because I was always rushing through the lessons. Frankly, I do not care for that name. Can you think of a better name?"

Cripple nodded thoughtfully. "*Eyo.* I think Ugly Eyes would be more appropriate."

"Appropriate for what?"

"Your name, of course. Mamu Ugly Eyes—yes, that is a good name."

"Are my eyes *that* ugly?"

"You must admit, *mamu,* that they are very pale, almost like water. They really are not in the least bit attractive."

"Cripple," Amanda said, allowing herself to use the word for the first time, "in America, where I come from, Ugly Eyes would be an offensive name."

"But we are not in America, are we?"

No, Amanda thought, not by a long shot. And we aren't in

Kansas anymore, are we, Dorothy? We aren't even in South Carolina. You could study about Africa until the cows came home, but without actually spending time there, you didn't know a thing. Not one bloody thing.

Unless it was raining or he was experiencing another bout of malaria, Husband loved the walk home from the post office. Although it was an uphill walk most of the way, the thought of home and hearth—the embrace of little arms, a proper supper, and above all Cripple—supplied him with the necessary energy.

Although his days were long, they were quite tolerable when compared to those of Husband's friends. The mine workers were locked away behind brick walls for three months at a stretch, cut off entirely from their families for the duration. Those not skilled enough to be sorters had backbreaking jobs such as shoveling gravel onto conveyor belts. Husband was lucky to have an easygoing boss like Monsieur Dupree. Every day between the hours of twelve and two in the afternoon, the post office was shut down so that the M. Dupree could have his main meal of the day at his house, perhaps even take a nap.

The two-hour hiatus was not long enough to accommodate a trip home for Husband, so he spent his time snacking on bananas and mangoes (fruit did not count as food), and napping on a *malala* mat in the shade of a mango grove. More often than not, he skipped the nap in favor of reading one of the books M. Dupree was forever giving him.

These strange books were called novels and written in French. Unlike the Bible or the geography and history books he'd studied in school, each novel was entirely the product of someone's mind. "Works of fiction," M. Dupree called them, "meant only to entertain." But without a religious doctrine to impart, or a science lesson to be taught, they were books without a purpose. They spoke of luxuries almost unfathomable, and of people so untouched by everyday problems that they had the time to do foolish things, such as squander their goods or commit indecent acts with, or upon, their neighbors. Yet Husband could not wait to share the stories with Cripple around the evening fire, while Second Wife muttered to herself across the flames.

Second Wife had no tolerance for foolishness, which was a very good thing in its own way, as she kept everything running. If not exactly smoothly, at least on course. If Second Wife had been one of the characters in these books—well, then it could not have been written.

Tonight Husband paused on the bridge, as he often did, to admire the view. To his right was the broad, red-brown Kasai River. It was an important river, one that formed a region and shaped its people. To his left was a gorge into which the river plunged, and with so much hydraulic force that it kept the European part of the city perpetually supplied with electricity.

Belle Vue Falls was the Belgian name for this geological feature, and from it they had taken the name for their town. The bridge had been built by forced labor, and although seventy-eight African lives were lost, as well as three European, the result was an architectural marvel. It was intentionally constructed as near to the lip of the gorge as possible, so that whoever crossed it might take full advantage of the view. But critics of the bridge—Europeans from other towns and cities, and engineers who hadn't been included in its construction—said that it was only a matter of time before erosion sent it toppling into the gorge.

Tonight, as Husband stood on the bridge, facing the gorge, he thought about the men who had died in the pounding waters below. The Africans had been expendable, their names of no significance to the colonialists. The three whites, however—two Belgian, one Greek—had their names carved into a rock pillar that stood as a memorial on the European side of the river.

Then Husband remembered, for the millionth time, that

Cripple had said she was going to work for the American *mamu*. If Cripple said it—well, it was almost as good as done. Husband couldn't wait to hear the news. When he arrived at his family compound, he was panting heavily.

His oldest son, Brings Happiness, ran to greet him. "*Tatu*, what has happened?"

"Happened?" Husband panted for a while before continuing. "Your foolish *tatu* just ran up the hill. That is what happened."

"Eh," Second Wife grunted, as she poked the slumbering fire back to life. "You will wear your heart out if you persist in doing such foolish things. Then who will feed and clothe the children?"

"Maybe Cripple," Husband said. "Has she returned from her job?"

"Job? What Job? Forgive me, Husband, but who would give a woman such as First Wife a job?"

"Wait, and you will see." Husband was well aware that there was no love lost between the woman he lived for and the woman who lived to serve him. It was the stuff of French novels, except that his family was not rich beyond dreams. Besides, it was the lot of the African to endure. Surely to ask more of life was to anger the spirits.

Husband knew that Second Wife would be happy to say more on the subject, so he turned his full attention to the children. Satisfied with his father's answer, Brings Happiness was playfully teasing a young sister, much to the amusement of the other children. Only Baby Boy seemed left out of the action, sitting quietly in the doorway of the house, sucking on something—something as large as a mango seed, but clearly not that. What could that be?

Husband walked over and scooped the child into his arms. "What do you have there?" he asked gently.

Baby boy was too young to speak, but he generously removed

the wet object from his mouth and held it out, as if offering it to his father.

"Second Wife," Husband called, trying not let the excitement show in his voice, "what is this our son chews on, as if it were a piece of sugarcane?"

"Just a stone he found in the manioc field. He is growing a new tooth, and the coldness of it is soothing. But do not worry, Husband, it is so large he cannot put it all into his mouth at one time."

"Then I will not worry," Husband said, but his heart was pounding.

CHAPTER EIGHT

The Bashilele were one of the few societies in the world which practiced polyandry—that is to say, a woman could have more than one husband. The cause of this was polygamy, which resulted in not enough women to go around. In brief it worked as follows: three or four men would band together and purchase one wife, whom they shared equally, but after several years the wife was given the privilege of selecting a single husband from this group. As for the others, hopefully by then they had secured private wives of their own, or else, if they still desired marriage, they'd have to go the group route again.

Second Wife had just finished stirring the stiff mush, and was in the process of shaping it into a smooth ball when Cripple hobbled into the family compound. That was just like her; wait until the real work was done, and then offer to stir the pot of manioc greens or poke at the chicken bubbling in palm oil at the fire's edge. Disabled or not, there was no denying that Cripple was a lazy woman who milked her husband's sympathy for all it was worth.

"Let me help," Cripple said. Predictably.

"No, all is ready." Second Wife turned her back and clapped her hands, ostensibly to call the children. In truth, she couldn't bare to look at her husband's eyes, to see the joy in them that Cripple's safe return brought.

"Cripple," Husband said, "how was your day? Did you get the job?"

"Of course, Husband. Did I not tell you I would?" She laughed. "I have already begun; that is why I am so late."

"Ah. What are your duties? What is the American like?"

The children, who always claimed to be starving this time of the day, were crowding around Cripple instead of the food pots. "Yes, tell us," they said in one voice.

"The American is as tall as a papaya tree, and her hair is as soft as the threads of green corn. But her eyes—they are the color of water, with maybe just a hint of sky reflected in them."

The children's gasps of pleasure annoyed Second Wife immensely. They were forever begging their other *baba* for her silly stories. Well, Second Wife could tell such stories too, if she had time to think. But who had time to think when there was always so much work to be done?"

"And the job?" Husband said.

"Oh Husband, I think you will be disappointed in me, because I am not her housekeeper."

"*Kah*," Husband said, "that is indeed surprising news. But I am not disappointed in you. It is the American woman who disappoints. Clearly she has no vision."

"Do not be hasty to judge her, Husband. I am not her housekeeper because—instead—I am her assistant."

"Her assistant!" Husband roared with laughter. "Do you joke with me?"

"I am telling you the truth. She said that a mind such as mine would be wasted on the tasks of a housekeeper. I am to be trained to use a typewriter and a sewing machine!"

"A mind like yours," Second Wife muttered, "is not deserving of such an honor."

Unfortunately Husband had ears as sharp as a jackal's. "What did you say?"

"I said that the food is ready."

"Yes," Cripple said, "it is time to eat."

Second Wife felt her cheeks burning with anger. How dare the woman come to her defense. It was nothing more than a ploy, a way to keep Husband convinced that his first wife was as generous of spirit as everyone believed she was—everyone, that is, except for Second Wife. Cripple was a fraud who manipulated others with her disability. The time would come, and soon, when Husband would see through her and discard her like a cracked gourd. Second Wife was sure of that.

The Nigerian felt strangely happy. The fish had given him energy, and last night he'd made *two* important discoveries, not just the one he'd anticipated. And all because of bats.

At first he'd been confused, mistaking the bats for swallows. But when he realized his mistake, he remembered that bats often live in caves and so there must be a cave nearby. He paid closer attention to their movements and was astonished to see that they appeared to emerge from behind the waterfall.

How could that be? The water was coming down with such force that the spray stung his face and chest. The Nigerian scrambled over slippery boulders, trying to catch the last of the dying light. At least there weren't any crocodiles to worry about going in this direction.

The roar of the falls was so loud that it seemed to suppress his other senses. It wasn't until the Nigerian gave up on the cave, and had turned his back to the onslaught, that he felt the cool breath of air against his neck.

For Senhora Branca Violante Cunha e Mao de Ferro de Sintra e Santos Abreu e Nunez, early morning was the best part of the day.

Fortune had smiled on the Nunez family the day they were given their housing assignment. All the houses suitable for Europeans were company owned, of course—the Consortium owned *everything*. Invariably the best houses were given to mining officials according to rank. Cezar Nunez, as the new manager of the Bell Vue grocery, was at the bottom of the hierarchy.

But the Vice President in Charge of Operations had recently retired to Belgium. His now vacant mansion was built on the edge of the breathtakingly beautiful gorge that had given rise to the town's name. His replacement had four small children and a wife who was paranoid that her children would climb over the low stone wall that enclosed the patio and tumble to their deaths. The wife happily settled for the only other empty house, which was located in the heart of town. Would the Nunez family be willing to live on the gorge?

As she sat there savoring her second cup of coffee and listening to the roar of the falls, Branca couldn't think of a sillier question. Both the house and its setting were the kind of things that only movie stars or crooked politicians ever got to enjoy.

She paused from her reveries to proofread the invitation she had just written. If its recipient understood her attempt at English and responded in the affirmative, then they would be having drinks together in the club restaurant on Thursday at four. If she accepted Branca's invitation, the American would unwittingly kill two birds with one stone. For one thing, Branca could use a new friend—no, be honest. Make that *any* friend. But to be friends with a missionary, maybe then the vicious tongues would stop wagging.

The self-righteous Belgian hausfraus had always thought they were too good for her, even before the rumor started. And what made them so special? They were only the wives of the white-collar mine workers. Instead of shoveling gravel, their husbands shuffled paper, or sorted diamonds. Yet these women had the temerity to look down upon Branca simply because she was Portuguese.

Portuguese. The word was more often than not hurled as an epithet amongst the Belgians, especially the Flemish speakers. It was like calling someone a nigger in the United States. True, the Congo was a Belgian colony, but if not for the Portuguese explorers, there wouldn't even be a European presence in the Congo. At least not to this extent.

Branca's many times great-grandfather on her mother's side, Joao Albergeheria e Mao de Ferro, had been an apprentice navigator on one of Vasco de Gama's voyages. Her father's family descended from minor nobility. Branca herself was red-haired and blue-eyed, the legacy of some Celtic ancestors who'd settled in the north of Portugal centuries ago. She certainly did not deserve to be classified as barely above a mulatto—unofficially, of course. But it may as well have been officially, given that both she and her husband were treated like lepers.

Satisfied with the accuracy of her invitation, Branca sealed the envelope before ringing one of the two little brass bells next to her. Immediately the head houseboy appeared at the doorway. His snappy uniform was so much more attractive than anything worn by the Belgians' servants.

"Yes, *senhora*?"

"Please deliver this to the American guesthouse. Make sure that the American woman, Mademoiselle Brown, gets it. Under no circumstances should that pushy housekeeper get it. As a matter of fact, wait for the reply and then ask for the original note back."

"But *senhora*, there are many variables. What if—"

"Francois Joseph, do you value your job?" For Branca it was a rhetorical question. Francois was an *évolué*, a man dedicated to the pursuit of evolving into the special class of educated Africans who would someday rule his country or, at the very least, shed his past as an ignorant bush person. To that end, the man had abandoned his birth name, answering only to his baptismal name.

The fact that Francois wished to emulate the ways of European civilization made him an excellent houseboy. He studied table settings, memorized recipes, and because he'd worked for more than one European, the keenly observant man was more cognizant of what went into running a proper household than was the *senhora* herself. That's why he'd been promoted to head houseboy three years ago.

"Yes, *madame*, I value my job."

Branca dismissed him with only the slightest of nods.

Husband hadn't slept at all. Cripple was snoring softly on one side of him, but even without checking to see if Second Wife's eyes were open, he knew she was staring at the roof of the hut, rigid with anger. It had not always been this way.

When he paid her bride price and brought her to his home, Second Wife had seemed quite happy to be the wife of a witch doctor *and* a man with a cash income. For the first time in her life she could purchase material for new clothes, as well as luxuries such as glass beads and brightly colored scarves. When there was no meat from the forest to be had in the marketplace, Husband bought cans of sardines or dried *makayabo* fish. When the babies started to come, there was a little money to treat them at clinic if need be. (Of course clinic visits were to be kept secret, lest Husband's reputation as a witch doctor suffer.)

But it had not been possible for Husband to conceal his special fondness for Cripple. It was as if her spirit and his spirit were two halves of the same seed pod. That she wasn't fertile was no longer important, now that Second Wife was producing heirs. Cripple's mind was fertile, and that pleased Husband greatly.

Yet even as he rejoiced in having Cripple, it pained Husband that Second Wife was so unhappy. He could see her point; Cripple did next to nothing to relieve Second Wife of the burden of caring for seven children *and* maintaining the manioc plot. Although now that Cripple had a job, things would surely change for the better.

Husband was not about to sell the manioc plot, which had been in his family for generations, but he would look into the possibility of hiring another woman to do the work, instead of Second Wife. And if what he had in his pocket turned out to be what he suspected it was, he might even be able to hire an entire village full of women to help Second Wife.

It was not going to be a simple matter, however, to sell what Baby Boy had found in the field. The mining Consortium owned the mineral rights to all of the land on the Belle Vue side of the river, a strip twenty miles long and ten miles wide. How the Consortium had come by these rights was a moot point; the Belgium government enforced their claim, and that's all that mattered. Any African found panning for diamonds, or even just fishing along that bank of the river, was subject to a harsh reprimand.

The land on the village side of the river was another situation altogether. Although the Consortium claimed the strip immediately adjacent to the water and extending for a hundred yards inland, they did not mine there. But that was only because few diamonds had ever been found on that side of the river. Still, the Consortium was not about to turn the land over to the Africans, in case the land ever yielded the precious stones. In what the Belgians thought was a generous move, Africans were allowed use of the shore for fishing, bathing, voiding, and for acquiring drinking water.

The manioc plot was at least half a mile from the river, but Husband knew that anybody willing to buy Baby Boy's discovery would naturally assume that the gem had been found on the Belle Vue side of the river. Such an assumption would undoubtedly lead to imprisonment, and probably severe beatings as well. Even if

Husband journeyed to another city, selling the stone would be fraught with danger. Where had he gotten such a thing? Had he stolen it? If no, then where had he found it?

Therefore until the enormous diamond could be sold, it was worth no more to Husband and his family than a piece of gravel. In fact, it was worth even less. At least a pebble that large could be used to give a stray dog a good thwack on the ribs.

If—and it would be a huge gamble—Husband could broach the subject with a trusted European, one who might even be considered a friend, and speak hypothetically about such a stone, then perhaps some useful piece of information might be forthcoming. If, after this conversation, even a glimmer of hope was offered, Husband would bury the diamond until such time as it was appropriate to act. If, however, there was absolutely no chance that the stone could be sold for a vast sum, then, in the dark of night, Husband would cast the stone into the gorge, and it would never again be seen by human eyes. No hole that Husband could dig would ever be deep enough to permanently hide something this valuable—especially from himself.

His heart pounding, Husband was the first to rise from the family sleeping mat.

CHAPTER NINE

The men in the Bashilele tribe were hunters and the women engaged in subsistence farming. They were semi-nomadic. Some villages would remain in the same location for as much as a hundred years, but other villages would pick up and move if hunting ceased to be productive, or if a disease began to claim lives, or in times of imminent danger. Using both the leaves and stems of raffia palms as building materials, the Bashilele constructed their lightweight houses in sections. When it was time to move, everyone in the family carried a wall, or roof panel, on his or her head. A village could literally disappear overnight.

Cezar Nunez cursed softly as he fumbled with the keys, trying to find the right one for the Yale lock that kept the groceries in his store safe from two-legged predators at night. There was a watchman, of course, an old man with a bowed jaw, who claimed to have fallen from the top of a palm tree while harvesting palm nuts. The fellow had come with the store, so to speak, and although he spent his nights drinking palm wine and dozing, Cezar had no intention of sacking him—or anyone else for that matter.

It was his head clerk, Kweta Daniel, who deserved a dressing-down. Kweta, he'd been assured, was 100 percent trustworthy, and as punctual as a Brussels streetcar. So far, in the three months since he'd taken over the Grand Market, Cezar had seen no reason to question the African's honesty. But if this is the way Brussels streetcars ran, then it was no wonder the Belgians had been such pushovers during the war.

Damn that man! He was supposed to open the doors to customers at half past seven on the dot, and it was already a quarter to nine. At the very least, if he was ill, Kweta should have sent a runner with a note, in which case Cezar would have opened the damn store himself. If this happened again, then Cezar's job might well be on the line. In the meantime, he had no choice but to deal with one very unhappy customer.

"Monsieur Nunez," the operations manager's wife said, murdering the pronunciation of a fine Portuguese name, "my husband wished to have milk with his morning coffee. We were out of it, so I sent the boy to buy some. He came back empty-handed, of course. I sent him back and again he returned with nothing. My husband was furious that he had to report to his office without his coffee. So here I am to sort things out. Why are you just now opening the store?"

The operations manager—OP behind his back (the P stood for *pissant*)—was the highest-ranking Consortium executive in the field. Since the entire town was owned by the Consortium, and everyone in it employed by the same (as were the inhabitants of the village across the river), the OP was nothing less than a dictator. As a person, the OP seemed fairly decent, so Cezar preferred to think of him as a benevolent dictator—or maybe just a king, who ruled without divine will.

"Madame, I am deeply sorry, and I apologize for your inconvenience."

"Monsieur Nunez, have you been up all night drinking?"

"No, madame."

"Then why are your hands shaking?"

"Uh—it's exceptionally cool out this morning?"

"Are you asking me?"

"No, madame."

"Here, give me those keys."

"Certainly, madame."

During the handover, Madame OP leaned close and sniffed. "You drunken swine," she hissed softly.

Cezar Nunez had no choice but to endure the indignity. It hadn't always been this way, Cezar licking the boots of Northern Europeans like he was a dog whose job it was to clean up their spilled porridge. When he married Branca, the most beautiful woman in Portugal, the young groom had been one of the richest men in the country—at least his father was. If things had gone right—well, they hadn't. The bulk of the family fortune had been made from owning a German munitions factory. When that factory was nationalized in the mid-thirties, shortly after his son's marriage, Cezar's father fell into a deeply depressed state and committed suicide.

Left with just a small tire-producing factory in Lisbon, the younger Nunez—with his wife's encouragement, it must be noted—gambled everything on a career as a retailer in the Belgian Congo. During the war years, it appeared to be a good investment, and Cezar and Branca started a family. When the children reached school age, they were sent to Portugal, returning to visit during the long school break, at which time their parents lavished affection upon them. For a while everyone was happy. But then for reasons Cezar could not explain, the chain of small stores that sold dry goods to Africans began to fail, one by one.

It felt like a curse had fallen on the Nunez family. In less than one generation their fortune had dwindled to nothing, and now this. The former heir to immense wealth and privilege was working as manager in someone *else's* store, and a Belgian hausfrau was accusing him of being drunk, whereas he hadn't had as much as a sip of wine since dinner the night before.

Somehow, someday soon, Cezar Nunez was going to stick it to the bitch, and everyone like her. Either he'd find a way, or die trying.

The morning after she'd hired Cripple, Amanda was up bright and early. She couldn't wait to see her newest employee again. Perhaps today she would ask Cripple to take her on a tour of the village—oh my, she should have done that yesterday. It would be downright inconsiderate to ask a handicapped woman—a cripple at that—to walk back up that horribly steep hill. Unless—she could walk Cripple home *after* work. That was it!

Amanda chased the last bite of scrambled eggs around on her plate with the last bite of toast. Then she savored her last sip of coffee. Protruding Navel was a presumptuous, irritating man, but he was also a fabulous cook. If only he wasn't forever popping up out of nowhere. You couldn't even think about him without the risk of—and there he was now!

"Mamu Ugly Eyes," he said in Tshiluba, having glided into the room completely unnoticed, "there is someone here to see you."

Amanda cringed. How fast that horrible name had spread. She should have been more emphatic yesterday to Cripple. Well, she hadn't, and it was too late now.

"Cripple is here, yes?"

"No, *mamu*, it is another African. A man."

"What does he want?"

"He will not say. Only that he must speak with you in person. But I have seen this man before. I believe that he works for the Portuguese woman whose house you see across the gorge."

Amanda folded her napkin into quarters and placed it on the table before rising. Without having to ask, she knew where to find her visitor. Whites used the front door, Africans the back—with, of course, the exception of Cripple. It was an unwritten rule here,

but hard and fast nonetheless. In fact, it was not that much different from the way things worked in South Carolina.

The staff at the language and orientation school in Brussels
had tried to prepare the young American for just about any situation she was likely to encounter in the Congo. Unfortunately, not
a word had been said about the possibility that Amanda might
even find one of the Congolese physically attractive. It was all
Amanda could do to keep her eyes on the man's face, just above
the bridge of his nose.

"Yes?"

"Mademoiselle Ugly Eyes, here is a message from my employer, Senhora Nunez."

The visitor spoke in French. Good for him. But from now
on, Amanda would only speak Tshiluba to the Africans—unless,
of course, she knew for a fact that they couldn't speak this major
trade language.

"How did you know my name?" she asked.

The messenger's eyes widened and he laughed. "So, you speak
our language."

"You sound surprised."

"*Mamu*, none of the white women in Belle Vue speak our language. Maybe just a few words, which they shout at their servants,
and all of which they pronounce badly."

"And the white men?"

"That is different. Some of them speak our language very well.
That is because they must work with uneducated villagers who
do not speak French. Perhaps a few Portuguese speak it as well. I
think they pick it up from their mistresses."

"Their *what*? I don't understand the word."

"The women who are not their wives. We say 'mistresses.'
Now do you understand?"

Amanda could feel the blood pour into her cheeks, undoubtedly turning them a bright pink. "Yes, I understand. Now please

tell me how it is that everyone knows my name is Ugly Eyes. Was it from my assistant, Cripple?"

"I do not know, *mamu*, for I heard it from my wife, who heard it from our neighbor. But we have a saying in the village: whisper your secrets only in the privy, but know that even those walls can hear you."

CHAPTER TEN

The OP was in a foul mood. He was fond of taking his coffee with milk, a custom he'd developed during the war, when milk had been far more plentiful than coffee. This morning there hadn't been any milk, and when you got down to the core of the matter, he had no one to blame but himself.

Why hire a Portuguese, his wife had demanded, when he'd first mentioned Senor Nunez as a replacement for Gilbert, that thieving scoundrel. Didn't the OP know that even a French-speaking Belgian, a Walloon, was more reliable than an Iberian, be he Spanish or Portuguese?

The truth is, the OP had met many fine Portuguese since coming to the Congo, whereas his wife stayed clear of them as if they were the plague. But the OP's wife was to be pitied, not berated on that account, for how could she help her upbringing? A Flemish girl through and through, she'd even balked at marrying him when he finally divulged that he had a Walloon grandmother. It was the way they were raised, those pure-blooded Flemings. Not so unlike the Germans when you thought about it.

At any rate, first it was having to miss out on a proper breakfast, and now this impossible demand placed on him by the home office in Brussels. The world would be a much better place if airplanes had never been invented. The telegraph as well. Make that all modern forms of communication. In the old days—much before his time, of course—it could take weeks for bad news to travel, and by the time it finally arrived, there was sometimes a slim chance that it had long since been negated by new information. Even if it hadn't, there was certainly no need to respond quickly. After all, it would take weeks for an answer to get back to Europe, so what difference would a few days make? None. Even a few weeks didn't much matter.

But this piece of bad news had arrived yesterday in the form of an aerogramme, flown in by Sabena Airlines. It was an unscheduled flight—one that brought an insurance inspector to examine the crash site—but it brought mail nonetheless. How unkind of fate to deliver trouble in this manner. Suddenly, if the OP expected to keep his job, the outgoing flight would have to carry his response to the letter in the Belle Vue mailbag.

The OP had put off opening the aerogramme until this morning because he knew it was going to be bad news. Bad news, taxes, and sex with Madame OP were three things it never hurt to put off as long as one could. Now he wished he'd put it off even another day.

Dear Monsieur OP,

I have just come from a meeting with the Directors, and I am afraid that what I have to report is not good. Profits are down for the third quarter in a row which, as you know, is directly tied in with decreased production at Belle Vue mine. At the same time production costs have risen.

The Directors are beginning to question my wisdom in offering you the position of OP. I have assured them that you are the most qualified person for the job, having grown up in the

Congo, as the son of the OP at our sister mine to the south. I also reminded them that, even though profits are down, they are still much higher than they have ever been under any previous OP. The problem, I told them, is that you started out with such a bang, you spoiled them by raising their expectations.

Nevertheless, we must figure out a way to get things back on track again. They say the sun is setting on the British Empire, and there is much concern here in Brussels that the sun will shortly begin to set on us as well. Rough estimates are that we will have to turn the colony back over to the Congolese in no more than ten years, possibly even as few as five.

That said, we must (as the American saying goes) make hay while the sun shines—instead, in our case, we will find and export diamonds. Monsieur OP, I respect you enough to let you make your own decisions. Therefore, I will not interfere in how you turn things around, but unless profits are significantly up for the next quarter, you will be relieved of your post and perhaps even forced to retire under less than optimum conditions.

In reviewing what I've written, it comes across as rather harsh. But Monsieur OP, my intent is merely to convey to you the Board's sentiments, so that you have the opportunity to exonerate your reputation, as well as mine. I shall expect a reply from you in next week's post, one that assures me that you understand the gravity of the situation.

Cordially,
Monsieur Lenoir, CEO

Monsieur OP felt his cheeks stinging with shame. The fact that production was down was entirely his fault, and one that could have been avoided.

Unlike the deep core deposits in South Africa, the Congo diamonds were found in alluvial gravel beds just below, or even sometimes directly on, the surface. By and large the diamonds were small, off-color, and heavily occluded. Nonetheless, they had many industrial uses, and there was a steady market for them. Approximately 10 percent of the stones were good enough to be sold to wholesale jewelry makers who produced gaudy trinkets for undiscerning costumers. Only 1 percent of the Belle Vue diamonds were of gem quality, but when these were properly cut in Antwerp, they brought in more money than all the other stones combined.

A year ago the OP, after several successful years in his position, decided to gamble the mine's resources on processing a new deposit that supposedly contained a higher percentage of gemstones. He based his decision on a report his geologist submitted a month before succumbing to malaria. The report detailed the location of a deposit some twenty kilometers to the north, but away from the river, that contained certain indicator gravels that are usually found along with higher-grade stones. The geologist had estimated that as many as twenty percent of the stones found there would prove to be of gem quality, and some would be of exceptionally high quality.

The OP had been twice to visit the site, located at the bottom of a box canyon from which flowed a powerful spring that soon became a fast-moving stream. The canyon floor was forested, but ridges and spirals of resistant rock rose above the trees like turrets of a castle. The keepers of the fortress were a pack of baboons that vocalized loudly whenever humans invaded their domain. On his second visit a pair of vivid blue crested plantain birds soared overhead. It was a magical place, and had it not been for its mineral potential, would have made an excellent spot to picnic.

In order to properly mine the gem-bearing gravel, a road had to be built, as well as a fence that virtually blocked off the open end of the canyon, thereby denying access to poachers. The road and the fence required months to build, and had diverted a large number of his African workers and a substantial portion of his operating budget. Not to mention that he'd secretly bought two dilapidated pickup trucks from some missionaries, on account of the fact that all the diamond-bearing dirt from the canyon had to be brought into the processing plant in Belle Vue. To build a new plant out there would have been impractical and way beyond even his ability to maintain by finagling resources.

But if the rains came on time this year—not early like last year—the mine could be in production as early as the end of August. Who knew, but by Christmas the mine might have produced the Star of Congo, which was the name he planned to bestow on the first flawless stone over ten carats, and which he personally planned to present to Their Majesties King Baudouin I and Queen Fabiola of Belgium. Now, just when things seemed to be coming together, there was this stupid ultimatum from the Directors.

What did they think he was doing? Picking his nose? Someday, when his gamble had paid off, more than a few of those men were going to be sorry for their no-confidence vote. As for the CEO, the man had a spine made of noodle dough. True, he was just doing his job, but . . .

The OP sent his fist crashing down on his mahogany desk. "Flanders," he bellowed.

"Sir?"

His secretary was a Belgian lad in his early twenties, a newcomer to Africa. He was the son of a friend of the CEO, and the OP was still not convinced that boy hadn't been sent to spy on him. He certainly looked the part. Claiming allergies, Secretary was never to be seen without a white handkerchief over his mouth and nose to keep out the ubiquitous dry-season dust. The Africans found this amusing, and on several occasions the OP had caught some of the office boys mimicking the new arrival by tying scraps of cloth over their faces. Frankly, it was funny, so the OP didn't have the heart to chide them.

"Flanders," the OP said, "make yourself useful and run down to the store and get some milk for my coffee."

"What if the store doesn't have any, sir?"

"Then find a cow and milk it."

"But sir, there aren't any cows around here."

"Then find a goat. Whatever you do, don't come back without milk. And I mean fresh milk, none of the powdered stuff."

"Yes, sir."

With the anteroom clear of spying eyes, the OP set about preparing his answer for the directors. They weren't going to like it.

Loving eyes watched Husband head in the direction of the thatch-walled privy. He disappeared for a reasonable amount of time, and upon emerging glanced in all directions before striding over to the clump of banana trees growing on the forest's edge. To loving eyes it appeared as if Husband had begun to search for something, poking around in the detritus and pulling at the loose sheaths of banana leaves. Weaving in and out of the clump of fat stalks, he spent almost as much time there as he had relieving himself. Then abruptly Husband began to walk at a fast clip, not back to the village, but in the direction of town.

CHAPTER ELEVEN

Because potential brides were at such a premium amongst the Bashilele (due to polygamy), baby girls were contracted into marriage before they were even born. A man in search of a wife would give a pregnant woman and her husband a down payment on the unborn child. If the baby turned out to be a boy, the prospective bridegroom got a full refund. If indeed a girl was born, a formal engagement would ensue, with the girl moving in with her husband at about the time she experienced her first menses.

Amanda was pleased to get the senhora's invitation. It would be wonderful to have a friend among the white community, she thought, and then immediately chided herself. Black, white, it shouldn't matter. What she meant to tell herself was that it would be comforting to have a friend who was also an outsider, and with whom she shared some cultural affinities. Of course it wasn't as good as an American, or even an English friend, but—oh stop it, she said to herself. You don't have to justify everything. It is what it is, and you will enjoy it. Or not.

But one thing she definitely would not enjoy was drinks at the club. It was wrong to drink alcohol because it destroyed one's body, which was the temple of God. And it was wrong even to just sit in the club and sip a glass of grenadine, because it gave the impression to others that she approved of their behavior. No, if Senhora Nunez really wanted to meet Amanda, and possibly be her friend, then she would agree to come tomorrow afternoon for tea. Say four o'clock?

She wrote her invitation on a crisp piece of rose-scented stationery while the houseboy waited, but when she gave it to him, he wouldn't budge.

"Madame, please, you must also sign the note I brought with me."

"Why?"

"My employer is very strict. If you do not sign it, she will be angry with me."

Hmm. Perhaps this Senhora Branca Nunez was not going to be compatible after all. Well, time would tell. She signed the note, and then on an impulse gave the servant a two-franc piece from a jar of coins she'd found on a top shelf in the kitchen. It was nothing, really, just four cents in American money.

"Madame, what is this for?"

"It is for you."

"But I do not work for you, madame."

"Yes, but you walked here with the message."

"It was my job, madame."

"Are you refusing the money?"

The man shifted feet, staring past her head as he thought. "No, madame, I am not refusing the money. But with this"—he held the coin—"I can buy nothing."

Amanda could hardly believe her ears. In Language and Orientation School, one of the staff had informed her that the average wage of a full-time servant was one dollar a day—or fifty Belgian francs. She had just tipped the man four percent of his daily wage, and he was unhappy?

"Here," she said, and handed him another two-franc piece.

He took the money and left without another word. Confused, Amanda stared at his retreating back.

"You have insulted the man, Mamu Ugly Eyes."

Amanda whirled. Protruding Navel was the last person she wanted to see today. The man had the ability to sneak up on you like a cat, but he had none of the redeeming qualities of a domestic feline.

"You were listening?"

"*Mamu*, it is my job to cook and clean this place. I had business in the kitchen."

"Protruding Navel, if it pleases you, tell me why this man was insulted."

"Because he is not your servant, as he explained. Therefore, you must either let him do his job without a *matabisha*, or else pay him what he is worth. Instead, you have treated him like a child. Like an errand boy."

"So you would have been insulted as well?"

"No, *mamu*, because I do not deliver notes."

"I see."

"Mamu Ugly Eyes, do you believe it is wrong to steal?"

"Yes, of course. It is one of the Ten Commandments."

"Then, *mamu*, why is it you have stolen from Mamu Singleton?"

"I beg your pardon?"

"The jar there—on the top shelf—that belongs to the *mamu*. She uses it to buy eggs and produce from the village women."

"I assumed as much. But I was only borrowing the money. I will replace it at once."

"Very well, *mamu*. May I speak frankly?"

"Yes, of course." There was no stopping him anyway.

"I do not think you are a very good example, Mamu Ugly Eyes."

"*What*? An example for whom?"

"The village woman who limps, she who is called Cripple. She is coming up the road; I can see her now. She is a heathen, *mamu*. But she will never believe in your Jesus if you are to be her example."

Amanda felt like there must be steam rising from her ears. Why was Protruding Navel pushing her so hard? What was his agenda? Or did he just enjoying sticking the knife in and turning it slowly? Like a corkscrew. Surely there were plenty of men in the village who could be trained to be housekeepers.

"Are you a Christian, Protruding Navel?"

"Of course, *mamu*. As was my father, and his father before him. My three mothers are Christians as well. There are no heathens in my family."

"Excellent. Then you will have to set the example for Cripple."

"But *mamu*, she is a woman!"

"Yes, but Jesus was a man—and so are you, yes? And only a man can accurately portray another man. Therefore you must act like Jesus."

"Does *mamu* mock me with her clever words?"

"No, she does not. In fact, she has never been more serious in her life."

Amanda turned her back on her housekeeper and smiled at Cripple.

Strategy. It was all about strategy, Husband mused, during his long walk to the post office. Life was like a game of soccer, or football, in which there were many players but only one goal per team. Husband had been an exceptional player as a student in the Catholic mission school, not because he was faster or more coordinated, but because he knew when to pass the ball and when to keep it. More often than not he passed it, but only when it gave his teammates a clear shot into the goal. Only on rare occasions did he run it all the way in. But for Husband to profit from a diamond that large would take a great deal of strategy, perhaps more than he was capable of engineering.

To say that Consortium was paranoid might be a bit overstating things, but nonetheless, the mine at Belle Vue amounted to a maximum-security prison. Ten-foot-high cement-block walls, surmounted with rolls of barbed wire, were intended to keep the uniformed workers in, along with any diamonds they may have pilfered. Three days before their shifts were over, the workers were fed a laxative and their subsequent bodily wastes were closely examined. They also had to undergo a personal cavity search, have the insides of their mouths examined, and had to submit to having greased combs dragged through their hair. Any cuts or scabs that had not been noted on their bodies when they first checked in had to be reopened, on the suspicion that a diamond might be concealed in the wound.

Husband breathed a sigh of relief to find M. Dupree alone at the post office. There was still some time before the flag had to be hoisted so that the doors could be officially opened. If Husband didn't act now, he would be miserably tense the rest of the day.

"Monsieur Dupree," he blurted, "may I have a minute?"

"Of course, Monsieur Their Death, but literally just one minute. I have to finish sorting the outgoing mail before the plane arrives."

"*Oui*. It is about a diamond, sir."

"A *diamond*? What about a diamond?"

"Let us say, Monsieur Dupree, hypothetically speaking, that someone found a very large diamond way out in the forest somewhere, far beyond the Consortium's land. Then let us say that the person who found it tried to sell the diamond—perhaps to a white man. What would happen to the person who tried to sell such a diamond if the man he approached turned him in to the authorities?"

M. Dupree stepped to the window and peered out before pulling down the shade and locking the door. "Monsieur Their

Death, would you like some coffee? Unfortunately there is no milk today."

Husband could not believe his ears. For fifteen years he had reported to work every morning, and he could count on one hand the days he'd missed: the day Cripple lost the only child she'd ever conceived; two days when Husband's fever was so high he couldn't stand, much less walk; and the day Middle Son was blinded by a spitting cobra. Although M. Dupree was a kind boss, never once, in all those years, had he offered Their Death even a glass of water.

"Yes," he said quickly, before he lost his nerve, "coffee will be very nice."

These were not words Husband used to describe coffee, because he had never drunk the beverage. These were words Husband had heard white visitors say when M. Dupree offered them coffee. But those occasions were rare.

M. Dupree took a blue enamel mug down from a shelf high above the coffeepot, which was kept warm on an electric heater. Then he made a great show of blowing the dust from the mug and wiping the inside of it clean by using his shirttail. He smiled as he handed the mug to his employee.

"Sugar?"

"No, *merci.*"

"Monsieur Their Death, how large is the hypothetical diamond?"

"Very large, monsieur. Perhaps as big as a chicken egg—a European chicken egg." Husband knew a man who once bought a European hen at a market in Kikwit. She was twice as big as a village chicken, and so were her eggs. Unfortunately she did not have the sense to abandon her nest when a river of army ants invaded the village one night. The next morning there was nothing left of the hen, not even a wattle or bone.

Too late, M. Dupree tried to suppress a gasp. "What makes

you think this is a diamond, and not just a common stone? There are many stones that resemble diamonds to the untrained eye."

"There is a fire inside this one, Monsieur Dupree."

M. Dupree considered this new information in silence. "A fire?" he asked at last.

Husband nodded. He'd taken a sip of the coffee, and it was vile stuff. Was he obliged to drink the rest?

"Not a real fire, of course, but the look of one."

"Are you telling me that this hypothetical diamond has already been faceted?"

Husband's knowledge of French had just been stretched to its limit.

"Cut," M. Dupree said, drawing a pair of rough sketches on the back of an envelope. "When they come out of the ground they might look like this. Just a stone—like any other. But then the diamonds are cut into fancy shapes and polished, so that they reflect the light. Like this."

"It is not cut," Husband said, "but there are some straight sides nonetheless."

"What color is the fire?"

"All colors, but mostly blue. Yet at the same time the stone is as clear as water."

M. Dupree was taking deep breaths, exhaling through his teeth. "Monsieur Their Death, where did you find this stone?"

"I did not find it, sir."

"Of course."

"But it exists, monsieur. You have my word on that."

The postmaster smiled. "You have never lied to me—unlike some of the others. So, you want to know how to turn this fabulous diamond into cash. Isn't that so?"

"*Oui.*"

"Well, I would be happy to make inquiries on your behalf—subtle inquiries, to be sure. But you must do your part as well."

"My part?"

"We whites have a saying, Monsieur Their Death. A picture is worth a thousand words. Do you understand what I'm saying?"

Just because Husband worked outside, cropping the *puspulum* grass with a scythe and whitewashing the trunks of mango trees, did not mean his was an outside brain. "Certainly, Monsieur Dupree. You desire to see the stone so that you can accurately describe it to those whose opinions you seek."

"Exactly! So, when can I see it?"

Husband had anticipated this, and was ready with his answer. "I will show it to you the day after tomorrow, but we must meet on the bridge."

"The bridge?"

"*Oui.* It is unwise to bring a diamond across the river, where the Consortium can claim it and accuse me of stealing."

"In that case, why don't I just come to your house?"

"Monsieur, how will that look? My neighbors will be frightened to see a white man in their village. They will think there are new taxes to pay, or that one of them is to be punished. Either way, they will be curious, and we will have no privacy."

"Perhaps you are correct on that score, but why can't I see the stone today? Or even tomorrow? Why must I wait until the day *after* tomorrow?"

Husband was ready for this question as well. "Because I need the extra time to get my affairs in order—in case you double-cross me."

"*Mais non*, I would never do such a thing! I am a man of—"

"Monsieur," Husband said, interrupting a white man for the first time in his life, "you will drive across the bridge at six thirty in the morning, the day after tomorrow, as if you are going somewhere on important business, and I will be waiting in the middle. You will stop, and I will show you the diamond. But if you want to hold the stone in your hand—to feel its weight, to turn it this way or that way in the sun—you must first give me ten thousand francs as collateral."

"You cheeky bastard!"

Husband had never felt so much power in his life. Perhaps it was a delusion, but even if M. Dupree and a cadre of gendarmes appeared outside his hut tonight and tortured him into handing over the jewel, it would still have been a life-changing experience. A moment from which he could draw strength for the rest of his life.

"Monsieur Dupree, I beg you to imagine what it would be like if our situations were reversed. Would you hand over a stone of this value before you had some sort of assurance?"

"Assurance? Fine! I am *not* a thief. Is that assurance enough?"

"Monsieur, perhaps I have made my inquiry of the wrong person."

The postmaster's snort reminded Husband of the horse he had once seen a Belgian girl ride through the streets of Belle Vue. The animal was supposed to be part of a breeding program that would eventually give the *évolué*, for whom cars were still way beyond reach, a means of transportation. But the climate at Belle Vue was conducive to the tsetse flies, which seemed particularly found of horseflesh. Three of the four horses imported for the project succumbed to sleeping sickness, and the fourth was fatally mauled by a leopard.

"Monsieur Their Death, if you think that any other white in this town would be more suitable, then please, be my guest."

"Very well, monsieur." Husband set his half-finished mug of coffee on the counter and headed for the door. He had no doubt—none at all—that before the door closed behind him, M. Dupree would call him back. This was, after all, the same way Second Wife tried to manipulate him, and it wasn't going to work. As long as he had the diamond, the power was all his.

* * *

Husband felt surprisingly calm as he watched Monsieur Dupree lock up the post office and disappear in a cloud of dust. The haste with which the man moved indicated his strong interest in the diamond. Although it occurred to Husband that his employer might simply be rushing off to get the authorities, he didn't believe that deep in his soul. Husband was at peace.

This same calm feeling had permeated him the day he married Cripple. She will never bear you children, his mother, and his mother's sister wives, had warned him. If sex is what he wanted, his best friend told him, then why not just sleep with one of the dowry goats, because any one of them was more attractive than Cripple. Husband refrained from hitting his friend because of the peace that came along with Cripple, but he was no longer friends with the man. That man, by the way, had married a nubile girl in the full blush of maidenhood, but after having given him two children, the woman ran away with a white man, a crocodile hunter from South Africa.

While Dupree was away, Husband swept the dirt walk that led from the road to the post office, using a broom made from split rattan stems. Then he dug up the beginnings of a termite mound that, by the natural order of things, should not have appeared until after the rains. The termites poured out, scrabbling in all directions, but Husband kept digging until he reached the queen termite. She was as long as his index finger and as fat as his thumb. When he swallowed her whole, she tickled his throat with her legs. Any day that started off with a tasty bit of protein was bound to be a good day. Husband knew it in his soul.

CHAPTER TWELVE

Wealthy chiefs often had many wives. Wives had their own little houses and some perks that commoners did not have, but being a chief's wife was not an enviable position. When a chief died, his wives were compelled to journey with him to the spirit world. A large pit was dug for the grave. The dead chief was laid to rest in the center, and his wives (their arms and legs had been broken) were positioned around him. The wives were then buried alive.

The Nigerian slept so well that for a minute, upon waking, he thought he was back home in Lagos. When he realized where he was, he sat up and stared. The cave was much larger than he could have imagined.

Last night, after much slipping on the rocks—yes, his knee was badly skinned—he'd managed to climb high enough up the wall to reach the source of the cool, relatively dry air. By then it was dark, so that every move was by feel.

All he could remember from then was that he'd been able to stand, and that he'd moved away from the roar of the falls. He'd held out his hands in front of him, expecting to bump into a rock face with every step, or to hit his head on the ceiling, but there had been nothing to stop him. It was only when he felt dry soil beneath his feet that he'd stopped, dropping to the floor of the cave and falling instantly asleep.

Silt. That's what he'd felt. At some time—perhaps many times—in the distant past the river had risen high enough to flood the cave, leaving behind a soft deposit of light topsoil and organic matter so fine that it felt like the petals of a frangipani blossom.

The Nigerian turned toward the mouth of the cave, which was delineated by only a dark gray patch. How far did the cave go? He could barely hear the falls from where he was. Weren't caves supposed to be damp? This one was anything but. With a fire—or better yet, electricity—one could almost imagine living . . . He stopped imagining.

It was suddenly obvious that he had not been the first man to think of this.

Cripple was pretty sure she was late for work. Neither she nor anyone she knew owned a working wristwatch. A few villagers—mostly cooks to the Belgians, and successful men like Husband—owned alarm clocks, which were gifts from their employers. Everyone else, Cripple included, used the sun as a general indicator of time, along with their personal body rhythms.

In fact, Cripple was very much against the European system of telling exact time; she saw no point to it. It imposed needless stress on people, and besides, it was arbitrary. Who had a right to assign numbers to the sun's journey across the sky, and by what reckoning did the first person to do so choose six as the time when the sun appeared on the horizon, and six again when it disappeared?

Clocks and wristwatches made people hurry, and hurrying was, in general, not a healthy thing to do. If not defined by the strictures of European time, events ran their due course. Naturally. As they were meant to. A palaver, for instance, was over when either the parties came to an agreement or the village council handed down a judgment. Dances were over when the dancers collapsed from exhaustion or the drummers grew too tired to lift their hands. A child played until it cried to be picked up or the sun, having run its normal course, disappeared, signaling predators to begin prowling. Even something lowly like making mush didn't require ownership of a timepiece. One stirred the cornmeal until it began to splatter, and then stirred in manioc flour until the mixture was too stiff to stir anymore. Did the Europeans, Cripple wondered, move their bowels according to timepieces?

By the look on her employer's face, Cripple was pretty sure *that* had yet to happen today. "*Bonjour*, Cripple. Where have you been?"

"*Bonjour, mamu*. I have been, first in my village, and then on the road that leads to here."

"I assumed that. What I mean is, why are you late?"

"At which hour was I supposed to arrive?"

"You were supposed to be here at eight."

"Then let us pretend that Greenwich Mean Time is one hour off. There, you see? I am just on time."

"You know about Greenwich Mean Time?"

"Of course. I am a heathen, and quite unattractive, but I am not stupid."

"You learned this from your classes at the Catholic mission school? I am impressed."

"No, *mamu*, I have never been to school."

"But you said—I'm sure I heard you say—that you studied at their school."

"Mamu Ugly Eyes, only boys are allowed in that school. I learned this while sitting outside on the grass. Believe me, it is more comfortable that way; the grass is softer than the benches, and the air is cool when the breeze blows."

"Still, it is a pity you have not gone to school."

"Why?"

"Because then you could have become a teacher, or a nurse. You could be doing something more interesting than working for me."

Cripple laughed till her sides hurt. She stopped only because the look on her employer's face—if one could accurately read such a pale face—told her that the joke had not been intentional.

"Cripple. In my country it is rude to laugh at another like that."

"But *mamu*, I thought you were only joking. Forgive me. I did not mean to offend."

"Joke? What could I possibly have been joking about?"

"A nurse, *mamu*. Or a teacher. That is men's work."

"Only men?"

"Yes. Is it not that way where you come from?"

"It is not. In fact, it's almost the opposite."

"Yours is a strange country, Mamu Ugly Eyes. Tell me more."

Much to Cripple's irritation, before the *mamu* could share more bizarre facts from the land beyond the ocean, the idiot Protruding Navel strolled into the kitchen with all the arrogance of a rooster. When he saw Cripple, his beady eyes narrowed to slits, and he made a clucking sound of derision by thrusting his tongue behind his lower teeth.

"*Mamu*," he said, "it is not wise to have a witch doctor's wife in the kitchen. The evil spirits she brings with her will curdle the milk and rot the eggs. And besides, the other whites will talk, accusing you of setting a bad precedent, perhaps even forcing them to admit heathens into their houses. Does the *mamu* not wish to make friends in the city? If that is the case, then I shall be happy to tell this village woman to wait for you by the woodshed."

The young—and woefully inexperienced—white woman actually seemed to consider this absurd suggestion. She looked from Protruding Navel to Cripple, and back again. Cripple, who'd endured enough sorrow in her lifetime to equal the lives of three

Protruding Navels, was not going to be humiliated again without a fight.

"Mamu Ugly Eyes," she said, pausing to choose her words carefully, "will not all milk sour, and all eggs rot, if they are not consumed in a timely fashion? But if, by chance, they spoil faster in this house than is normal, it might well be because of their proximity to a man who beats his wife until her eyes are swollen shut, and whose son limps like I do, yet who was not born that way."

"This one lies!"

"*Nasha*. Ask anyone in the village, *mamu*."

Cripple, whose only experience with white women was seeing a Belgian nun pass within fifty meters of her at the Catholic school, was fascinated by the *mamu*'s reaction to stress. The young American's face turned red, like the blush on a ripening mango, and her eyes welled with tears. Then the lips began to quiver. Cripple marveled at a society that allowed its women to exhibit so much vulnerability. Didn't they know that action begat experience which, in turn, begat action? America must be a very unhappy place.

"I have heard enough from both of you," the missionary finally said. "Protruding Navel, please go sweep the verandah while I show Cripple how to help with some chores."

"No, *mamu*, I will not go. Not until this woman apologizes for the insults she has heaped on me."

Cripple's heart pounded. "I would sooner apologize to the mamba that killed my mother as she gathered mushrooms after the rain."

"Then I will stay here."

"Go!" the American barked.

"*Mamu*," the horrible man said, "I can no longer work for you."

Mamu Ugly Eyes gasped. "You can't quit! If you quit, Mamu Singleton will be very unhappy with me."

"That is not my problem."

The scene that was unfolding before her eyes horrified Cripple, but she found herself unable—or at least unwilling—to come to the young missionary's rescue. Why should she? She was perfectly willing to coexist with a wife beater, and a child beater, just as long as she did not have to humble herself to such a man. But to apologize for having merely stated the truth? That would happen only when the Kasai River ran dry, which, by the roar of the falls outside, was going to be never.

"Very well, Protruding Navel, you may quit. I'm sure Cripple will appreciate getting your salary as well as hers."

What a foolish thing for the *mamu* to say. Did she not understand the mind of a man?

"Mamu Ugly Eyes," the housekeeper said, "you cannot fire me. I was hired by Mamu Singleton. Only she can fire me upon her return—but she will not, for she respects my work. In the meantime, there is much I can teach you about running a guesthouse."

"So you agree to stay?"

"Of course, *mamu*; that was always my intent. Now please excuse me while I sweep the verandah, or have you not noticed that it is dirty?"

Cripple watched him go with mixed feelings.

CHAPTER THIRTEEN

Some tribes welcomed the birth of twins, but not the Bashilele. For them it was a great tragedy. Since single births were the norm, it was believed that an evil spirit had been born along with the baby. As evil spirits are tricky, it was impossible to figure out which was the real baby, and which was the spirit. In order to punish the evil spirit and discourage it from returning at a later date, both infants had to be tortured and ultimately destroyed. The common practice was to stuff hot chili peppers up the infants' noses and bury them alive in an ant-hill. This sounds very cruel to us, but for the Bashilele it was a matter of survival.

Amanda's pulse was still racing when Captain Jardin walked into the kitchen. Walked right in from the dining room, no less, like he owned the place. Of course she was glad to see him, but shouldn't he have knocked first? She must look a fright.

"Is everything okay, Amanda?"

"What? Yes, everything is fine. Why do you ask?"

"I thought I heard loud voices."

"It was only me giving instructions to my housekeeper."

"Be firm, yes? From what I hear, Protruding Navel can be very difficult to manage."

"I have come to that conclusion as well." She turned to introduce Cripple to the captain, but her new assistant had disappeared. Oh well. It would probably have been improper anyway. Although she certainly would have introduced her parents' maid in Rock Hill.

Pierre gently touched her forehead. "How is that bruise healing?"

"It's fine." But why did he bother to ask now? For all he really cared, she could have died two days ago.

"Amanda, may we sit down?" He patted a brown leather briefcase that reminded her of scuffed shoes.

"By all means. Would you like some tea? Coffee?"

"No, thank you. Perhaps another time—soon."

"Yes, soon," she said, but couldn't quite keep the sarcasm out of her voice.

He followed her into the living room and they both sat, as far away from each other as possible without moving the furniture.

"I've come on official police business," he said, looking her straight in the eye.

"Police business? I haven't broken any laws, have I?" It was a stupid thing to say, a knee jerk reaction that could ruin everything.

He chuckled. "His Majesty's Colonial Government has no laws against beauty, I assure you."

"Then what is it?"

"It's about the plane crash."

"Oh?"

"There were twelve passengers on your plane when it left Leopoldville, but only eleven could be accounted for following the explosion. I've conducted a thorough search of the area around the plane, but I can find no trace of human remains. I was hoping you could help me."

"*Me?* I can't identify a wishbone once it's been broken."

Pierre laughed as he pulled a stack of papers out of the briefcase. "It seems that our missing passenger is a Nigerian who sometimes goes by the name of Daniel Ogunde. He is listed as being two meters and—well, approximately seven feet tall. Do you recall seeing him?"

Amanda nodded. "I couldn't believe how tall he was. And I loved his orange robes. I remember he sat several rows behind me, and then—although I really can't remember the actual crash, I do remember that it was this man who pulled me from the plane."

He stared at his papers. "I hadn't thought of that."

"What?"

"The other passengers gave me detailed descriptions of their last minutes on the plane, and how they got off. Madame So-and-So says that Monsieur What-Is-His-Name pushed her from behind, and so forth. But no one has mentioned helping you."

"That's so rude!"

"Forgive me, Amanda, but it was not my intention to insult you—"

"And I mean that it was rude of the others to just leave me there, so that I could get blown to smithereens."

"Smith Ereens?"

"Tiny pieces. Pierre, I thought for sure I told you this before—that a man pulled me from the plane."

"Yes, but somehow you neglected to tell me that he was seven feet tall."

Amanda laughed softly. "Details, details. I didn't realize his height was so important. Or his skin color, either."

"Perhaps they are not. But Amanda, life in the Congo can be very complicated." He stuffed the papers back into the briefcase, and muttering some excuse in rapid French, made a beeline for the door.

It was a beautiful August morning: not too hazy, and just cool enough to remind one that south of the equator the seasons are reversed, and this is what passed for winter. Outside the OP's window, small black-and-white birds, with tails four or five times the length of their bodies, flew in jerky motions across the lawn in search of food. The OP loved those birds, although he didn't know what to call them. They reminded him of the adage, You can catch a bird by putting salt on its tail. Someday, when he had time to breathe, he'd ask his sister in Brussels to buy him a book on African birds. Someday, if he really had time, he might even chase one of those birds with a saltshaker.

The loud rap of knuckles on the door may as well have been on his head. What the hell was Flanders thinking? If he knew it wouldn't get him in trouble, he'd kick that kid's butt out the door and chase after him with a saltshaker—maybe right over the edge of the waterfalls.

"What is it?"

"Sir, there is a gentleman here to see you."

"An official?"

"No, sir."

"Then tell him to get lost."

"Sir, he says it's urgent."

Only then did the OP tear his gaze from the window. *Merde.* It was only the whiny postmaster. The fellow was always complaining about something. Just last week he'd come whimpering that he needed funds for another employee, because his workload was getting to be too heavy. It's not like the guy had to actually deliver any mail. All he had to do was stick a few letters into numbered slots, one for each of the eighty-three Belgian households, plus less than a dozen miscellaneous holders of post office boxes. The latter included the Nunez family, the American guesthouse, the Catholic mission, and some of the *évolué*, who seldom, if ever, got any mail.

"Yes, Monsieur Dupree?" The OP could feel his jaw clench.

"I need to speak to you alone, sir."

"We are alone."

"With the door closed, sir."

What the hell did the guy want, to jump his bones? He'd always felt there was something different about Dupree, something he couldn't quite pin down. Of course he thought that about any man who came to the Congo without a wife and neglected to get a mistress. Tit for tit, these African women were far better-looking than the pasty women back home. Perhaps not as beautiful as Madame OP had been in the beginning, but her looks had gone to hell ever since she got him to walk down the aisle in Liege. That didn't really matter though, because the bitch had stopped sleeping with him three years ago, upon discovering his penchant for the local beauties. The incident on the savanna really had nothing to do with it.

"Close the damn door, Flanders."

"*Oui, monsieur.*"

The second it closed the OP slapped his desk with an open palm. "Don't just stand there, Monsieur Dupree. Tell me what you need to say."

"Sir, it's about a diamond."

"This whole operation is about a diamond—hundreds of them. Be more specific."

"Well, sir—uh—does the Consortium own all the diamonds in the Congo?"

"What kind of silly question is that?"

"So, it doesn't. Am I right, sir?"

"You are quite right. But what the Consortium doesn't own, Belgium owns. And if Belgium wishes to mine diamonds, then they have to go through the Consortium."

That shut the postmaster up. But not long enough.

"Monsieur OP, suppose an exceptionally large and beautiful stone—of gem quality—was found on crown land. What would become of it?"

"Is this a riddle? Who put you up to this?"

"Monsieur, it is not a riddle."

"Then it's nonsense. Now please, have Flanders see you out. And don't return unless I send for you."

"But sir, there is such a stone."

The OP felt a twinge of excitement. This business, more than most, was not unlike a night in a gambling parlor. With luck you broke even, some extravagant sallies aside. With exceptional luck—well, there was always that slim chance that someday you'd be the one who struck it big. Ultimately it would be the Consortium that scored, but it would be under your watch. If you played your cards right to the end, that could mean a weekend chalet in the Ardennes, or a town house in Brussels, complete with a mistress. At the very least he could dump that wrinkled old crone of a wife—ah, that was a terrible thing to think. But it was true. Heilewid had let herself go since the incident, and in more ways than one. She'd once been a scintillating companion, a gracious and clever hostess, but now she did nothing but lie around the company pool, smoking Camel cigarettes and drinking Johnny Walker, while feeling sorry for herself. Yes, she had ample reason to feel sad, but enough was enough. Wasn't it? Hadn't he been patient long enough? What man . . .

"Monsieur, did you hear me?"

"Of course! Monsieur Dupree, is it you who discovered this diamond?"

"No."

"Then who?"

"I'm not at liberty to say."

"*Merde!* You work for the Consortium, the diamond belongs to either the Consortium or the crown, which means whoever has it is a thief, and anyone protecting this thief is a criminal as well."

The postmaster was shivering like a malaria patient. This

pleased the OP immensely. He was not really a mean person—ask anybody—but he was only human. If he didn't enjoy the fringe benefits of power, then he'd lack the motivation to keep his job, and then someone who really was mean would take his place. Then what would happen to cockroaches like Dupree?

"Monsieur OP," the cockroach said, "it was only a theoretical question. I am sorry to have wasted your time."

"*Au contraire*, Monsieur Dupree. You said there really was such a stone. If you won't tell me who your contact is, at least tell me more about the stone."

"*Oui, monsieur.* It is perhaps eighty carats in size—this is just a guess, monsieur—with a full color spectrum, but leaning towards blue. Ah yes, and it is as clear as water."

"But that's impossible! We've never had a gem-quality diamond exceed five carats, even in an uncut state. And that happened only once. A diamond like the one you describe might end up being fifty carats or more. It would be practically priceless."

"Those are my thoughts as well, monsieur."

Forget a chalet in the Ardennes, and screw the mistress in Brussels. A find such as this could mean a yacht, or a villa in the Italian lake country. And that is only if he went through the Consortium. For someone with his experience, and contacts in the cutting industry back in Antwerp—well, there would be risks. As it stood, the Consortium had to constantly watch its back, due to fierce resistance to its very existence by the South-African-dominated cartel. But the bigger the prize, the greater the risk. That's how it had always been since the dawn of time. No matter how this played itself out, the OP was certain that it would get him out of the Congo, and away from that mummified woman he'd become embarrassed to call his wife.

"Monsieur Dupree, what were the circumstances under which you saw this stone? In the daylight? By lantern light? What?"

"*Monsieur*, I have not seen it."

"What the hell? But you—"

"Monsieur, I have an appointment to see it."

"When?"

The postmaster was more devious than the OP had expected. He stood there silently, staring at his shoes as if they were the most interesting thing on the face of the planet. Well, at least he wasn't entirely stupid.

"Very well, keep that information to yourself. But as soon as you've seen the stone, report back to me. *If*—and I think it's a huge if—this turns out to be true, you, my friend will be rewarded handsomely."

"Monsieur OP, my grandfather had no teeth and four chins, yet my grandmother thought he was handsome—if you get my meaning, monsieur."

The OP laughed. "Don't worry. The reward will be based on a percentage of the stone's retail value. Say, one half of one percent?"

"Oui, monsieur. Merci, monsieur."

The man darted for the door like a frightened rabbit. "One more thing, Monsieur Dupree. How much do you know about diamonds? Have you ever even seen one close up? An uncut stone, that is."

"Monsieur OP, before I came to Africa, I worked for six years as a cutter in Antwerp. It's in my file, sir."

Now *that* was interesting. "But you don't wear glasses, Monsieur Dupree."

"Correct, Monsieur OP. When my vision began to be compromised, as happens to most cutters, I asked for a transfer to another branch of the business. The only opening was here. I could hardly pass it up, could I, monsieur? It being Africa—every young man's dream."

"Right. What you're saying though, is that you would know a diamond if you saw one. And that you could estimate its cut and weight."

"*Oui, monsieur.* As well as its color and clarity. These are all things one learns in cutting school."

"*Bien.*" The OP stood. He would personally escort the postmaster to the front door. When he swung open the door to his office, he almost gave young Flanders a broken nose.

"What the hell are you doing, Flanders?" he roared.

"*Rien*, Monsieur OP. Nothing. Just putting these files back into the cabinet by the door."

The boy sounded scared enough to be innocent. Or he could just be crafty. If he really was a spy, implanted by the Brussels brass, you can be sure he'd been well trained.

"From now on, Flanders, when I have a visitor, you remain at your desk. Is that clear?"

"Yes, monsieur!"

The OP stood on the verandah, watching the postmaster drive away. It was indeed a beautiful day. What the heck, maybe he really would chase after one of those long-tailed birds with a salt-shaker, or better yet, he'd close up the office and join his wife at the pool. After all, her condition wasn't really her fault, was it?

His name was Wilhelm Van Derhoef, not Flanders, although he was indeed from Flanders. But that puffed-up, pigeon-chested runt could call him any name he wanted. In fact, the more names the better. It was all going into the special report the CEO had asked him to write.

It wasn't Wilhelm's idea to volunteer for the position of secretary when it opened up. He had no desire to live in the Congo. The previous secretary died of yellow fever. In fact, one out of four whites never made it back out of that country alive. But the young Wilhelm was promised a promotion to junior management if he'd agree to a three-year stint. In this postwar economy, who could pass that up?

It seems that the board was not thrilled with the OP's performance. The Belle Vue operation had been carefully sited by a team of skilled geologists, yet the profits from the mine were somewhat less than had been predicted. Now, with the prospect of an independent Congo on the horizon—and nationalization invariably following independence—the mine needed to be producing a good deal more than the initial prediction.

Yes, it was possible that there were mitigating circumstances responsible for the low profit margin, factors that were out of the OP's control. *That*, precisely, was why Wilhelm had been dispatched to the Congo.

Wilhelm Van Derhoef had arrived with an open mind, but he had immediately taken a dislike to the arrogant OP. Walloons were like that, weren't they? Just like the French in that regard. And that's exactly what they were when you came down to it—French. The political union of Walloons and Flemings that constituted the modern state of Belgium was no more a natural nation than was the amalgamation of almost two hundred ethnic groups that comprised the Belgian Congo.

Wilhelm—no, from now on he would proudly claim the name "Flanders"—slipped a small disk from the pocket of his trousers. It was a cheap mirror, purchased in the native market. One side was glass; the other side bore a portrait of Belgium's King Baudouin I. How ironic was that? When an African held up a mirror to see his face, what others saw was the visage of their pasty monarch who was living in untold luxury on another continent.

Flanders glanced around the outer office, to make sure no one was watching, before picking the pimple that was on his neck. The pustule popped easily, causing him to smile. That's exactly how the OP's career was going to end.

CHAPTER FOURTEEN

The Nile crocodile (*Crocodylus niloticus*) is found throughout most of Africa, not including the Sahara. They can grow up to twenty feet long and weigh over a thousand pounds. They feed on whatever fish or animals they can catch, including man. They reproduce by laying eggs in a nest near water. When it is time for the eggs to hatch, the parents assist by cracking the eggs open and carrying the babies to the water's edge.

The postmaster couldn't wait to tell his lover about the morning's events. Yes, it was broad daylight, and yes, it was a terrible risk, but it might also turn out to be the opportunity of a lifetime. News like this demanded to be shared.

Rich, rich, rich—they were going to be rich. And screw that offer of a reward. Not that he'd refuse it, but he didn't think, not for a second, that the OP would follow through with it. Screw the reward because there was enough money to be made by selling the stone directly. With his contacts, he was just the man to do it.

The idea had popped into his head as Their Death was still talking. Ideas like that weren't manufactured; they were slipped down from the cosmos, gifts from those who had passed on ahead. The stone the yardman had described, even with subtracting a chunk due to exaggeration, would be well over a hundred carats. Maybe as much as two hundred. And a diamond that size—not that Dupree had a lot of experience with stones of quite that caliber—always presented several possibilities to the cutter.

That is to say, only the Brits, with their shamefully ostentatious royal regalia, and a few Middle Eastern potentates had any use for a diamond that exceeded thirty or forty carats. Therefore, the practice was to cut exceptionally large diamonds into more saleable sizes, generally keeping them in the five-to-ten-carat range. That way, the market was much broader, and in the end one actually made more money, as the sum of the parts was greater than the whole.

Dupree would be happy to "make change" for a fifty-carat diamond. All he needed was to be in possession of the yardman's stone for one evening. The next morning he could present the OP with a fabulous diamond of approximately eighty carats, while he pocketed a handful of "chips" that he would later sell for millions of dollars.

"Why not just pocket the entire diamond?" he could hear his lover ask. "Why tell the OP anything?" Ah, but in the answer lay the genius of his plan.

He'd remind his lover that anyone leaving Kasai Province was rigorously searched for diamonds. There were ways to get around this, but they weren't comfortable, and could backfire—you should pardon the pun. Yet, as the man responsible for handing the OP a priceless gem, what point would there be in searching him? None, of course; a smuggler would never have parted with a jewel like that. *Au contraire*, the OP himself would probably see Dupree off on the plane, possibly even with an African band playing on the runway. With all that racket, the dirt strip might finally be clear of pigs, which were an anathema to bush pilots everywhere in the tropics.

And since no one suspected that they were lovers, the object of Dupree's affection could also be on the plane. Sure, the post-master's sweetheart would have to be strip-searched—or maybe not. Maybe everyone would get a free pass that day. Only time would tell.

Madame OP had a first name—Heilewid—but pity the person who dared get chummy enough to call her anything but Madame OP. Even the three women at Belle Vue she might have called friends knew better than that. One was either in awe of Madame OP or afraid of her, but never on an equal footing.

That fine dry-season morning, as her husband contemplated chasing long-tailed birds with saltshakers, Madame OP plopped her sun-ravaged body into the deck chair that was hers alone, if only by unwritten decree. She snapped her withered fingers, and although it was barely past ten, a few minutes later a tall glass of vodka mixed with guava juice appeared on the glass-top table next to her. It wasn't magic, of course, although it may have looked like that to any observers, ones who may have glanced away for the few seconds it took the black waiter to set the drink down and disappear.

Yes, it might appear that the OP's wife was a drunk who wasted her life lying about a pool and turning her body almost as dark as the Africans whom she presumably deplored. The previous OP's wife had at least made a pretense of visiting the workers' village, spending several generous minutes distributing pamphlets, albeit in Flemish, on the benefits of feeding babies formula instead of breast milk. Well, tough titties, said the kitty. She wasn't that OP's wife and she'd never be like her. Didn't want to be like her, in fact. At any rate, there wasn't anyone in Belle Vue, black or white, who had the right to judge her, not after what had happened that awful day.

She'd been in the Congo almost two years when her identical twin sister, Geete, and her husband arrived for a visit. It was the longest the sisters had ever been apart in their forty-plus years on the planet. One of the many activities planned for the holiday was to take Geete and her husband to witness the annual burning of the savanna over in Bashilele territory.

Both Geete and her husband, Günter, had taken to the idea at once. "It sounds so exciting," Geete had said. "Can I bring my camera? If I get a really good picture I'm going to enter it in the summer art festival."

Heilewid nodded in her deck chair, as the memory of that day became her reality for the umpteenth time. "Of course, bring your camera."

Günter's eyes shone. "And guns too, yes?"

"I'm afraid not," the OP told his brother-in-law. "Bows and arrows only. You see, the Bashilele light this vast circle of fire—maybe five kilometers across—and force it to burn inward. As it burns, any animals that get trapped are forced to escape through the flames. Either that, or die trying. You wouldn't believe what they manage to catch that way: antelope, warthogs, porcupines, hyenas—even leopards. But if you were to shoot, there is too much danger of hitting one of the hunters on the other side of the circle."

"Sometimes even people get trapped inside the circle of flames," Heilewid said. "Last year it was a little boy. He couldn't have been more than five years old."

Geete grimaced. "A boy? What was he doing there?"

"The women and children have a part in this hunt as well. Their job is to swat down the giant grasshoppers that the flames stir up. They use pads woven from palm fronds and mounted on long poles. It's quite something to see them at work."

"But what on earth do they want with giant grasshoppers?"

"I bet I know," Günter said. "They eat them, right?"

"Ugh, Günter!"

"He's right," the OP said. "For the natives it's just another source of protein. Besides, it's all a matter of culture, isn't it? We eat cows and pigs, but not cats and dogs."

Geete shook her head adamantly. "That's different; those are companion animals. Anyway, there isn't enough money in the world to get me to eat a grasshopper."

Günter's eyes twinkled. "What about a cruise to America?"

"You're serious?"

"Absolutely. But you have to eat an entire grasshopper."

"Except for the wings," Heilewid said. "Nobody eats the wings.

"Deal!"

They were all still in high spirits when they arrived at their prearranged viewing site. But almost immediately Geete spotted a tall anthill poking above the dry elephant grass. It appeared to be less than a hundred meters away.

"Let's climb up," she said. "We'll get a much better view."

"Nothing doing," the OP said. "This site's been cleared by the Bashilele headman. It's in the safe zone."

"Yes, but you already see which way the fire is headed. That anthill is every bit as safe."

"We don't know that for sure," Heilewid whispered. She should have shouted. She should have leaped on her sister and pinned her to the ground, while the men tied her up with the winch chain they always carried in their vehicle.

"Look, I'm a grown woman; I can do what I want. And yes, I may be adventurous, but I'm not stupid. From up there, on that anthill, I'll be able to see if the fire changes direction—in fact, long before you do. Who knows, I might save *your* lives."

"Then I'm sending our tracker with you," the OP said.

"Watch out for mambas," Geete said. It was the last thing she ever said to her sister—at least while she was alive.

Their charred bodies were found two days later, by which time the ashes that covered the savanna had cooled enough to permit recovery. By then a hungry hyena was defending the human remains from a pack of jackals. The OP shot and killed the hyena and two of the jackals. Geete was subsequently buried in the small white cemetery on the village side of the river, and the tracker's body was returned to his people.

At least that's what Heilewid was led to believe. The awful truth was that neither the OP nor the Consortium doctor could definitively identify the remains. It was quite possible that the tracker's people buried Geete, and a black man was buried in the white cemetery. But ashes to ashes, what did it really matter?

At any rate, from then on Heilewid loathed: she loathed her husband, she loathed Geete's husband, she loathed Africa, she loathed the Africans, she loathed the animals, and most of all she loathed herself. As a veteran fire watcher, she had known that the hunts were dangerous, but she had given in to Geete's pleas to get a better view.

They say that losing a twin is like losing half of yourself. Surely, then, losing an identical twin was like losing all of yourself. But not so. Enough of you remained to feel pain, so that when you weren't hating, you were hurting. It was an unbearable situation in which to be. If one chose to drink oneself into a stupor, it was nobody's business. Nobody's business at all.

Branca couldn't believe the American's audacity. She was both appalled and delighted. To not just refuse an invitation, but to turn around and issue one of her own—now there was a woman she might actually like. And although she would miss out on showing off at the club, she would finally get to see the inside of the guesthouse.

Situated as it was, above the falls on the Belle Vue side of the river, the Nunez villa was directly opposite the missionary facility.

Just yesterday she'd seen the American woman pick a flower and tear off the petals one by one and let them flutter on the breeze generated by the mighty torrent of water. Branca had been able to identify the flower as a zinnia, thanks to the high-powered binoculars she kept on the patio at all times during the dry season. One never knew when the glasses would come in handy. Once Branca had witnessed a fisherman in a dugout canoe plunge over the edge, both craft and occupant disappearing forever.

At night the lighted rooms of the guesthouse offered even more entertainment. Under the mistaken idea that no one could see into the rooms facing the falls, the American couple who'd built it had seen no need to spend money on shutters and draperies. What they hadn't counted on was the fact that a powerful pair of binoculars could deliver startlingly detailed glimpses of naked missionaries as they prepared for bed.

At last Branca was going to get to see the house close up. As far as she knew, this was a privilege that none of the Belgian wives could claim, with the possible exception of the OP's wife. It was possible that, before the fire incident, which preceded Branca's arrival in town, the OP and his wife had been invited there for a meal. But that invitation, had it even been issued, would have been out of obligation. It scarcely counted. Tomorrow afternoon . . . Branca adjusted the focus with her right index finger.

What the hell? There was a short African woman hobbling about in the kitchen, following the American around like a puppy. Leaning against a wall, his lips pursed in obvious disdain, was that mean-tempered housekeeper the Singletons had hired years ago. Belly-Button Hernia. Was that his real name? At any rate, Branca's housekeeper called him that, and said that because of his foul disposition, he had many enemies in the village. At the moment he looked like he wanted to scoop up the crippled woman and throw her over the falls. Well, well, this was certainly something to investigate when she went over for tea. Finally, life in Belle Vue was beginning to get interesting—although Branca would pack her bags and head back to Portugal in a heartbeat, if her ship came in.

She chuckled hoarsely as she lit another cigarette. With her luck the ship would come sailing up the Kasai River and plunge over the falls before delivering its precious cargo. But ship or no ship, things were looking up.

CHAPTER FIFTEEN

The Belgian Congo was home to two elephant species: the commonly known large savanna elephant (*Loxodonta Africana*) and the pygmy forest elephant (*Loxodonta cyclotis*). Until recently these were classified as subspecies, but DNA studies have shown them to be quite distinct from each other. Traditionally, elephants were hunted for their meat, as well as for ivory.

Amanda felt like she'd waited her entire life for this moment. She'd wanted to see Africa ever since she was eight years old, when a missionary had described her experiences to Amanda's Sunday-school class. To be truthful, she hadn't ever really wanted to be a missionary herself—maybe an adventuress—but after the accident she'd set her own desires. The middle of the Belgian Congo was where God wanted her to be; it was the hardest life she could imagine.

Except that it wasn't so hard after all. She'd decided to take a walk before breakfast to experience the real Africa, and was having a wonderful time. The air was crisp and clean, the scenery stunning, and the people—the vast majority of them—couldn't be any friendlier.

There was a steady stream of villagers, mostly men, headed

toward the Belgian side of the river. They greeted Amanda with cheery *bonjour*s, until she answered in Tshiluba. Then, more often than not they laughed before greeting her in kind. A very few refused to make eye contact, and only one was openly hostile.

As she neared the village, children seemed to pop out of nowhere. They seemed as surprised as she. Some gasped, some cried, others laughed, but invariably they ran away or simply disappeared again. Then one small boy, naked except for a string of tiny blue beads around his waist, stood his ground.

"*Muoyo webe*," Amanda said softly.

The child stared up at her, his brown eyes wide but serious. After a few seconds, he removed a wet finger from his mouth, tottered over to Amanda, and touched her arm. Amanda smiled and squatted. This time the child touched her hair. Then he grinned.

Amanda didn't see it happen; the children swarmed around her, almost knocking her on her backside. They touched her arms, felt her clothing, tugged at her hair, all the while jabbering a blue streak. Although they spoke a variety of languages, Amanda caught words like "ugly" and "ghost woman." One precocious girl demanded to know if the missionary was white all over—even "down there?"

"*Eyo*," Amanda said, as she struggled to her feet.

The children gasped in astonishment, and then burst into giggles and fits of whispering. The precocious girl was pushed at Amanda.

"They want me to ask how many children you have."

"I have no children."

"Surely you must, *mamu*. Because you are already an old woman."

"I am not an old woman; I am only twenty-three." Then Amanda remembered that for many Africans life was so tenuous that chronological age was simply not important. In fact, it was probable that none of the children surrounding her even knew their own ages, much less had a basis for comparison.

"Ask her," another girl said, "how many children her sister wives have."

Amanda turned and smiled. "Ask me yourself."

"But I do not speak your language, *mamu*," the dear child said, completely without guile.

"Yes, but I am speaking to you in *your* language."

The children murmured amongst themselves as they took this bit of information under consideration. Amanda surmised she was perhaps the first white woman they had ever talked with, and since it was well known that the Belgians did not bother to learn local languages, it would seem logical to these children that she didn't either.

"*Mamu*," a boy said, tugging on her sleeve, "please say something else in our language."

"Very well. The river below is very loud."

"No, *mamu*, it is not the river that is loud; it is the waterfalls."

"*Toh*, she is right," a taller, and presumably older, boy said. "The river is still the river when it falls over the rocks."

The girl who'd asked the very personal question grabbed Amanda's left hand. "Truly, it is so."

Another girl grabbed her right hand. "Truly, truly. What is your name, *mamu*?"

"Her name is Ugly Eyes," the older boy said.

Amanda stiffened. "Why do you say that?"

"Because it is your name, *mamu*. There is much talk of you in the village. But these girls"—he spat to the side, narrowly missing another child—"are hardly more than babies. They know nothing."

"Aiyee," the girl on her right cried. "*Mamu*, will you let him speak like this about us?"

"Boys can be very mean," the girl on left said, and began to pull on Amanda. "*Mamu*, will you come to my house? I want to show you to my mother. She has never seen a white woman close up."

The little girl who'd initially raised the language issue pushed her way to the front of the pack. "But Mamu Ugly Eyes, we still do not know if you speak our language."

Amanda laughed inside. Never had she felt happier.

Cripple was a keen observer, which made her an apt student. Nonetheless, the American followed some strange customs, the rational for which eluded her. Second Wife either carried the family's water supply up from the river or fetched it from the village's one communal tap. No one ever questioned its drinkability. Mamu Ugly Eyes, on the other hand, insisted that her water (she had her very own tap!) be boiled for twenty minutes before being strained through a white cloth. It was then cooled in a machine that produced air colder than even the coldest dry-season morning, which invariably came in July. Although it had another name, Cripple decided to henceforth refer to this machine as "July Morning."

July Morning also produced "ice," which Cripple recognized as a cousin to hail. Ice was put into drinking containers and then the cooled water poured over it. The result was a liquid so cold it stung the tongue and set one's teeth on edge. What was the point of such a cruel ritual?

"Cripple," Mamu Ugly Eyes said, "what's wrong with the water?"

"Nothing, *mamu*."

"Then why aren't you drinking it? You said you were thirsty."

"Yes, *mamu*." From having spent years living with Second Wife, who could be very critical, Cripple knew the value of dissembling. "*Mamu*, today you wear a different dress. Is it true, as

I have heard, that white women own enough dresses to wear a different one each day of the week?"

"Yes, I think so."

"Is it also true, as I have heard, that you do not bathe?"

The young white woman had a pleasant laugh. "What? Of course we bathe."

"But *mamu*, then why so many dresses—unless it is to cover the stench."

"We stink?"

"Not too bad, *mamu*, I assure you. No worse than a wet dog."

The stranger laughed even harder. "But a wet dog stinks!"

"Perhaps, but not to another wet dog. So you see, *mamu*, it is possible you may still be able to find a man willing to marry you. But of course he would have to be white."

"Cripple, I refuse to be offended by your words because I know you mean no harm. But for your information, most white people—at least we Americans—bathe every week."

"Perhaps it is unwise for me to disagree, Mamu Ugly Eyes, but I do not think this is the case."

"What? How can you possibly say that?"

"Because there are many of your kind living in Belle Vue, and not once have we seen a white person naked at the river's edge. As a result there is much debate about a certain matter. It would please me, *mamu*, if I could be the one to inform the others of the truth."

"What matter? What truth?"

"Does the color of your skin extend beneath your clothing?"

"*What?*"

"Are you white all over, *mamu*?"

"Of course!"

"Even the men?"

The *mamu* laughed now. "Yes. Although I have never seen a naked man—of any color—I assure you. But I am positive that everything about them is white."

Cripple shook her head in wonder. "What a strange sight it must be to see a white *lubolo* on a man. There will be many people who do not believe me."

The ugly eyes sparkled, rendering them almost attractive to behold. "I'm glad to be of service, Cripple."

"But *mamu*, if we do not see you bathe, then when do you? In the dark of the night?"

"No, Cripple. You do not see us bathe because we do so inside our houses."

"Truly?"

"Truly, truly," the white *mamu* said. "Come, I will show you."

Cripple followed her employee into a little room she had not seen. It was a crowded space with bizarre furnishings. Cripple recognized the sink, for she had seen a similar device in the kitchen.

"What is that?" she asked, pointing to a large white object that she thought might be a chair of some sort.

"We call that a toilet. One sits upon it to do their—well, I am not sure of the Tshiluba words for what one does."

Cripple thought hard, but for the life of her couldn't come up with a reason to sit on such an uncomfortable-looking piece of furniture. "Is it a white custom?" she asked.

"Not just for whites!" The *mamu*'s ugly eyes were sparkling with mirth. "It is where one makes—uh, water. And the other thing."

Cripple felt a wave of nausea, for at last she understood. "You save *that*?"

"No, no!" The *mamu* was laughing so hard she could barely speak. "It goes into a large hole. Deep into the ground."

Cripple shook her head. It never ceased to amaze her how people with such strange, and often backward, customs had been able to subjugate her people—and not just her people, but almost two hundred other tribes. It must be the guns they brought with them. Machetes and bows and arrows were no match for guns, which could fire their ammunition a long, long way. Yes, it was the guns, coupled with deceit. One could not fully trust a white person—not fully. Not ever.

"But there," Mamu Ugly Eyes said, pointing to a giant white cooking pot, "is where we bathe."

"Who carries the water, Mamu? Is that to be my job?"

"No, it is no one's job. For there is a faucet here too, similar to the one in the kitchen. We fill this—uh, I shall call it a pot—with water, and then we sit in it and wash with soap. That is how we bathe."

"Forgive me, *mamu*, but you sit in your own filth?"

"Yes, but—come along, Cripple. I will show you where I sleep. Perhaps you will approve of that."

But when Cripple saw the bed, she did not approve. "Who sleeps with you, *mamu*?"

"What sort of question is that? I am a Christian. Until I am married, I will sleep alone."

"Then there is much wasted space, *mamu*. You will get very lonely. And with so much emptiness, it will be quite tempting for snakes and scorpions to join you. Then you will roll over—and well, let us hope you are not stung."

"Cripple!"

"Yes, *mamu*?"

"Do you always speak so directly?"

Cripple was about to tell the white woman what was really on her mind, when she sensed the presence of another. She turned just in time to see the sneer before it disappeared from Protruding Navel's face.

Protruding Navel was the second son of a Lulua chief. His birth name was He Who Grabs, because he was born with the grip of an infant baboon. The midwife had to pinch him in order to pry open his tiny hand, which had curled around her finger. His name was changed to Protruding Navel for obvious reasons, when he developed a serious infection in an already herniated navel. Fortunately, there was a Protestant mission nearby with an American doctor who was not only able to get the infection under control, but also to diminish the appearance of the infant's navel. Somewhat.

Grateful for his son's life, the chief returned the doctor's kindness by allowing the male children of his village to attend the mission school. Protruding Navel proved to be an excellent student, capable of becoming a civilized person, an *évolué*, if the right circumstances presented themselves—which they did in the persons of Muambi and Mamu Singleton.

But for Protruding Navel, being a housekeeper was not the end of the road. Someday he would realize his dream of moving to the capital city of Leopoldville, where he would earn a degree from Louvanium University. He would become a doctor, of course, so that he could help others, just as he had been helped. But he would also be rich, and maybe someday he would even have his own housekeeper.

There was just one glitch; Protruding Navel was a member of the Lulua tribe, not the Baluba. It was the Baluba who were Belgium's golden boys. They were perceived to be more intelligent, more industrious—in other words, more European. The Belgians even noted that the facial features of the Baluba were more like their own. The irony was, in Protruding Navel's opinion, that the tribes spoke the same language—although the Baluba did slaughter the pronunciation of some words. And yes, at one time the Lulua did oppress the Baluba, although perhaps that was too strong a word for benign slavery. Still, none of that should have given the Baluba favor in the Belgians' eyes. And surely Protruding Navel, as an individual, had done nothing to deserve the burden of being doubly discriminated against.

"Protruding Navel!" the white *mamu* practically shouted. "Why do you spy on us?"

"I do not spy on anyone, Mamu Ugly Eyes. I have merely come to inquire what it is you desire for today's big meal. There is chicken in the freezer, and I have a pineapple that has ripened to perfection. Mamu Singleton has taught me how to make a Chinese dish that is both sweet and sour. Will the new *mamu* be wanting that?"

"Yes, that sounds very good."

"Would you like me to teach her to prepare this meal?" Protruding Navel used his chin to point at the irritating little Muluba woman.

"That's a wonderful idea!"

"And shall I also teach her how to kill the snakes?"

"What snakes?"

"Every morning I search the house for snakes. In this season, when everything is dry, the toads come in where it is cool and damp. In the privy room, in the kitchen, and elsewhere. Do you not see them under the bathing tub?"

"Yes, I've seen toads—"

"Snakes eat toads, *mamu*. Yesterday I killed a cobra that was under the bathing tub."

"Truly? I did not see that."

"I did not show you, *mamu*, because I knew it would frighten you. But as this little one is an African, she will not be so afraid. Together it will not be so hard to keep the house clear of snakes."

"*She* has a name, and it's Cripple."

"Very well, if it pleases the *mamu*, I will call the little one by her name."

"How about now?"

"*Mamu*?"

"Call her by her name *now*."

Protruding Navel had, in his role as housekeeper, observed that white women were harder to please than their men. But nothing in his years of working for Mamu Singleton had prepared him for this. Yet if he wished to keep his job, he would have to bend like bamboo before the wind.

"Cripple," he said, pushing the word from his lips like it was the membrane of a corn kernel that had lodged between his teeth.

CHAPTER SIXTEEN

The spotted hyena is one of the few mammal species in which the female is substantially larger than the male, and dominates him. Even the lowest-ranking female outranks the highest-ranking male. Females seem to have taken role reversal one step farther, in that they have developed a pseudo-phallus, five to seven inches long, and very convincing pseudo-testes. Also, females have been frequently observed engaging in sexual activity with other females.

When his lover walked in through the front door of the grocery store, Cezar Nunez couldn't help but smile. His lover was getting bolder and bolder. The first time they'd made love was after the store had closed for the evening; they did it among the paper goods. Thereafter his lover would come in the back way, sneaking unnoticed into his office, where they would tryst during the long midday siestas. But to just walk through the front door, during prime morning shopping hours, was not only bold, it was also utterly dangerous. The thrill, thought Cezar, was immensely erotic.

"Cezar, we have to talk," the postmaster said, coming straight to him.

"*Now?* It's the middle of the morning."

"Not that. This really is talk."

Cezar's heart beat faster. What if Dupree had come to break it off? Their affair—was one allowed to use that word? Well, their time together was the only thing that made life worth living. He didn't enjoy being a manager of a Belgian grocery store, not any more than his wife enjoyed being the wife of a lowly grocer. And he certainly didn't enjoy his wife any longer. In the beginning he'd found Branca wildly attractive, but in the beginning she was also unavailable: a nobleman's daughter who consented to marry him because of the money he represented.

It was obvious now that she found him as attractive as a bag of potatoes, and to be entirely truthful, he would choose the potatoes over her in a heartbeat. Their marriage was held together only by inertia, and maybe just slightly by their mutual stubbornness, their unwillingness to admit defeat.

And then along came Dupree. Cezar had been attracted to boys for as long as he could remember. But with the exception of one drunken night during his university days, he'd never acted on those urges. With Dupree, caution went out the door. The Belgian postmaster fit his fantasy perfectly, as both a lover and a friend. The "love that dare not speak its name" begged to be shouted from the treetops—although of course that couldn't be done. Yet the three months they'd been seeing each other were the happiest in Cezar's entire life.

"Dupree," he whispered—never using his lover's Christian name was his last line of emotional defense—"can't it wait? My job, you know."

"Screw your job, Cezar. We're going to be rich. So rich, you can buy this store and give the merchandise away for free."

"What are you talking about?"

"Not here. In your office. Let's talk there."

Cezar bit his lip as he considered the possibilities. Perhaps Dupree really did know what he was saying; perhaps a wealthy aunt in Belgium had died and a telegraph had just arrived informing him that he'd inherited her estate. But it could also be another harebrained scheme, like the time Dupree had suggested they raid their tills and run away to America, to San Francisco, where men like them were tolerated. Or the time, when they lay spent in each other's arms, that Dupree had suggested buying a fish farm on which they could raise Nile perch, a tasty fish known locally as *capitain*. They could ship it by air back to Europe, a plan that would make sense only to an entrepreneur whose goal it was to lose money. It was one thing to risk everything for sex, for intimacy, but for a pipe dream? If it was pipe dreams he wanted, Branca had more than enough for him to choose from.

"Cezar, you've got to trust me on this."

"Okay," he said. "Let's talk about last week's soccer game as we walk back to my office."

Mid-morning was a particularly busy time, and the two African clerks seemed to have everything under control. Nonetheless, Cezar Nunez flinched when Dupree slammed the office door behind them.

"It's a diamond," the postmaster blurted.

"And?"

"And nothing! Didn't you hear what I said?"

"We're surrounded by diamonds, Dupree. They're in the gravel used to make the concrete blocks of our houses. Here"—he kicked the outer wall of his office—"there are diamonds here as well. What about diamonds?"

"There's this fellow that works for me. He goes by the unfortunate name of Their Death. He's a good man, worked for me for years. He came to me yesterday morning asking me for help with a problem. Turns out the problem is a freaking diamond the size of a mango seed. Supposedly gem grade. He asked me for advice on how to sell it."

Cezar's mind flicked about the edges of this tale like a serpent's tongue searching for traces of its prey's warmth. He loved Dupree, and was pretty sure Dupree loved him in return, but could he really trust the man? Perhaps love and trust didn't necessarily go together. If this was a trap of some kind—no, it couldn't be that. Cezar's caution collapsed as greed took over.

"What did you tell Their Death?"

"I hinted that I might consider making inquiries. He said that if I want to see the stone, I should meet him tomorrow morning on the bridge. If I want to actually touch the stone—feel its weight, examine it from all sides—I must first give him a deposit of ten thousand francs."

"Whew, that's a lot of money! Cheeky, isn't he?"

"Yes, but I can't blame him. If the stone is real, it will be worth millions."

Cezar whistled sharply and then, remembering where he was, whistled a few bars of a popular Portuguese ballad. "So now what? Even if you got your hands on the stone—permanently, that is—you wouldn't be able to get it out of the province, much less this damn country."

"Ah, but you see, I plan to cut this stone first. I'll turn over a sizeable chunk to the OP, who will, no doubt, make a big deal about shipping it back to Belgium. I'll be the one accompanying the stone, and since I'll be doing it openly, no one will bother to check me." Dupree smiled, which never failed to render him devilishly handsome. "And because they won't be checking me, they won't find the rest of the stone either."

Cezar smiled back at his lover. It was a clever plan. But what else would Dupree come up with? Talk about gems.

"What about me?" he asked.

"You will be sitting next to me on that plane. I was thinking that Tahiti might be a nice place to settle down. It has the advantage of being very far away from both here and Belgium, but still they speak French." He paused. "Does that sound okay? I mean, any place in particular appeal to you?"

"Tahiti is supposed to be hot. How about Brazil? They speak Portuguese there."

"And Brazil isn't hot?"

They both laughed, but Cezar was unable to quiet his mind. "What if the OP doesn't go for it? What if he arrests you for producing the diamond? Remember Madame Flaubert?"

It was a rhetorical question, of course. A heavy woman who loved to eat, Madame Flaubert had been one of Cezar's best customers—until she'd been arrested at the airport just six months ago. She'd been caught with twenty carats of small gem-quality diamonds surgically inserted into her prodigious rolls of abdominal fat. Her accomplice was her husband, Dr. Flaubert, who had served as the physician to Belle Vue's white community for the past fifteen years.

Upon getting arrested, Madame Flaubert and her disgraced husband claimed the gems were a parting gift from the OP, who had cautioned them to keep his generosity a secret. The OP denied his involvement and the Flauberts were now in Brussels awaiting sentencing.

"No need to worry about the old goat this time. He's desperately trying to turn the mine around. The pressure from headquarters has got to be intense, now that the prospect of independence is looming on the horizon. Get as much as you can, while you can, seems to be the idea."

"When will you try and float this plan?"

"I already have. Came straight here to tell you."

Cezar hoped the burn in his cheeks didn't show. Dupree had done it again; he'd made decisions for the both of them. It was getting to be a habit, just like it was with Branca.

"You could have told me first."

"Sorry. But I didn't want to get your hopes up."

That seemed reasonable. "Hey look, I really have to get back to work."

"Cezar, there's just one more thing."

"Not until siesta, Dupree. Not until the clerks leave."

The postmaster laughed. "No, not that! You see, I've got to come up with ten thousand francs by tomorrow morning, but I'm a bit strapped for cash at the moment."

"It figures."

"What is that supposed to mean?"

"That you're always short on money. Don't they pay you for being postmaster?"

"I don't have that much at the *moment*."

"But I do? Because I manage a store? Look, you have your own till over there at post office. Why don't you borrow from it?"

Dupree lowered his eyes, which told Cezar all he needed to know. He knew his lover had a fondness for—no, was addicted to—playing poker with other lower-echelon Belgian employees of the Consortium. Cezar had bailed him out before with a series of small loans.

"How much this time?"

"One hundred and fifteen thousand."

"Blessed vision of Fatima! You're joking, yes?"

Dupree said nothing.

"Damn it! Tell me you're joking."

"I had a winning hand, I just knew it. And the only way I could clear up my debts was to bet it all."

"What *all*? You had nothing. What did you use for collateral?"

"My mother's apartment in Antwerp. My name is on the deed."

Cezar cursed, using words and languages in combinations he had never heard. When he was through venting, he was out of breath.

"Okay," he finally said. "I will get you the money, but we will do more than just succeed in this diamond venture, because we will do it my way, and we will do it flawlessly."

Dupree managed a weak smile.

CHAPTER SEVENTEEN

There are at least two, and perhaps as many as four, subspecies of go-rillas (*Gorilla gorilla*). The western lowland gorillas are slightly smaller than their mountain cousins, with shorter fur, and are more likely to climb trees to feed. They also live in smaller groups. All gorillas make temporary nests each evening—either on the ground or in the trees—which they abandon each day. Gorillas can live to be more than fifty years old in the wild, and even more in captivity.

The Nigerian stared at the object in his hand; it was a bone. A human bone. He was sure of that. In Lagos he'd once worked as the cleaning man for a morgue. The coroner, an Englishman, had been a pompous ass, insisting that everyone in his employ, even the mop wielders, know something about anatomy.

By the time his job ended, the Nigerian knew exactly how to strangle a man in the shortest possible time. Of course it would have been easier to use a knife or a saw, but cutting implements created messes, and he wasn't about to clean another up mess—even if it meant covering his tracks.

They say that practice makes perfect. After he joined the Circle of Cobras, the former janitor was given the opportunity to hone his skills, proving that the axiom was indeed true. The Circle of

Cobras was considered by many in the trade to be Lagos's most successful smuggling ring, but of course it was a risky business, one that did not suffer fools gladly. It was the Nigerian's job to silence those who couldn't be bought, or who otherwise caused trouble for the ring.

Because of his intimate knowledge of the human body, the Nigerian knew that the femur he held in his hand was quite old. Perhaps even thousands of years old.

Branca had been educated by Portuguese nuns, and now here she was preparing to visit an American nun—well, a nun of sorts. Any woman who would throw away the younger years of her life in tropical Africa either had the personality of a nun or else was crazy. Probably both.

Because it was a nun she would be having tea with, Branca chose to wear an off-the-shoulder white cotton peasant blouse, a wide black belt that cinched the waist and emphasized both hips and bosom, and a colorful gypsy skirt that flirted playfully with her knee caps. Before donning beaded sandals, she painted her toenails a blazing orange red.

"Hey there, Miss Nun," she said aloud to her reflection in her full-length mirror, "take that. Now guess what? You're not allowed to smack me with your ruler. Or whip my legs with that willow branch in the corner. Or even just complain to my parents. How do you like that, Miss Nun?" Her reflection scowled back at her in a typical Sister Mary Angelina fashion.

Because she was a redhead who burned easily and freckled at the mere suggestion of the sun, Branca carried with her a white silk parasol, a gift from her *duenna*. It was as pleasant a day as any, and Branca marveled at how comfortable Bell Vue could be during the dry season. It was almost like being in northern Portugal in early autumn, or perhaps late spring—except that here everyone was black, and when she got home she'd have to have her feet inspected by one of the houseboys.

Chigger mites, which lived in the dirt and then burrowed into exposed skin, were the bane of the tropics. Left alone they laid eggs, which then hatched and laid more eggs, until one's feet were riddled with them. In the meantime they itched unbearably, so that their host was driven to scratch. That invited infection, which often lead to crippling. Most whites engaged in a weekly ritual during which an eagle-eyed servant dug out the critters with a sterilized pin and then daubed the open skin with kerosene. One way to cut down on infestation was to wear socks and closed shoes, but how then could one taunt the American nun? No, painted toenails were the only way to go.

Branca paused to check her lipstick before knocking on the door. But both to her surprise and annoyance, the door was flung open before she could put away her compact mirror. How very American of her hostess.

"*Bon soir, madame.*"

Branca found herself staring at the young woman. Sure enough, she was as plain as rice without gravy. Not a smidge of makeup on, hair pulled back into a bun—not even a chignon, like the French, but a bun! And her dress! It covered just about every centimeter of her skin.

Oh well, the American would soon learn that when the rains came they brought with them a clothes-clawing humidity that made you want to rip every shred from your body and sit under the waterfall. Of course you couldn't do the latter, which meant you had to immerse yourself in the tepid company pool, made even more tepid by the urine of ill-mannered Belgian urchins.

"Good afternoon," Branca said, in BBC English. She'd learned the language in school from Portuguese nuns with horrible accents, but had been able to improve her own accent through hours spent listening to her shortwave radio.

"I'm Amanda Brown. Please come in."

"You may call me Senhora Nunez—for now."

Branca followed the young woman into a very disappointing salon. It may as well have been Belgian; it was sparsely furnished with those heavy wooden chairs with wicker backs and bottoms, hideous floral cushions, cheap area rugs, and nothing on the walls except for religious plaques and needlepoint mottoes.

"Reverend and Mrs. Singleton will be retiring shortly—as soon as I've been properly trained."

"Yes, I know."

"Perhaps then I will do some redecorating. Shall we sit?"

As soon as they were seated on those horrible chairs, the young hostess rang a small bell, informing the servants it was time to bring out the tea. Well, at least she had learned something since arriving in Africa.

When the repast arrived, Branca was pleased to see that it was indeed English tea, and served English style with sugar biscuits and various small cakes. The cream, alas, was only evaporated milk.

"Senhora Nunez, I'm so glad you could join me today."

"Yes, but if you will recall, the idea was initially mine. Tell me, what is it you Americans have against alcohol?"

"Well—and it's not *all* Americans—we as Christians believe that our bodies are temples of the Lord, and that we should take care of them. Alcohol is bad for one's health, you know."

"No, I don't know. To the contrary, a glass of sherry or perhaps port actually aids in digestion. And tell me, if bodies are so special, then why are so many missionaries fat?"

"Uh—they are?"

"Indeed. I have observed many fat missionaries stay at this guesthouse. Are Americans generally overweight?"

"I don't think so."

"Well, you certainly are not. But it is a shame that you so thoroughly cover what God has given you. And believe me, my dear, the Almighty has been very generous with you."

"I am saving myself for my husband."

"Ha!" Branca could say a great deal more on the subject of husbands, but now was not the time. "Are you aware that the club serves excellent food? One need not consume alcohol during the meal, either."

"Yes, I have heard good things about the food."

"So then you will agree to meet me there for lunch tomorrow?"

"But I can't. You see, I make it my policy never to eat in places that serve alcohol. I'm very sorry, Senhora Nunez."

"That is ridic—" Branca caught herself just in time. "Miss White, don't you want to save my soul?"

"I beg your pardon?"

"Well, I am a Catholic. In your eyes, I am not a Christian. Correct? And you must answer this, Miss White. I am not going to budge until you do."

Once while hunting, Branca had seen an antelope that had been cornered on a small peninsula that jutted out into a lake. It had the same look in its eyes. In the end, the antelope had chosen to swim out into the lake, where it drowned.

"Senhora Nunez, it is not my place to judge you. But if you insist on an answer, then yes, I don't believe you are a true Christian."

"That's what I thought. Well, now we're getting somewhere."

"But I—"

"No excuses. You want to save my soul, am I right? Then I will give you a chance to save it tomorrow at the club. And who knows, perhaps others will be similarly moved."

Branca was pleased to hear the young woman's sigh of resignation.

* * *

Second Wife thought about what she'd seen and heard that morning. She thought about it as she trudged to the village spigot to get water to rinse out the morning's dishes. She thought about it as she swept the family compound with her rattan broom. She thought about it as she peeled manioc roots and split them to be dried in the sun. She thought about it as she took other roots, ones that had already been dried, and put them in the wooden mortar. She thought about it as she pounded them into flour with a heavy wooden pestle. She thought about it as she sifted the flour and pounded the remnants again. She thought about it as she wiped mucus from Baby Boy's face with a corn husk and shooed away the flies that were drinking the moisture at the corners of his eyes. She thought about it until she could think no more.

Tonight she would have words with Husband. Tonight she would issue an ultimatum. Either he must make Cripple help with the chores or marry a third wife. Husband made a salary; not as high as the mine workers earned, but still quite respectable. And now and then he received a chicken—or maybe a duck—as payment for a potion or an amulet. Once he was even given a goat by the village council of elders for putting a mild curse—a cessation of activity, so to speak—on Farts Too Much. But the main reason Husband could now afford a third wife was because Cripple was finally doing something useful; Cripple was earning money.

But what if Cripple objected? Cripple had been forced to get used the idea of a second wife because she'd been unable to bring forth living children. She might not, however, tolerate a third. And that's where the problem lay: Cripple. Cripple had too much power. She acted like a man, and instead of being outraged, Husband was amused. Never had Second Wife known such a woman.

Short, almost dwarfish, and deformed, Cripple exuded an aura of someone ten times her size. When she first met her co-wife,

Second Wife had fully expected the strange little woman to be picked on unmercifully by the other village women—like a sick hen is pecked to death by others in its flock. She had also expected Husband to be mocked for his choice. But neither of those things had happened. Instead it was "Life to you, Cripple. How are you today?" And as for Husband, he was now referred to as "Cripple's Husband," as if that was his name.

But the incident that had seared an indelible mark on Second Wife's soul was the time Brings Happiness, her very own son, went temporarily missing on an excursion to pick mushrooms. Then it was, "Cripple's son is missing. Have you seen him?" They were words of concern, spoken by kind neighbors and friends, but for Second Wife, each syllable was like swallowing a hot coal. Cripple had not endured the pain of childbirth, it was not her breasts that nourished Brings Happiness. Why should she get any of the credit?

Yet what if Husband refused to be reasonable? It seemed likely that he would refuse; men in general were not inclined to be reasonable. Yes, she would have to come up with a backup plan, one that effectively eliminated Cripple from the picture.

Second Wife hummed to herself as the beginnings of a plan flitted through her brain, like a long-tailed bird skipping over a sea of elephant grass.

CHAPTER EIGHTEEN

The hippopotamus (*H. amphibious*) and the pig developed from a distant common ancestor. Of course the hippo is much larger, weighing up to six thousand pounds. Hippos are extremely territorial, and possess tusk-like teeth, making them one of the most dangerous animals in Africa. Once, while on a picnic by the Kasai River, the author's family witnessed a hippo overturn a dugout canoe and then bite the occupant in half.

Amanda smiled to herself. The tea with Senhora Nunez had gone remarkably well. The woman was obviously in need of friends, and although she was by no means a perfect fit, it was nice to know she was there. Also, the soul-saving challenge the Portuguese woman had used was as good an excuse as any to visit the club.

In fact, the woman had a point. Just because the club served alcohol was no reason to stay away. How could she share her faith with the European population if she had virtually no contact with them? Although saving souls was not her official assignment in Belle Vue, it had been Amanda's personal reason for going to the Congo in the first place.

Amanda's soul had almost been lost for eternity, the night of her high-school prom. At that point in her life, although she was forced to attend both church and Sunday School on a regular basis, the teenager had not yet given her heart to Jesus. In the wee hours of the morning she snuck out of bed and rendezvoused, first with some girlfriends, and then some male friends. Soon there were three cars full of teenagers headed for Gaffney, South Carolina, where, it was rumored, a bar existed that served alcohol to minors. Plus, it had a dynamite rhythm-and-blues band.

The stretch of State Route 5 between York and Gaffney has more ups and downs than the ridges on a dragon's back, and as many twisting turns as a dragon's tail. A road like that is best experienced by driving fearlessly, turning the challenges into adrenaline-filled moments. And what better way to do that than to play "automobile leapfrog," a game in which drivers constantly try to zoom around each other?

Because of the late hour and the fact that the road wound through forest for most of its length, no one expected a car of "civilians" to be traveling the other way. But that is exactly what Mr. and Mrs. Homer Johnson were doing. Homer and Loretta had married late in life, and when they finally tied the knot, they both decided to quit their jobs and take a motor trip across the country. Rather than follow a map, they thought it would be more fun to follow the back roads, choosing their destinations on a whim. They'd begun the trip in their home state of Vermont, driving only during the day to avoid hitting deer. Why they decided to drive after dark this one fateful night will probably never be known. But it is doubtful that they even saw the car full of teenagers long enough for the image to register, because there was no sign that Homer, who was driving, had tried to avoid the crash.

Homer was impaled on the steering column, dying instantly. Loretta was not so lucky. She sailed through the windshield, landing in the piney woods several yards from the car, where she bled to death from internal injuries. All six of the teenagers in that car that smashed head-on into the Johnsons' car were killed. The car immediately behind them ran off the road to avoid a pileup and hit a tree, killing three of the occupants. Trapped inside with the bodies, only Amanda survived. The third car slowed only enough to turn around before heading back home at the speed of light.

The accident was not discovered until approximately six in the morning, when a logging truck appeared on the scene. Amanda was unconscious when she was discovered, more from shock than from bodily injury; apart from a broken arm and some facial contusions, she was remarkably uninjured.

Physically, she recovered quickly, but emotional recovery took the rest of the summer. In September a traveling evangelist came to town, setting up a large white tent on the dusty county fairgrounds. Amanda attended three nights in a row and on the third night heeded the altar call. To the soft strains of "Just as I Am," she turned her life over to the Lord. The fourth night the preacher talked about venturing to the far corners of the earth to spread the Gospel, and that's when Amanda first felt that the Holy Spirit was directing her to go to Africa.

Now here she was, stuck managing a retreat for exhausted missionaries and dealing with an arrogant housekeeper, instead of being in the trenches winning souls for Christ. Then out of the blue this Catholic woman calls upon her and practically forces her into a den of iniquity, where souls were ripe for the plucking. If that wasn't the Holy Spirit moving in her life, well—well, then nothing. It was indeed just that. Amanda could feel it in her bones.

"Mamu Ugly Eyes."

Amanda jumped. "Yes?"

"I did not mean to scare you."

"I am fine."

"Certainly. *Mamu*, may I have your permission to return to my village?"

"Now? But there still many chores to be done."

"Forgive me, *mamu*, but do you not still employ the angry one?"

"Who? Oh yes, but that is not your concern." She lowered her voice. "The truth is you were hired to replace him. How can you replace him if you don't take over his duties?"

"I will, *mamu*, I promise. It is just this one night that I must leave early."

"And why is that?"

"Because my sister wife is having a baby and I must catch the child as it is born."

"Isn't there a midwife?"

"So there is. But the midwife has a terrible temper, even worse than that of Repugnant Navel. She does not—"

"Protruding."

"*Eyo, mamu*. The baby protrudes, even as we speak."

"No, I mean that your coworker's name is *Protruding* Navel, not Repugnant Navel."

"Must we quibble over details, mamu, while my sister wife screams?"

"Screams?"

After closing her eyes and clenching her fists, Cripple let loose with a scream that would surely have brought the cops running in South Carolina. "Like that, *mamu*. Unfortunately the midwife does not tolerate such noise. She would beat my sister wife at the slightest sound, as already she dislikes my family. So you see, there is no plan to use her services."

Surely Amanda had heard wrong. "*Beat* her? You mean, the midwife would hit her?"

"Oh yes." Cripple's eyes shone as she mimicked striking the nearest chair. "Aiyee! Aiyee!"

"But that's terrible!"

"Indeed it is, *mamu*. Would you care to see me demonstrate the beating again?"

"No, thank you. Tell me, Cripple, has your sister wife gone into labor already? And if so, who's attending her now?"

"*Mamu*, I do not know how it is in your country, but here the women choose the hour when they give birth. They say, 'I will give birth at such and such a time,' and then they do it. My sister wife has chosen this hour."

Amanda had to clamp her hand over her mouth to keep from laughing. The clever little woman was trying to pull the wool over her eyes.

"Go," she said. "But tell her that next time she needs to check with me first."

"Yes, *mamu*."

Instead of returning to the village, Cripple crossed the bridge that led to the European sector of Belle Vue. She could count on one hand the number of times she'd made the trip alone since becoming an adult, and all were to deliver some urgent message to Husband at his place of work. The falls terrified her and the sight of so many white women and children, with skins the color of water lily petals, repulsed her.

She was not the only African that day, by any means, walking along the main arteries of the town, although most of them were men. Still, there were nannies pushing devices that held babies—a bizarre way to transport an infant when you thought about it—and vendors carrying bunches of bananas on their heads, or enamel basins filled with delectable things to eat, like palm nuts, dried caterpillars, salted fish, and chili peppers. The banana sellers were hoping to unload their wares on Belgian housewives, while the rest had in mind the servants and their families who lived in small brick houses behind the mansions.

This afternoon Cripple headed in the opposite direction, away from the post office. She walked resolutely along the edge of Boulevard des Allies, which had been named after the recent tribal war in Europe. As long as she kept out of the way of bicycles and the very occasional automobile, she was essentially invisible. Once a snarling dog lunged at her, but a thick chain prevented it from getting close enough to do harm. Had it gotten any closer Cripple would have been forced to whack it with her walking stick, just as she had mimed beating the *mamu*'s chair.

As Cripple approached the airport the large mango trees that lined the dirt boulevard gave way to spindly acacias, and finally just elephant grass. The road ended in front of a cement-block building that sheltered the ticket agent and his passengers on days that planes were scheduled. At the moment there was no sign of life except for a herd of black pigs, sprawled on the runway like so many breathing boulders.

Cripple had heard about a footpath that skirted the landing strip, and much to her relief she found it easily. At this hour of the day, when the sun was low in the sky but still in full view, the only animals that one needed to watch for were the omnipresent snakes. Cripple, believing she could lesson the threat by making noise, thrashed at the elephant grass that bordered the left side of the path. This made the walking slow, but kept her anxiety level at a reasonable level.

Finally, there it was, what remained of it. Cripple had been hoping to see enough of the airplane to enable her to imagine what it must be like to be inside one. She had read a little about these marvelous machines, and seen them fly low over the village, but had never had the privilege of talking to someone who had actually been in one. Therefore she couldn't quite picture how it was the people managed to fit inside. And how did they position themselves once they got in? Did they lie on their stomachs—perhaps one above the other—or did they squat on their haunches?

How very disappointing to find nothing but small pieces of twisted metal and scattered cinders. Husband had described it as thus, but Cripple had needed to take it in with her own eyes. Perhaps if she'd been able to get to the wreckage the day it happened, there might have been more to see. Anything that could be put to use had surely been carried off: large metal scraps for roofing; smaller scraps for blades, knife blades, even false teeth; rubber for sandals and slingshot strings.

Cripple had already concluded that the trip had been a waste of time—and much-needed energy—when she found a piece of molten glass that looked very much like the diamond Husband had hidden in the banana grove. For surely the oddly-shaped stone was a diamond; she'd lived in a diamond-mining village long enough to know that the gems did not pop out of the earth faceted and polished.

Just why it was that Husband had chosen to lie to her with his silence, she did not know. But she would soon enough. After a while, like children, men invariably felt the need to confess. In the meantime, it would serve him right if he thought he'd made a mistake, or better yet, realized someone was onto him.

Ah, there was another suitable glass "diamond." And another. And yet another. Cripple gathered five in all, and tucked them for safekeeping under her turban, where they lodged securely in her densely coiled hair. They were not perfect, by any means, but they would be adequate for the job. She could not help but smile. The spirits had played a cruel joke on her parents, giving them a daughter with limbs twisted like liana vines. But these same spirits had been so occupied with distorting her body that they'd left a perfectly sound mind alone.

It did not even the score, as far as Cripple was concerned, but it did give her a reason to live. She would live well. As would Husband. That was not too much to ask, although it would mean a lifetime of outsmarting the spirits. And therein lay a conundrum;

a logical mind could not believe in unseen things like spirits—and this is why Cripple could not accept the Christian god either—but on a visceral level, she knew that to ignore their power was to court disaster.

In the far distance, where the elephant grass met the setting sun, a hyena laughed. Cripple gripped her walking stick tighter.

CHAPTER NINETEEN

Leopards (*Panthera pardus*) were found throughout the Belgian Congo, where they were strongly associated with witchcraft, and believed to be endowed with magical powers. Although much smaller than lions, leopards are incredibly strong for their size, capable of hauling antelopes high into trees for safekeeping. They are solitary, which, along with their spotted fur, ensures that they are seldom seen by humans. As with lions and tigers, there are confirmed cases of leopards becoming man-eaters. Black panthers are merely a melanistic form of the regular leopard.

The OP, by rights, should be living in Belle Vue's largest house, but that damn Portuguese, Nunez, had finagled his way into it, and until his lease was up, there was nothing the OP could do. But, if one kept things in perspective, what the OP did have wasn't half bad. No, it was a lot better than that. He'd lived in a two-bedroom apartment back in Brussels. Here he had four bedrooms that were twice as large as those.

There was a lot to be said for colonial living—well, as long as you were white, and preferably Belgian. Labor was cheap and so were house servants. A comparable villa in the South of France would cost fifty times as much, and as for the servants—well, if they were French servants, forget it. The French had attitudes. They looked upon the French-speaking Walloons, not as cousins, but as imposters. No doubt the Dutch felt the same way about the Flemings.

"Screw the French," the OP said aloud, and tossed back what remained of his gin and tonic. "Screw the Dutch too."

Heilewid, who'd been sitting back in her chair, as quiet as a corpse, stirred.

"What did you say?"

"I said we should be going in soon. It's getting chilly."

"Claudia says it might actually frost tonight. Do you think that's possible?"

The OP nearly dropped his glass. His wife hadn't said that many words since the day she'd lost her twin. Even more astounding was the fact that these words were arranged into an intelligible sentence.

"Uh—frost? I don't think so. Not at this latitude. Although we are up a thousand meters. I heard on the shortwave this morning that Elizabethville had a frost—their first in recorded history."

"It makes me think of Belgium. This cool weather, I mean."

The OP stared at his wife, whose face was half in silhouette. They'd taken their dinner of roast guinea hen, buttered new potatoes, and haricots verts on the verandah, as they usually did unless there was wind-driven rain. They'd eaten in silence, the only conversation between him and the table boy, who'd asked if he could have the bones when they were through with their meal. The lad had concocted some story about using the bones as bait to catch a particular species of forest rat that was said to be delectable, but the OP knew better.

"I understand there is another whole guinea back in the kitchen," he'd said.

"*Oui, monsieur.*"

"Take it instead. Maybe your forest rat prefers meat."

"*Merci, monsieur, merci.*"

The OP had dismissed the boy before he'd gotten maudlin. The OP had meant to be kind, not softhearted. There was a difference.

"I can't believe you're talking about the weather," he said now to his wife. "What happened? Did I miss anything?"

"Probably not. I haven't changed my mind, if that's what you're thinking. I still hate it here. I still hate you. But for a minute, when you spoke to the table boy, I caught a glimpse of the man I married. I was speaking to him."

"Am I so terrible now?"

"You're obsessed with your work."

"Can you blame me? I feel like I've been living in an empty house. Besides, after the—uh, the accident, I offered to send you back to Belgium."

"That would have been the end of your career. You know that. The OP has to have a wife, who has to entertain, keep the other wives busy—you know how it goes. If you've forgotten, just give yourself the same speech you gave my father when you asked for my hand in marriage."

"I was beyond nervous then. I had to come up with reasons why I would want to drag his daughter off to the colony. And anyway, what entertaining have you done since the fire?"

The OP wished he could have another gin and tonic without ringing for a servant. But the liquor was inside, and if he left the verandah now, he might return to find that it had been all a dream. Gin and tonics were as British as steak and kidney pie, but they were a habit he'd picked up while on safari to Kenya during his first year in Africa.

"Heilewid," he said softly, "what happened that day was not my fault, any more than it was yours. So why do you hate me?"

"That's just the thing; I don't hate you any more than I hate myself. Neither of us should have allowed Geete to leave the group."

He couldn't stand to hear her say that, although he knew it was true. She'd been killing herself with sun, booze, and cigarettes just as surely as if she'd held a gun to her sunburned head and pulled the trigger.

"You could go back now. Everyone expected you to do so after the funeral. The brass would have understood. I'm sure they still will."

"Geete is dead. What do I have back in Belgium to go home to? A father whose chief pleasure in life is controlling everyone around him? Girlfriends who cry when they chip their fingernails? Eight months of rain and cold? No, thank you. I plan to stay here, where I can sit out on the patio on the coldest night of the year and speculate about the likelihood of a frost—which, of course, will never happen—and then tomorrow I'll lie out by the pool again. Oh and by the way, should we throw a party soon?"

If it wasn't for the hollowness in her voice, the OP would have been overjoyed by what he heard. He felt instead like the keeper of a small wild animal that had been caught in a trap and must be nursed to full vigor. Heilewid had done that once with an antelope fawn—or she'd tried to. A hunter from the village had brought in this shivering little thing, hardly bigger than a Chihuahua. His wife had fed it with a bottle, and at night would put it to bed in a cardboard box, in which she placed a hot water bottle wrapped inside a towel. The tenderness she exhibited toward this frail, exotic creature was heartbreaking to watch, knowing, as he did, that she could never have children.

The antelope fawn lived for almost a week, and seemed to be thriving, possibly even growing, and then one morning Heilewid woke up to find her tiny charge cold and stiff, its large brown eyes glazed over. That was the first time that the OP observed his wife retreat into a shell of protective silence, one that lasted about a month.

There had been one previous episode of silence, or so he'd been told by her father. When Heilewid was twelve, her mother had drowned herself in one of the many canals that crisscross the Low Country that is Flanders. But by the time the OP met Heilewid, she seemed to have recovered to the point that she could play the part of Ophelia in a community production of *Hamlet*.

The night song of a jackal brought the OP back to the present and he shivered, suddenly finding himself too cold to stay outside any longer. He stood, his glass in hand.

"You coming in soon?"

"Soon. I want to enjoy what it feels like not to be hot. October will get here before we know it. And you still haven't answered my question about having a party."

The OP was at a loss for words. Working on the party might be therapeutic for her, but what if, when the event actually came to pass, she snapped? On the other hand, everyone already knew she'd had a nervous breakdown. What was there to lose? If only by default, Heilewid was still the alpha female of the pack—those socially starved, and sometimes bewildered, European housewives who suddenly found themselves living in the middle of nowhere. To the best of the OP's knowledge, as of yet none of the company wives were jockeying for that position—well, except for Branca Nunez. But Branca didn't really count; she was Portuguese and her husband was not directly connected with the mine. She was, however, a real looker. A spitfire too, but strictly off-limits.

"*Well?* What about the party?"

"Sure," he said. "A party would be great."

"Thank you."

A second jackal began to serenade the moon. Soon there would be choir of them. Their high, plaintive yips, followed by extended howls, were alarming to newcomers to Africa. For old hands like the OP, it was music to sleep soundly by.

"When they stop," he said to Heilewid, "come inside."

"Yes, I know. Because then it's hyena time."

The Nigerian had heard of the ancient men, the ones who'd lived in caves before the time of the forefathers. The missionaries had rebutted these legends with their own stories from the Bible. Yet men of science—including the dead, pompous Englishman—said there was truth in the tales of the ancient ones.

Of course it didn't matter now who was right or wrong; what mattered was that there were the remains of a campfire. *Somebody's* campfire. And there was flint. And logs that had been washed deep into the cave during a flood and that were now as dry as the bone in his hand.

That evening the Nigerian ate cooked fish, and that night he was warm and comfortable. At daybreak he would search for a way to climb up the opposing side of the gorge. Perhaps he would fashion a ladder of some sort. This time nothing, and no one, was going to stop him from completing his mission.

CHAPTER TWENTY

It has been said that 90 percent of African snakes are poisonous, and the other 10 percent hug their victims to death. This is an exaggeration, but there are more than ninety species that are harmful to people. Poisonous snakes include the gaboon viper, the puff adder, the death adder, the black mamba, the green mamba, and the spitting cobra. The African rock python is not poisonous, but strangles its victims. It can grow to twenty-five feet and is capable of swallowing an antelope whole—even a small person.

Husband found sleeping impossible. It wasn't just because of the jackals, which had set the village dogs howling, but worry over how the morning would play itself out. The white man always had the advantage.

That was a fact as old as recorded history, even history as told by the white man. The early Portuguese explorers had discovered a land governed by powerful kings and less powerful chiefs, but black men all. Less than four hundred years later the Congo was in the sole possession of Belgium's King Leopold II, whose method of ruling was so brutal, the League of Nations forced him to cede the land over to Belgium Parliament. During his reign of terror, approximately a million people were put to death, yet history would never record Leopold II as one of the most evil tyrants of all time, because his victims were mainly black people dwelling in the heart of darkness.

The Congo was a land of almost unimaginable riches: ivory, rubber, gold, titanium, uranium, copper, hardwoods. The greedy king, stoked by the newfound use for rubber during the advent of the automobile, levied a "rubber tax" on the male populace. Raw rubber is a tree sap, and any man failing to collect his daily quota from the wild would have his right hand chopped off with a machete. Husband could remember that, when he was a small child, there were a number of old men in his village with only one hand, a legacy of this cruel dictum.

Yes, conditions had improved since the days of King Leopold II, but neither a black man's worth nor his word were equal to that of a white man. What if M. Dupree, whom Husband believed to be an honest man, turned out to be a liar and a thief? And if that was the case, what was to prevent the postmaster from simply taking the diamond by force and telling everyone that he, M. Dupree, had discovered it? Husband could even be killed in the process. Then what would happen to Cripple? To the children? To Second Wife?

But especially to Cripple. As the mother of sons, Second Wife need only eke out a living until they were young men, and then her old age was assured. Even now the oldest was capable of doing some things that could help out financially. Already the girls helped their mother in the fields. And although by custom they all were obligated to take care of Cripple, as she was their sister wife and sister mother, sadly, that was no longer guaranteed. The world was changing at a dizzying rate, and the only thing one could count now was change—well, that, and the fact that one needed to use the privy sooner or later.

Taking care not to jostle anyone, Husband rose from the sleeping mat, slipped into his work clothes, and moved stealthily to the door. Already the morning was bright enough to dim the stars. When he stepped outside the cold air felt like a slap across the face. When he breathed out through his mouth, he could see steam. He did it again, and then again, pretending that he was smoking a cigarette. Only once before, when he was a small boy, had such a thing happened. That year many had died from the cold, because there were very few among them who'd owned blankets. But enough of the games; one had to keep in motion to endure cold such as this.

Husband jogged along the narrow path to the outbuilding. Halfway there he stopped abruptly, and then stepped back. Lying across the path was a stout gaboon viper, one of the deadliest snakes in Africa. Husband stood motionless as long as he could, waiting for the viper to move. When Husband could tolerate the standoff no longer, he backtracked to where he could find a stick. When prodded the snake finally moved, but sluggishly. Showing no interest in Husband it slithered slowly into the elephant grass, stopping even before its tail disappeared.

Having wasted precious time, Husband skipped the privy and headed straight for the banana grove.

Loving eyes watched Husband pause halfway to the privy. What could be the reason? Was he suffering from the cold? Never had she experienced cold this intense. It was almost unbearable. If she darted back into the hut and grabbed a blanket, she might not loose track of Husband. But she would definitely wake the others. She shivered, her teeth rattling, as she waited for Husband to move. What was he doing now? He'd turned and appeared to be searching for something. Was that a stick? A moment later Husband began to run, passing the privy and not stopping until he reached the banana grove.

With her arms folded tightly across her body in order to preserve heat, she waited until Husband emerged, and then, as before, followed him on the road to town.

* * *

Husband hadn't even made it as far as the bridge when he saw a truck coming. Perhaps it wasn't an official rule, but cars and trucks in the Congo had the right of way. Both pedestrians and cyclists were expected to throw themselves to the side of the road, while the vehicles barreled on unimpeded. Animals either fled in terror or died under the wheels. The drivers never stopped to see if the people were okay, but sometimes, if they hit a pig or other large animal, they might stop just long enough to check for dents before speeding off again in a torrent of swearwords.

This truck was moving slowly, and the driver seemed to be scanning the throng of workers crossing over into the white sector for the day. When the truck was just a few meters away, it stopped, and a white man jumped out.

"You there!" he barked. "Are you the fellow who works for the postmaster?"

Husband's heart raced. This could only be bad news. Perhaps M. Dupree had gone to the police, or the OP, and he would now be arrested. Or maybe it was something less sinister, such as the fact that M. Dupree had found a new man to raise and lower the flag, and to keep the stones and tree trunks whitewashed. In any case, why had M. Dupree not come in person?

"*Well?* Are you that fellow?"

"*Oui, monsieur.*"

"I thought so, based on that poor excuse for a uniform you're wearing. Do you know who I am?"

"*Oui.* You are Monsieur Nunez, the manager of the white people's store. Monsieur Dupree has sent me there to buy things for him on occasion."

"That is correct, but in addition to being the store manager, I am also Monsieur Dupree's close friend."

Husband nodded. He knew that the men were friends, and he thought that they might even be more than just friends. The clerks at the store had spread stories through the village—stories about how frequently M. Dupree visited their boss, and about what they thought was really going on in the back office. Of course none of this was Husband's business, and besides, M. Dupree had always treated him with kindness.

"Monsieur Leur Mort"—the merchant translated his name into French, which, admittedly, sounded strange—"your boss regrets that he cannot make the appointment this morning."

Husband could feel the cold beads of sweat that were breaking out on his forehead. "I see."

"But not to worry, yes? Because I am here to pick up the parcel on his behalf."

"Parcel?" Husband's hand gripped tighter that same small parcel made of a young banana leaf in his right hand.

"That one," M. Nunez said, pointing.

"Ah, this! But you see, sir, I am under strict orders not to give this to anyone, except to Monsieur Dupree."

"*Oui*, but of course. Still that was before Monsieur Dupree took ill and had to be flown to Luluaburg."

"Ill?" Yesterday his boss had been the picture of good health.

"*Oui*, it is very serious. Something to do with his heart."

"That is bad news indeed. Please tell him that I will think positive thoughts today on his behalf. I will perform a ritual as well."

"Ritual? What kind of ritual?"

"I am a witch doctor. I will offer some gifts to the spirits."

"How fascinating, and how kind of you. Now, if you please, hand me the parcel."

"I cannot, monsieur."

"Of course you can. Just extend your right arm. Then open your fingers."

Husband turned and began walking rapidly the other way.

"Monsieur Leur Mort!" The white man jumped back into the

truck and resumed driving—slowly, but directly at the grounds-keeper.

Husband began to walk at a fast clip.

"I'll run you down. Don't make me run you down! A lot of innocent people could be hurt."

Husband glanced around and spotted Cripple hobbling down the hill from the village. She too must have gotten an early start. He stopped, and so did the truck.

"You have made a wise decision," M. Nunez said. He sounded vastly relieved.

It occurred to Husband that the man might be bluffing. But he had lived long enough, seen the white man do enough inexplicable things, to know that one could never be sure what they would do next. After all, it was within their power to do anything they wished—if not to themselves, then to the African. One man's word against another did not apply if they were not of the same color.

Husband reached out and dropped the parcel into the waiting palm of the Portuguese store manager. "Someday it will no longer be like this," he said.

"I won't be here when that day comes," M. Nunez said, and the truck roared up the hill, straight at the people coming down.

CHAPTER TWENTY-ONE

African civet cats (*Civettictis civeta*) are not really cats, although they do share some distant ancestors with the cat family. In general, they are small spotted omnivores with long muzzles and bodies that give them a mongoose shape. They secrete copious amounts of scent (also called civet), which was historically used as a fixative in fine perfumes. The scent was scraped from the perineal glands, a process that was painful to the animal. Today most perfume manufactures use a synthetic substitute.

It was a miracle no one was hurt—that's what the village Christians said, the ones who'd been spared death beneath the wheels of the store manager's truck. Cripple grimaced when she heard that sort of talk.

"Husband," she said, leaning on his arm as they walked together to the missionary rest home, "let us suppose that the incident that just happened was indeed a miracle."

"Which it was not."

"At any rate, this spirit, whom the Christians call God, chose to spare the people in the truck's way."

"That's right. Baba Esetah said she saw an angel, with his back to the truck, spread his wings in order to slow it down enough to allow the people time to jump into the drainage ditches."

"Was the angel a black man, or a white man?"

"If he was an angel, then he was not a man at all."

"But were his feathers black like a vulture's or white like those of a cattle egret?"

"Do you mock the Christians, wife?"

"Of course not! I am a very curious woman, Husband. You know that."

"Indeed."

"So this is what I really want to know; instead of just slowing down the truck, why did the angel not disable it altogether? Perhaps even make it roll backwards and over the falls?"

Husband laughed. "Wife, you are trouble."

"I will not deny that. But now that we are alone, Husband, tell me the business you had with that white man?"

She could feel him tense. "Me? I had no business with him! He stopped to ask where he could buy some of our local palm wine—as if I should know such a thing. I tell you, I was deeply offended by that. Tell me, Wife, do I look like the sort of man who drinks palm wine?"

"Truly you do."

"Wife," he said, and then laughed.

"Husband, what is it that you gave him?"

"Nothing."

"The white man hurt your feelings, so now you hurt mine."

He pulled away from her, freeing himself from her arm. "What do you mean?"

"You do not trust me, Husband, so you lie to me. This man—the one who almost ran over us—is the same man who manages the store for whites. He has many Congolese employees. If it is palm wine he wants, he needs only to send one of them to buy it for him. And do not lie to me any longer about the parcel. My body is weak, but my eyes are strong and clear. So I will ask you one more time. What did you give him?"

Husband sighed dramatically. "All right. But you must promise not to be angry."

"I promise."

"And you must tell no one."

"Of course."

"As I said, I gave him nothing. It was he who took from me. He stole it right out of my hand."

"What could he steal from you, Husband? You own nothing but a good heart and a keen mind." Flattery was something men craved, just as surely as they craved air.

"And potions. Do not forget those. Some of the potions I make are very powerful. They are of great value to some."

"As you say, Husband." The truth be known, Husband's medicine was no stronger than the faith his patients brought with them. "So? What was stolen?"

"A diamond."

"What?"

"A very large diamond. As big as a hen's egg and as clear as a glass of spring water."

It was time to pretend that she was as innocent as Baby Boy. "Truly, truly?"

"Yes."

"Aiyee!" Cripple clapped her hands to her temples and commenced wailing like a mourner. "Aiyee! Aiyeeeeeee!"

Husband had no choice but to put his hand firmly over her mouth. "Hush, Wife! Others are looking this way. What I am telling you must remain secret. Do you understand?"

Cripple nodded vigorously, but when Husband removed his hand, she felt compelled to say *aiyee* just one more time, although almost inaudibly. "Where did you get this diamond?"

"Baby Boy found it."

"*Our* Baby Boy?"

"Yes. Apparently he found it somewhere in the manioc field and was sucking on it when Second Wife returned to the village from chopping weeds."

"Does my sister wife know about this?"

"She saw the stone briefly, but I am sure it did not occur to her that it could be a diamond. It is too big, for one thing. And where would Second Wife have seen a diamond?"

"Husband, how is it that you know this stone is a diamond?"

"Cripple, do you not recall that I once worked in the mines?"

"Yes, before our marriage. But that was many years ago,"

"One does not forget the look of a diamond, or the feel of one."

"Where were you going with this diamond when the white man took it?"

"I was on my way to sell it."

"To whom? Is it not true that the Consortium owns all the diamonds in this province?"

"It is true, but it does not own the desires of individual men. I was to meet another man on the bridge, a man whose desire for wealth exceeded his loyalty to the company. Now what am I going to tell him? He will accuse me of selling the stone to someone else. He may even tell the police about our arrangement, but lie about his own involvement. I could be arrested and put into prison."

Cripple reached for his arm again, and gave his bicep a good squeeze. "Nothing could be farther from the truth, Husband. They cannot put you in prison for a stone that does not exist."

"But it does!"

"Then where is it? It is not hidden on you. If they search you, they will not find it. This buyer you spoke of will look foolish in the eyes of the police. Trust me, Husband. He will say nothing."

Their Death placed his hand over hers. It was as intimate a

gesture as he had ever shown her in public, bordering even on the scandalous. Such displays of affection were engaged in only by Europeans, who often did unseemly things. Cripple had heard stories about Belgium women who worshipped the sun, lying on long, flat chairs, with their *thighs* totally exposed, while they said their prayers. And to think that white people—especially Americans—had a problem with seeing uncovered breasts!

Well, there can be enough of a good thing. Deftly, Cripple slid her hand out from beneath Husband's, lest her own reputation fall even lower than that of the European harlots. Life was already almost as much as she could bear without adding sexual impropriety to her long list of faults.

When they reached the narrow dirt road that skirted the falls and led to the guesthouse, Cripple invited Husband to continue walking with her.

"You are still early for work," she said, trying hard not to sound overly anxious.

"Yes."

"And your heart is heavy."

"Truly, truly."

"Husband, if it is well with you, I would like you to meet the new *mamu*."

"Why?"

"Because she is a good woman—a good white woman."

Husband stopped walking. "Cripple, I do not believe that all white people are the same. My boss, Monsieur Dupree, has always been fair to me."

"Yet you long for the day when we will have our independence."

"And you do not? Why is it, Cripple, that you do not wish us to have our own nation?"

"I do, Husband, I do. But I think that it will be like giving birth, and that is a painful process. And, as you above all others should know, sometimes the child does not survive. Husband, I fear for you."

He grabbed her hand, squeezed it, and dropped it just as quickly. "Come, take me to meet your *mamu*. One can never meet too many good women."

The postmaster was at a loss as to what to do. At precisely half past six he'd driven onto the bridge, but Their Death was nowhere to be seen. The transfer had to be quick, seamless in its execution; he couldn't very well park the truck and wait. This was unbelievable! Their Death had always been so reliable.

At a loss for what to do next, the postmaster kept driving until he reached the white cemetery, where he turned the truck around. Then it was back down the hill and across the bridge again, as slowly as he dared, as he searched the swelling ranks of African workers for a familiar face. His second time across, the postmaster stopped and pretended to admire the view.

Any other day there would have been no need to pretend, but this wasn't any other day; this was the beginning of a fabulous life, one that would be shared with the love of his life, Cezar Nunez. Damn Their Death for causing him so much unneeded stress. It wasn't like the man. If there ever was a stand-up, solid African who could be counted on, it was Their Death.

Finally, at ten minutes to seven, the postmaster gave up on waiting and drove straight to his employee's house. He'd been there before, when Their Death had been struck with a severe bout of malaria, and once when one of Their Death's middle sons had been temporarily blinded by a spitting cobra. He'd driven the child and his parents to the nearest Protestant mission station, one that maintained a hospital. Ironic, wasn't it, having to drive a witch doctor to a hospital? But in Congo that was par for the course.

There was a Belgian doctor living in Belle Vue—a real doctor whose job it was to care for the health of the Consortium employees and their families. That included the eighty-seven whites, but excluded the five hundred plus villagers. For the villagers, a male nurse was driven all the way over from Luluaburg every Saturday to hold a four-hour clinic. If there were still patients to see at the end of the four hours, well, that was too bad. The road to Luluaburg passed through Bashilele territory; it wasn't safe to drive there after dark. Villagers unlucky enough to become seriously ill the other six days either recovered on their own, resorted to treatment by witch doctors, or walked to the nearest Protestant mission, which was fifty kilometers away.

But having been to Their Death's house was not the same as knowing where it was. The village was a maze of mud wall, thatch-roof huts, built higgledy-piggledy along narrow lanes that were obstructed by chickens, dogs, and most important, bands of naked children. Dupree was not averse to running over the occasional chicken, and he'd grazed a dog or two in his time, but children were strictly off-limits.

"*Pardonez mois, monsieur,*" he said to an old man standing near the entrance to one of these lanes, "can you tell me the way to Their Death's house?"

The old man grinned, displaying a paucity of teeth. It was clear he didn't understand a word of French. He probably hadn't even understood Dupree's pronunciation of the African name.

Dupree drove along the road to the beginning of the next lane. "*Muoyo webe,*" he said in halting Tshiluba to a young woman who'd just emerged from a hut with a floor space no greater than that of his truck bed. It was a wonderful greeting, meaning "life to you," but they were the only words of Tshiluba he knew.

"Life to you," the woman said in return.

Dupree had no choice but to switch back to French. "I'm looking for the home of Monsieur Their Death. Can you tell me where it is?"

She made a clucking sound against her front teeth, which Dupree recognized as the universal "no." But then she squinted in thought.

"Monsieur, I think maybe there are five people with that name." Thank God she spoke excellent French!

Dupree grinned. Now he was getting somewhere.

"This man is tall, and he—" Damn it. What else could he say? That his employee had brown skin, black hair, and dark eyes? All these years and Dupree had not really looked at Their Death close enough to adequately describe him. Damn it, damn it, damn it. "Ah, yes! He's a witch doctor, and his wife is crippled."

"Yes, yes, now I know this man. He lives over there." She pointed up the road, and then indicated that he would have to make a left turn.

"Can you please be more specific?"

"No, monsieur. There are many paths into the village, as you can see, and the way to their house is complicated. I, myself, have only just moved here from Djoka Punda."

"But you said you know them!"

"*Oui.* Everyone knows them because he is the witch doctor. 'Look at Their Death and his wife, Cripple,' they say, when these two pass. 'If he is such a good witch doctor, why can he not cure her?' Then they laugh. But not me, monsieur. I am a Christian. I do not believe in witch doctors. Besides, it is not right to—"

"*Excusez mois!* I only want directions to their house."

"But I have never been to their house."

Dupree had no doubt the woman was lying. She'd started telling him the truth, then had second thoughts. You couldn't blame her for wanting to protect one of her own kind, but it was frustrating as hell. And it was getting more and more like this every day. Africans who had once been obedient and compliant now had sniffed the air of independence, of self-actualization, and answered only when they pleased, and then had the audacity to lie.

What was the Congo going to be like when independence finally did come? Would the blacks start ordering the whites around as if they were—well, black? If that happened, he would be long gone. At least that was the plan. Had *been* the plan. If only he could locate Their Death.

Dupree decided—but not without some regret—that his plan needed reworking. He would turn around and head back across the river and to the post office. If he did not spot Their Death along the way, he would remain at the post office. All night even, if he had to.

But it was only an hour later when Their Death appeared, and practically shaking with emotion, related his far-fetched tale.

CHAPTER TWENTY-TWO

The pied colobus (*Colobus angolensis*) is a spectacular large monkey. The body is black, but the face is framed in white fur, the shoulders are draped in long white fur epaulettes, and half of the tail is white. This animal is prized by the locals for both its meat and its fur. The latter is used in ceremonial headgear and to decorate the tips of a king's—or a chief's—scepter. Baby colobus monkeys are born pure white and look as if they belong to another species altogether.

I don't believe it!" M. Dupree said, his eyes flashing with anger. "I don't have time to hear your filthy lies."

"Monsieur, I am telling the truth."

"*Merde.* Tell me, why did you feed me those lies about a diamond, when you knew you'd get caught?"

Their Death could feel the vein on his left temple throbbing. He wondered if his boss could see it.

"Monsieur, if you please, I didn't know I'd get caught, because there really is such a stone."

"Then where is it? Oh, I get it now! You're holding out for more money."

"*Pardonez mois?*"

"You want a bigger cut of the deal; a larger percentage. That's pretty cheeky, given that I haven't even seen the stone."

Their Death decided not to honor the accusation with a response.

M. Dupree stared at him, looking helpless, as if unsure how to proceed. "So," he finally growled, "I'm right, aren't I?"

Still Their Death held his tongue.

"Look, you will confess sooner or later. Wouldn't you rather tell me than the *Bula Matadi*?"

It was not even a veiled threat. Their Death knew exactly what was at stake. The *Bula Matadi* would beat him with the dried hide of a hippopotamus which, being three centimeters thick, was more like being hit with a stout stick than with a whip. Cripple's husband knew many men (and a few women too) whose backs bore permanent keloid welts thanks to the infamous *Bula Matadi* and their hippo-hide whips.

It was time to speak, but not to give up. "Monsieur, are you not curious to know the identity of the man who stole the diamond?"

His boss sighed dramatically. "Proceed. I'll listen to your story, and then I'll be even more pissed, because you'll have wasted more of my time."

"Monsieur, it will not have been a waste, if you take my word as truth. The man who stole the diamond is the same man who manages the food store for whites here in Belle Vue."

The postmaster's mouth opened and closed several times, without producing a sound.

"It's true, Monsieur Dupree. I was on my way to meet you at the appointed hour, but this man—I don't know his name— approached in a car. He said he recognized me because of this uniform." Their Death referred to his blue shorts and shirt that were *de rigueur* for the job, even that of whitewashing stones.

"Go on," the postmaster croaked.

"He said you couldn't make it to our rendezvous and had sent him in your place. Then he demanded that I give him the small parcel I was carrying. I tried to refuse, monsieur, but he grew angry and snatched it from my hand. Then he drove away so fast he nearly hit some villagers, including my wife."

"Which way did he go?"

"Past the village, and toward Luluaburg. Are you not angry that he nearly killed people?"

"Yes, yes, of course. Are you absolutely *positive* the man was Senhor Nunez? The manager of the store?"

"Absolutely, monsieur."

The postmaster buried his face in his hands. "Go," he said sharply.

"*Oui, monsieur.* Today I will sprinkle the path with water, so as to keep down the dust—"

"I don't care what the hell you do. Just get the hell out of here and leave me alone!"

"Very well," Their Death said, but he meant just the opposite. The diamond had been his discovery, yet to hear M. Dupree, it had been *his* to lose, not Their Death's. That was so typical of the Europeans, was it not? They came, took what they wanted, and then if they lost something, they wept like children.

What if it were the other way around? What if Their Death was in Belgium, working as—that's as far as he got. In fact, he couldn't even imagine himself arriving in Belgium because, despite all his years in a Catholic school, taught by a Belgian priest, Their Death did not possess the visual tools required to mentally place himself there. He had never seen a picture of Belgium. Not one. The best he could conjure up was a sea of white, featureless faces, which still somehow managed to convey their deep displeasure at his being there.

Since his boss didn't care what the hell he did, Their Death decided that a nice long nap should precede the ground sprinkling, and then after that, perhaps another nap. Sleeping was the only way to dull the sharp sense of disappointment he was feeling, the pain of having his dreams literally snatched away.

Soon a new day would dawn in the Congo. When that day came the Monsieur Duprees, the OPs, all of the whites would be guests in *his* country. If they wished to remain here, they would have to treat everyone with dignity and kindness.

Second Wife had not slept well; the night had been far too cold for one thin blanket spread over three people. In fact, Second Wife had almost gotten up and sought heat amongst the bodies of her children, who shared another blanket. But it was Second Wife's night in the marriage bed, and she was not about to forfeit a minute of it. After he'd performed his husbandly duties, Husband had lifted the blanket and invited Cripple to sleep next to him and share his body heat. And with Second Wife lying just on the other side of him!

Second Wife, who had been born and raised downriver near Charlesville, where the land was low-lying, had never experienced anything near this cold. Neither had she heard of a husband who invited a wife into his bed on a night that was not hers. And the nerve of that little woman. Did she not see the pain she caused her sister wife?

Besides, Cripple—who had been reared in Belle Vue village— was more accustomed to such cold. But if she was uncomfortably cold, she should have remained in the family bed with her sister children. After all, it is children who sprawl over their mother when asleep, unlike husbands, who roll in the other direction. *Eyo*, Cripple would have been much warmer in the children's bed.

But Cripple was not known for her acts of kindness, nor for women's intuition. The woman was selfish to the core, and needed to be cut down a notch or two before the family's reputation was irreparably ruined. Perhaps it was already too late. For years neighbors had been making jokes about Husband, calling him *Mukashi-mulume.* "Woman Husband." Didn't he know he was the laughingstock of the village? As the old adage went, It is easier to grow a stone than to restore a reputation.

Well, there was one in the village who might be able to help. And yes, it was taking drastic measures, but the time had finally come for that, *nasha*?

This was the last straw. The camel's back was broken, and there was going to be no calling in the veterinarian. As soon as he could be located, Nunez was going to be dragged in—hopefully kicking and screaming—and the OP was going to give him a piece of his mind before handing him his severance papers.

This morning had started off with Heilewid still so pickled from last night's turn with the bottle that she couldn't have shown up to join him for breakfast, had she even tried. And although there was coffee, there were no fresh croissants, and not enough butter to spread on the stale ones leftover from yesterday's breakfast. When the OP questioned Cook, he smelled palm wine on the man's breath.

Always stubborn, but not always practical, the OP ordered Cook to whip his fat butt over to the store and buy butter, and whatever pastries goods had been baked that morning. If he didn't return in twenty minutes, he no longer had a job. Would he really hold Cook to such a strict timeline? Perhaps. But at least pondering the question kept his mind occupied until Cook returned. That, and watching the long-tailed birds flit across the lawn.

Cook was back in eighteen minutes, tears streaming down his face. "*Pardonez mois, monsieur,*" he stammered, "the store is locked and there is no one about. Not even the night watchman."

The OP slammed the patio table with his fist. "Damn that Nunez. Damn that man all to hell and back."

"*Oui, monsieur.*"

"I should have trusted my gut instinct; I should never have hired a Portuguese."

"Monsieur?"

"What?" the OP snapped.

"Am I still employed, monsieur?"

"Barely. The next time I catch you drinking, the next time you can't haul your fat butt into work in time to make fresh croissants, for certain that is the day you can say *adieu* to your job."

"*Oui, monsieur. Merci!*"

"Go back to the grocery and wait. When Monsieur Nunez arrives, tell him I want to see him, *tout de suite*, at my office."

"*Oui, monsieur.*"

"That is all, Cook. Ah—just one more thing. When I come home for my dinner, I expect it to be ready."

Anyone with a modicum of brains would have known that now was the time to follow orders to the letter. Cook, who had been trained by the prior OP's wife, was adept at making French sauces, but was woefully lacking the obedience gene. The fool didn't budge.

"I said, *That is all*. Are you hard of hearing?"

"No, monsieur. But I think I may know the whereabouts of Monsieur Nunez."

"At home in bed? With his wife? That is hardly news."

"Monsieur, I think it is possible he is with Monsieur Dupree?"

"What? The two of them gone off hunting again?"

Cook shrugged. "Monsieur, there are rumors in the village."

The OP formed a fist with his right hand and pushed hard the palm of his left. Now he was really pissed off. One of the least savory legacies of colonialism was the product of the conquerers' loins. Half-caste children didn't have a place in either society. The OP had seen children almost as white as he was, raised like Africans, but taunted by their playmates and adults alike. Of course the reverse could happen as well, with the children being exceptionally dark-skinned. But even these never felt fully accepted, never quite achieving parity in their mothers' tribes.

What was going to happen once their fathers retired back to Europe, and were no longer able to keep an eye on their offspring? What if the worst predictions came true and the Africans kicked all the Europeans out of the country? Would they kick the biracial children out as well? If so, the children certainly weren't going to be welcome in lily-white Flanders, that much was for sure.

"Where are the children?" the OP roared. "In the workers' village, or tucked somewhere back in the bush?"

Cook was a genius at looking confused. "Children?"

"Don't give me that nonsense, damn it. Answer now, and answer truthfully."

"But monsieur, this—this sort of activity . . . does not produce children."

It was the OP's turn to look confused. Gradually the meaning of Cook's coded answers became clear. As it did, it answered other questions that had occurred to the OP, but which he'd pushed from his mind, telling himself it was all imagined. Well, this put a different face on things, didn't it? It was one thing to father illegitimate children—colonialists did it all over the world—but this . . . this was of a more sensitive nature.

The OP was, at least in his opinion, a sophisticated man, who knew some homosexuals back in Brussels. Not being a particularly religious man, and quite secure in his own manhood, he had no truck with their lifestyle. But that was in Belgium, where people were racially homogeneous—not counting, of course, the Walloon-Flemish rift. Indeed, no doubt there were many Belgians who would rather their children be homosexual than take up with "the other sort of Belgian." But here, in Congo, a Belgian of any stripe was supposed to maintain a certain standard of behavior, so as to set an example for the "less-evolved" African. It was merely a fact of life that homosexual relations fell several notches lower on the morality pole than miscegenation.

"Go to the post office," he said quietly. "If he is not there, go to his house. Tell him to meet me at my office in five minutes. And don't repeat what you just told me to anyone. Is that clear?"

"*Oui, monsieur.*"

CHAPTER TWENTY-THREE

The scientific name for the ostrich is *Struthio camelus*, which means "sparrow camel" in Greek. Ostriches are the largest living birds, and males have reached nine feet in height, with the record weight 350 lbs. Ostrich have the biggest eyes of all land animals, including elephants, and their eggs are the largest single cells on earth. Their legs are very powerful and can eviscerate large animals. It is a myth that ostriches hide their heads in the sand. It probably stems from the fact that they keep their heads low to the ground when feeding.

Dupree drove slowly along Boulevard des Rois. The wide dirt road only qualified as a boulevard because of the strip of flower beds down the middle, but when the jacaranda trees that lined it were in bloom, it was as impressive as any street in Brussels. If Belle Vue could lay claim to a city center, this would be it. The grocery store, the club, the mechanic shop, the petrol station, the primary school for white children—these were all located along Boulevard of the Kings, as the American missionaries called it.

Dupree accelerated when he saw the mixed cluster of whites and black servants waiting outside the entrance to the grocery. Their Death was right about one thing: Cezar Nunez was not at work. He wondered if he should be the one to the break the news to Branca, but just as quickly discarded the idea. Branca Nunez was nobody's fool. She knew what was going on—she had to. Cezar had compared her to a dead fish: cool, slippery, and totally unresponsive.

Let the OP be the one to tell the bitch. The OP didn't have to deal with his own sense of loss, coupled with feelings of betrayal. Dupree would tell the OP that Nunez had absconded with the jewel, but nothing else. What the OP and his wife did behind closed doors was none of Dupree's business, and what Dupree did was none of theirs.

Upon arriving at the OP's house, the postmaster parked under the shade of a mango tree and sat quietly for a few minutes, in order to regain his composure. He needed to appear outraged—which he was on some level—but only that. Still, the smirk on the face of the houseboy who answered the door was enough to knock him off stride.

"I'm here to see the OP," he said, but his inflection betrayed him, turning the statement into a question, and shifting the power to the servant.

"Wait here, monsieur," said the boy, and then closed the door in his face. Imagine that! Closed the damned door right in his face, as if he were a door-to-door salesman or, worse yet, engaged in one of the street trades, such as rag collecting or panhandling.

Dupree was prepared to the give the boy a piece of his mind, but when the door opened again, it was the OP standing there.

"Come in," said the OP. "Actually, come right through the house. We can have coffee on the verandah. But I can't offer you any croissants, because the cook is lazy and the store is closed."

"*Tres bien, monsieur.*" Very good. Although things could hardly be worse for Dupree.

The OP gave him the seat with the best view, along with a

demonstration of mind reading. "The view isn't as good as the one from the Nunez verandah. Have you been to their house?"

"*Ah oui—mais non.*"

"Which is it? Yes? Or no?"

"I have been to the house, monsieur, but not to the terrace."

"So it is on the terrace that one gets the best view?"

Dupree wasn't so stupid that he didn't know the bastard was toying with him. "Monsieur OP, I have some terrible news."

"*Oui?*"

"Monsieur, I was unable to make the rendezvous on the bridge this morning."

The OP's expression changed from playful to deadly. The cat meant business.

"What the hell happened?"

"I was there on time, sir. And my employee brought the diamond with him as he promised. But you see, Monsieur Nunez beat me to it."

"I still don't understand. Make some sense, man!"

"As my employee—Their Death is his name—was coming down the hill to the bridge, Monsieur Nunez happened across and stopped to chat with him."

"*Chat* with him? What about?"

"The weather, monsieur—how cold it's been lately. And then Monsieur Nunez noticed that my employee was carrying a small packet, and asked him what was in it. Of course Their Death refused to show him, but Monsieur Nunez became agitated— you know how volatile those Iberians can be—and so the poor man had no choice but to show him. And that is when Monsieur Nunez grabbed the parcel and drove off."

"*Merde*! Are you *sure*? How can you be certain that this 'Their Death' man isn't lying?"

"Monsieur, he is devastated—as am I! He had his future riding on this stone. Now he has nothing."

"Where did Nunez go?"

"Most probably to Luluaburg. It is the closest real city, monsieur, with many Portuguese, and other foreigners, some with shady reputations. And then there is the possibility he abandoned the truck and walked across the border to Angola. That is a Portuguese colony—"

"I am not an idiot, Dupree! I don't need a geography lesson. It's also seventy kilometers to the border, and bush all the way. Most of it lion country. He would be eaten alive—if snakes didn't kill him first."

Betrayed though he was, the postmaster could not bare the thought of his lover dying alone in the bush. And the image of a lion tearing him limb from handsome limb was too much to bear. But if Cezar was in Luluaburg, there was always a chance of reconciliation. Someday. And if Cezar made it out of the country with the gem—well, wealth *and* reconciliation were even better.

"Monsieur OP, begging your pardon, I think the authorities in Luluaburg should be notified and—"

"Shut up, Dupree! Quit telling me my job."

"*Oui, monsieur.*"

"You do realize that this diamond would have done more than just line your pockets, don't you? It would not be exaggerating to say that it might have changed the future of this company. I can tell by that look in your eyes that you don't believe me. I'm sure you thought I was just looking out for my own interests. But it just so happens, Dupree—and I don't expect you to have known of this, because you work in the post office, not the mines—that production has dropped to the point that we are in danger of being shut down."

Dupree said nothing. After all, he'd been told to shut up.

"Boy!" the OP shouted. "Bring whiskey, not coffee, and bring it now!"

Almost immediately the smirking servant appeared, bearing a tray with a bottle of malt whiskey and two heavy glasses. He set the tray on the table and picked up the bottle, but the OP stopped him from pouring.

"That's all, boy."

Dupree cringed. The OP, in his opinion, was not an evil man, but the way he treated the Africans was beyond patronizing. It was humiliating. The servant, rude and condescending as he was, was still a man.

But treating servants this way was something all the colonials did; boy this, boy that, it was boy, boy, boy for them. Except for Nunez. He treated his employees as equals. That was one of the many things Dupree admired about the man . . .

"Dupree! Aren't you going to drink?"

The postmaster realized with a start that his drink had been poured, and the OP was waiting to make a toast of some kind. Or, worse yet, the OP had already made a toast, and was waiting for Dupree to respond.

"*Oui*," Dupree said, as he raised his glass.

"I want you to get started on it immediately. Forget about the post office."

"But sir, with all due respect, as postmaster I answer to His Majesty's Colonial Government, not the Consortium. I cannot, as you say, 'forget' about it."

The OP blinked with surprise, a reaction that Dupree noted with pleasure. Everyone agreed that the OP ruled Belle Vue like a dictator. Yes, most of the time he was a benevolent dictator, but he was never a man to be crossed. Even the Catholic fathers who ran the African school and the Americans who operated a guesthouse were always careful to stay on his good side.

"Look, Dupree," the dictator said, "you run the post office, but it is on Consortium land. It has just been brought to my attention that there are diamonds under your stinking building, so I am ordering you to move it."

"You must be joking."

"I never joke about diamonds."

Dupree was only briefly tempted to call the OP's bluff. Then he remembered that the OP had made good on his threat to fire two of his Belgian employees if they couldn't stop their teenage son from shooting, with a homemade slingshot, the long-tailed birds that flitted about on the grassy lawns. "Boys will be boys," the parents had said when warned about their son's behavior, but were sent packing the next day when the kid shot three of the ungainly but spectacular creatures.

"Monsieur OP," Dupree said, "you have my full attention. What is it you wish me to do?"

"Give me back that whiskey, man. I had no idea you were a teetotaler." The OP waited while Dupree set down the glass. "You are to find out from this 'Their Death' fellow exactly where it is he found that diamond. And I mean exactly—within a meter."

"Monsieur, what if he refuses to divulge this information?"

"Dupree, during the war I fought with the Resistance. Believe me, there is always a way to get a man to talk."

The postmaster swallowed hard, wishing he'd slugged back the whiskey when he'd had the chance.

"*Oui, monsieur.*"

"You have twenty-four hours, Dupree. After that, your job won't be the only thing on the chopping block. Do I make myself clear?"

The bastard was referring to his reputation. He was threatening to expose the postmaster's private life, if he didn't somehow persuade—or force—Their Death into revealing his diamond's provenance. And it *was* still Their Death's diamond. No money had changed hands. Not a single franc.

But even if the man could be made to talk, who in their right mind would pass that information back to the OP? Not Dupree, that's for damn sure. There were ways of smuggling diamonds out of the Congo—drastic ways, to be sure, but . . .

"Dupree! Do I make myself clear?"

"*Oui*, Monsieur OP. Very clear."

CHAPTER TWENTY-FOUR

The Cape buffalo (*Syncerus caffer*) is a large wild ox found in many areas south of the Sahara. Adult males can exceed two thousand pounds and are armed with thick horns, making them one of Africa's most dangerous game animals. Buffalo calves form very strong bonds with their mothers and their clans, a fact that often enables handicapped members of the herd to survive.

From where he lay on his back, Their Death could trace a mud tunnel, built by red ants, that began at the base of the mango tree and zigzagged up the trunk and an extended limb until it disappeared amongst the dark green of the lance-shaped leaves. Red ant bites were painful, but the ants weren't aggressive like driver ants.

When the rains finally arrived, the driver ants would be begin their migrations. By the millions. More than that. What came after a million? Their Death would ask Cripple; she knew everything.

Their Death was trying to fathom the limits of his wife's knowledge when a small green mango bounced with force off his nose. He sat up and looked around. The postmaster was standing not ten paces away, a grin on his face.

"Is this what I'm paying you for?" the Belgian said.

Their Death stood slowly, and then quite deliberately brushed the leaves and twigs from his clothes. "Monsieur, you said that I should do whatever I wanted."

"So I did! Well, what do you say that we both do something enjoyable? Monsieur Their Death, I am inviting you to my house for lunch."

Their Death wasn't sure if he'd heard right. What could such an offer mean? Their Death had never eaten lunch. One ate cold cassava mush in the morning, and then fresh mush in the evening. If one was hungry during the day—an unlikelihood, since the heavy mush sat in one's stomach like a rock—then one ate bananas, or some other light snack. Such as *mikata*. These pancakes, made from mashed plantains and fried to a crisp in palm oil, were a favorite of Their Death.

But there was more to concern oneself with than the menu. Would he eat with the servants in their compound, or by himself somewhere on the lawn? What if Mr. Dupree's servants were of another tribe, and treated him badly—maybe even tried to poison him? There were too many variables in this offer to make it the least bit attractive. Yet if he refused, it could cost him his job.

"Monsieur Their Death, I didn't ask you for the secret of eternal happiness. So I'll tell you what; I'm going to take your silence as a 'yes.'"

"But—"

"No, no, too late. Now come with me."

The postmaster was grinning foolishly now and gesturing to his automobile. Reluctantly Their Death climbed into the backseat.

Although she was married to a witch doctor, Second Wife had never sought the professional services of one—other than Husband's, of course. Second Wife was a woman of no concern who, up until now, had lived a life of no concern, one that was more or less expected of her, and one that she understood. Witch doctors were for the seriously ill, or those women who could not bear children, or anyone who suspected that they were under a curse. But who would place a curse on a woman of no concern, one whose life was no more, or no less, eventful than that of anyone else in the village?

Witch doctors put curses on people like Kadima Andrew. He was an *évolué* who thought himself better than everyone, and who went so far as to slaughter a goat, which he roasted in full view of his neighbors, who were then forced to smell the tantalizing aroma until their stomachs begged for mercy. Someone, or perhaps even a group of people, paid a witch doctor to put a curse on Kadima. They must have paid very well too, because the curse went into effect the very next morning, when Kadima, who was a clerk for the Consortium, slipped his foot into a shoe that contained a very large, and exceptionally venomous, scorpion.

Because Kadima was a rich *évolué*, the Belgian doctor was sent for. However, before the white doctor could get there, Kadima's house mysteriously burst into flames, causing the already stricken man to suffer a heart attack. Unfortunately the arrogant villager's family suffered as well, losing everything to the fire. But whose fault was that? Not the witch doctor's; he was only administrating justice. And as for the person, or persons, who ordered the curse, were they not justified in their actions? After all, Kadima's wives had assiduously fanned the aroma of roasting goat so that it pervaded their neighbors' hearths. As for Kadima's children, who lost their father and their home—ah, they should be grateful for having learned such a valuable lesson so early in life.

But today the children involved would not lose a working father. At the most, if all went well, they would lose only a useless sister mother, a crippled woman who barely counted as one. What's more, they stood to gain more of their father's time, as well as see their true mother blossom in happiness. First, however, there was the case to be made to the witch doctor. Might he refuse to even hear her case?

Strictly speaking, Much Medicine and Husband were not rivals, because they belonged to different tribes. One would no more seek the services of a witch doctor who belonged to another tribe than would a zebra wish to marry a lion. It simply wasn't done—although lack of trust had a lot to do with it.

But there are times in life when the zebra must at least flirt with the lion, lest it become his dinner. Second Wife had never seen a zebra, and only the tail of a dead lion, but she thought her analogy was a good one. The risk she was taking was immense, but it was also a matter of survival. What else could she do?

Needless to say, the lion was surprised when the zebra came to call. "Who is the woman," he demanded, "and what is the nature of her request?"

Second Wife, who was kneeling outside on a mat, had a mother's ears and could hear every word being spoken inside the witch doctor's hut.

"She is a woman of no account—except that she is also the wife of Their Death, the Muluba witch doctor."

"Eh," the old man grunted. "What does she want with me? I have put no curses on her family."

"She desires to buy medicine."

"For what purpose?"

"She will not say."

"What is she prepared to pay me?"

"She refuses to say that as well, *mukelenge*. But she has many children."

"Boys?"

"*Eyo*, I believe so."

"Then tell her to come in."

The witch doctor's hut was large and constructed of the finest *malala*, but there were no windows. As she stepped inside, Second Wife was reminded of a womb. It took her eyes several seconds to adjust to the dim light, and when they had, she slowly made out the form of the *muena tshihaha*. He was an old man, as wrinkled as an overripe guava. He was sitting cross-legged on a leopard skin and was clad only in a loincloth made of palm leaf fibers. Around his neck hung a string of leopard claws interspersed with charms.

"Sit," the witch doctor ordered.

Second Wife squatted on her haunches, which was the true meaning of sit when no chair was offered. She pretended to study the dirt floor of the hut.

"If your husband is a witch doctor," he said, "why have you come to me? Is his medicine not powerful enough? Do his curses fail to achieve the intended results?"

The zebra must pretend not to be offended by the lion, even if his breath smells of other zebras. Second Wife hung her head meekly.

"*Eyo, mukelenge*. My husband is a poor, incompetent witch doctor compared to you. He does not even possess a leopard skin."

"What? No leopard skin? Then where does he get the power to do magic?"

"That is the problem exactly, *mukelenge*. Can you imagine a witch doctor with only a goat skin?" The truth is Husband did not even own a goat skin, relying instead on traditional herbs to fix bodies, and the response of his patients to tribal legends to fix minds. It was also true that husband had a very low success rate.

The old man laughed uproariously, displaying a paucity of teeth. His attendant laughed loudly as well.

"A goat skin lacks the power to cure even a chigger bite," the witch doctor said at last. "It is no wonder then that you are here. So now tell me what it is you want."

"I want happiness. This I cannot have because my husband has room in his thoughts only for his first wife."

"I see. So you are a *mukau*." A second wife.

"*Eyo.*"

"How long have you been with this man? How many years?"

"Ten long dry seasons, and ten short."

"That is ten years, as the white man reckons. Do you have children by him?"

"I have seven."

"And they are healthy?"

"Every one."

"How many boys?"

"Four boys."

The witch doctor smiled. "Then the spirits have been kind to you."

"*Eyo*, but not in everything. There remains the problem of that troublesome woman."

"Your sister wife. Has she any children?"

"Not a one! But still, his love for her is beyond reason."

"Is she cruel to you?"

Using her tongue, Second Wife pushed air through her upper teeth. The resulting sound was a cluck of disapproval that was understood by many tribes in the area, not just the Baluba and Bena Lulua.

"She does not beat me, but neither does she help with any of the work."

"Explain further. Does she help in the fields? Does she pound manioc in the mortar?"

"To be fair, *mukelenge*, this woman is a cripple, so nothing is expected of her. Yet she finds it in her being to work for a white *mamu* across the river."

The witch doctor was silent for an unnerving length of time. "Do you truly wish to eliminate this problem in your life?"

"Truly, truly." With reason, Second Wife told herself. And surely that is what the witch doctor meant as well. But if he meant more than that—well, it is known to all that a curse has no effect on an innocent person.

"What can you give me in return?"

Second Wife smiled. She'd been waiting for that question. Keeping her eyes on the witch doctor, she undid the knot of her wraparound skirt, removed some coins, and then made herself decent again.

"I have fifty francs here. It is a lot of money, but you may have it all—*if* you remove this woman from my life forever."

The witch doctor snorted, and his assistant, who had been lurking in the shadows, laughed as well. "Fifty francs will not even buy a potion to rid you of bedbugs. Spells are very expensive, as the ingredients are rare and there is much risk to the one who chants them. The spirits who do the work of my bidding do not like being insulted. Do you understand this?"

"*Eyo*. What then is your price?"

"Your youngest son."

"*What*? Baby Boy? Never!"

Now the witch doctor laughed heartily. "Trust me, I do not want your son. I was only joking. Nor do I want your fifty francs. I want only what you have already given me."

Second Wife was immensely relieved, but she couldn't yet show it. "What is that?"

"Only the satisfaction of knowing that I am the best witch doctor in the village. Otherwise you would not have come to me. I will give you the help you ask, but you must report back to me when the potion works. Do we have an agreement?"

"We have an agreement," Second Wife said, trying to conceal the joy in her voice.

The witchdoctor grunted and clapped his hands. Immediately the assistant bent low so that the medicine man could whisper in his ear. Then he disappeared toward the back of the hut, emerging shortly with a small gourd. The witch doctor took the gourd and mumbled something into the open neck before handing it to Second Wife.

"See that she drinks this. It is practically tasteless, but it is best if it is poured into palm wine."

Second Wife's hands trembled. "But First Wife does not drink palm wine. No woman does."

"You speak the truth. In that case you may wish to mix it with a special treat. Does she like *mikata*?"

In her twenty-six long dry seasons, and twenty-six short—or thereabouts—Second Wife had never met a person who did not like the plantain pancakes, fried in palm oil until crispy around the edges. And never had she met someone who liked them quite as much as Cripple did. It was only a joke, to be said by Husband when First Wife was not around, but the woman would even steal a pancake from Baby Boy's hands—if given the opportunity.

"*Eyo*, she does indeed like them."

"Good. That is all. You may go now."

Second Wife rose, but she was not about to take her leave yet. "Please tell me, *mukelenge*, what will this medicine to do my sister wife?"

CHAPTER TWENTY-FIVE

The Congo gray parrot (*Psittacus erithacus erithacus*) is thought by many to be the most intelligent of all birds. Some of them have learned more than five hundred words, and are able to repeat complete sentences. Some researchers claim that these parrots are sometimes capable of associating words with their meanings. Although not as colorful as some parrot species, this gray bird has a bright crimson tail that is eye-catching. Keeping any parrot, but especially the Congo gray, takes a great deal of commitment.

The cool dry-season mornings were a balm to Branca's soul. She liked nothing better than to snuggle under an extra blanket—maybe two—and pretend she was a girl again in northern Portugal, her whole life still before her. What would she do differently if she knew what she knew now? She wouldn't marry an impotent man, no matter how handsome and virile he was in the beginning. And if she did agree to live in Africa, it would have to be one of the Portuguese colonies, like Angola or Mozambique. At least there she would be an equal among whites. But wait, a girl shouldn't even be bothered with such thoughts. All she need concern herself with today is that she keep her school uniform tidy so that the nuns wouldn't give her demerits—not to mention the dreaded switch—and after school she would head straight over to her friend Angelica's house, where they would sip hot chocolate together on the balcony while they watched the fishing boats come in. Then later, Angelica's family cook would prepare some fish for dinner, because tonight was the sleepover they'd been planning so long.

"*Senhora!*"

Branca looked over shoulder, and then sat up, clutching her blankets around her. "Francois Joseph! You are supposed to knock."

"I did, senhora, but you didn't answer."

"If that's the case, it's because I didn't want to be disturbed. Now leave."

"But senhora, it is Monsieur le Presidente."

"*Excusez moi?*"

"He is here to see you."

"Are you drunk?"

"No, senhora." The pompous man had the temerity to sound offended, even though she'd caught him tippling some fine Port only last week.

"Then which president is it? The American president, or the French?"

"It is neither, madame. It is Monsieur le Presidente de Belle Vue."

"He's not a president, you idiot! And why didn't you say who it was right away?" Branca shooed the man by flapping the blanket at him like a bullfighter's cape. Then she rushed to her armoire to find something suitably sexy to wear for her uninvited visitor.

The dress she finally settled on wasn't warm enough for such a cool day, but it was scarlet, with a cinched waist and a plunging neckline. There were those who thought redheads shouldn't wear red, but Branca strongly disagreed. One should wear whichever colors made one feel good, and that's exactly what scarlet did for her; it made her feel good *and* naughty.

Despite some shortcomings Francois Joseph was a competent head houseboy. Branca emerged from her boudoir to find the OP settled on the terrace with a cup of coffee in one hand and a slice of Cook's homemade biscotti in the other. He attempted to rise when he saw her, but she waved him down.

"No need for such formalities among friends." Noting his raised eyebrow, she added, "Or among fellow Europeans in the Congo. We are like family, yes?"

"*Oui, madame, c'est vrai.* And speaking of family, do you know the whereabouts of your husband?"

"At the store. He rises much earlier than I. He's a very hard worker."

"I quite agree. I've been very impressed with the range of products and services he's been able to supply. Last week I was in the store and saw cauliflower in a tin. And not just cauliflower bits, but complete heads. Who even knew such a thing was available?"

Branca was quick to pretend wonder. "Certainly not I."

"And frankfurters in a tin."

"Marvelous." But had she heard sarcasm in the OP's voice?

"We colonials no longer have to exist on beans and rice. But alas, if importing a variety of preserved foods was worthy of a medal, I would have brought one with me. Unless, of course, I knew for certain that the man to be honored was not a common thief."

"I beg your pardon?"

"Senhora, I will ask you one last time; do you know where your husband is?"

Branca's heart pounded, and her ears rang. At his finest, Cezar had been a mediocre husband with mediocre skills. But to her knowledge, he had never been dishonest. He wasn't bright enough to spin lies. As for stealing, the man didn't have the ambition needed to alter financial records, and there simply was never enough cash on hand to support a life on the run.

"Please, Monsieur OP," Branca said, trying hard to control the timbre of her voice, "tell me exactly what my husband has done wrong."

The OP set coffee and biscotti down and stared at her. It was the kind of stare meant to intimidate and force one to crack under pressure. Well, the arrogant Belgian could do that all day if he pleased. You can't squeeze blood out of a turnip.

"Senhora," he finally said, after rubbing his face with his hands as if erasing a chalkboard, "I have received a report that your husband, Cezar Nunez, robbed one of our African workers of a very large and valuable diamond."

"*C'est impossible*! The Africans aren't even allowed to own diamonds, and Cezar may not be the most clever man, but he's not entirely stupid either. What would he do with a diamond? You can't even take them out of the province, much less the country."

"There are always ways, senhora."

Branca had heard of some of these ways. Smugglers had been known to swallow diamonds, insert them into body cavities, place them behind glass eyes, tuck them into self-inflicted wounds, or sew them into hemlines of bulky clothing. There was even a Danish man who almost got away with a million dollars' worth of uncut diamonds he'd taped to the inside of a prosthetic leg. Unfortunately for him, the tape tore loose, and his leg began leaking diamonds as he climbed the ramp to board the plane that was to fly him back to Europe.

"Monsieur OP," Branca said, still unconvinced her husband could be involved in such a ridiculous scenario, "how has my husband responded to this accusation?"

"He hasn't said anything. You see, madame, he fled the scene. By now he could be on his way to Luluaburg. Or even Angola. I am hoping you will cooperate and tell us where he is. Perhaps something could be worked out—I'm sure you know what I mean."

"No, monsieur, I do not!"

"Look, I am prepared to offer a handsome reward for any information leading to the recovery of this gem."

This *gem*. The Bell Vue mine produced primarily industrial diamonds, although a small percentage ended up in mass-market jewelry. But for the OP to use the word *gem* when describing this stone could only mean that it was a groundbreaking discovery. Ha! Now there was a pun that would have amused Cezar—that son of a bitch—wherever he was.

"What does the word 'handsome' mean to you, Monsieur OP?"

"One hundred thousand Belgian francs."

The nuns hadn't forced math down her throat for naught. One hundred thousand francs was two thousand American dollars, the only currency, besides the pound sterling, that really mattered these days. It wasn't a fortune, by any means, but it would go a long way toward buying a simple white house in the Algarve, where Branca could hear Portuguese spoken in the street but still enjoy the warm weather she'd gotten used to during her years in Africa.

If it was true that Cezar was involved in this jewel heist, then it was a fact that he no longer trusted her, and that their marriage really was over. And if that was true, then turning him in would not be violating a trust.

Now that the children were grown, what was supposed to keep them together? Not sex. Not even friendship. Just habit—that and the recognition, on her part, that Branca Violante Cunha e Mao de Ferro de Sintra e Santos Abreu e Nunez was not trained to be a professional, just as she was not cut out to be a charwoman. An adulthood spent in Africa had accustomed her to servants, to having her whims catered to. For that she would need more than two thousand American dollars.

"For half a million Belgian francs and not a centime less, I can guarantee you return of the diamond and Cezar Nunez's head on a platter."

The OP's mouth opened and closed repeatedly, but not a sound came out. It was like trying to carry out a conversation on the lower garden terrace closer to the falls. Cezar had always taken guests there and delighted in their frustration as he pretended to share with them important and confidential news. They were invariably hoarse by the time they ascended back to the main terrace.

"Monsieur OP, may I remind you that, as manager of a store, my husband has many contacts. If we don't act quickly—well, this diamond of which you speak could soon be hanging around the neck of some fat Flemish hausfrau with the disposition of a rottweiler and a face to match."

"Get that diamond back for me," the OP growled, "and you can have your damn money."

Branca could barely believe her good fortune. Last night she'd gone to bed a lonely "business widow" in a virtually sexless marriage, stuck in a backwater colonial town with no friends. Today she was married to a jewel thief, with a chance—slim, though it might be—to vastly improve her situation. But astounded as she was, she needed to present a cool and confident façade.

"*Tres bien*, Monsieur OP. Although I will need more information to aid me in my investigation."

"You're not the damn police, Senhora Nunez. I'm not asking you to investigate anything; I merely want you to deal with that rat husband of yours."

"Ah, so you *have* gone to the police?"

"This is not police business; it's Consortium business. Didn't I explain to you that this has to be handled quietly?"

Of course he hadn't, but the rest was just as Branca had surmised. The OP ran the show only as long as the police didn't have to be involved. There was power in this knowledge, whether or not the OP realized it. Yes, it was better not to remind him of this.

"I understand. However, I can tell you now that my jewel-thief husband is a consummate liar and possibly dangerous—he stabbed a man in a bar fight in Lisbon. Killed him. It was a fight Cezar himself provoked. In fact, he didn't even know the man—just that the man had rooted for a different soccer team. That's why we're here. This, by the way, is also confidential." My, how easy it was to lie when half a million francs were at stake.

The OP smiled. "It is clear that we understand each other, Senhora Nunez. I rather like that. And since you've gone to so much trouble to fabricate this story, I will tell you that it was your husband's special friend, Monsieur Dupree, who told me about the robbery. He, in turn, was told by his groundskeeper at the post office. It was the groundskeeper who was robbed."

The term "special friend" stung like a nest of wasps because Branca knew exactly what he meant. At the same time it came as a shock. She'd been laboring under the impression he'd taken up with a village woman; such was the timbre of gossip amongst the servants. Although far from being proficient in the local language, Branca had picked up a few words of "kitchen Tshiluba" over the years. My, this certainly shone a new light on things.

This also explained the cold shoulder she'd been getting from the Belgian women. Interracial dalliances they could understand; many of their husbands were guilty. But this—this was beyond the pale of taboos. There was no point now to be seen at the club with that dowdy American woman. At her first opportunity, Branca would send the missionary a note canceling their luncheon engagement.

"Monsieur OP, I have, of course, seen the groundskeeper many times, as I am a frequent visitor to the post office. And if I recall correctly, I have also seen his wife there on several occasions. She is a small crippled woman, am I right?"

The OP shrugged. "There. You seem to know more about this case than I do. *Excusez moi,* senhora, but I need to be going now."

He popped the last bite of biscotti into his mouth, followed it with the coffee, and swallowed loudly. "Thank you for the refreshments. And remember: no police."

"No police," Branca said, her painted fingers crossed behind her back. But all was fair in love and war and diamond smuggling.

CHAPTER TWENTY-SIX

The king of the beasts is not king of the jungle. The African lion (*Panthera leo*) prefers to hunt in the open or in scrub forest, where charging at prey is not impeded by thick vegetation. Lions live in family groups called prides. It is the lionesses who do most of the hunting, often in elaborate cooperation. The male's job, besides fathering the cubs, is to defend his family against other males—although males do hunt occasionally, and their exceptionally large size enables them to pull down comparatively larger animals.

Wilhelm Van Derhoef, as of late known as "Flanders," made it a point to be the first one at the office each morning. The OP seemed to appreciate this—he could spend more time with that cold, shriveled wife of his—and Flanders didn't mind. What else was he going to do with his time? There wasn't a single European he considered a friend, and since he wasn't fond of reading, he was in bed most evenings by eight. *Most* evenings.

Flanders was, after all, a virile young man. When late one afternoon a very attractive village girl showed up at his door on the pretext of selling bananas, Flanders invited her inside. She'd come to the door before, selling mangoes and pineapples, but the houseboys soon clued him in on the fact that selling fruit was not the main source of her income. When he'd first invited her in, as on all subsequent occasions, the houseboys were gone for the day.

The woman said her name was Monique. She told him she was the daughter of a Belgian surveyor and his *Bashilele* mistress, but her father refused to acknowledge her existence. Although her mother's people, who were very traditional, were kind to her, they didn't consider her one of the tribe. One day, when she was about fourteen, Monique walked away from the village of her birth and to the nearest town, where she hoped to find a mingling of tribes. That town was Belle Vue.

Monique was tall, with prominent cheekbones and a long, slender neck. Her flawless skin was the color of toffee, and the light blue clothes she favored flattered her immensely. To Flanders she was the most beautiful woman to walk the face of the earth, and he promptly fell head over heels in love with her.

As smitten as he was, Flanders was very much aware that he had come to Belle Vue for a specific reason: to gather information for the top brass in Brussels. A *spy*. That's what Flanders really was, and in the beginning he had reveled in that knowledge. He'd come to spy for the corporate office, and even if he was found out—or just failed to uncover anything newsworthy—what did he really have to lose? He was still young enough and bright enough to start over again. Possibly even in America. But the day he realized he was in love with Monique was the day everything changed.

Now he *had* to succeed. If he was successful, he might be able to take Monique back to Belgium with him and not have it matter so much. That was the best he could hope for. If he kept Monique very much in the background, there was a remote chance that his personal life might be ignored—not accepted, of course, but ignored. His mother, however, would never accept the woman he loved.

Enough worrying about the future; it was time to act. Yesterday he'd heard snatches of conversation revolving around a huge diamond of exceptional size and brilliance. Then this morning as he was driving to work, he'd spotted the store manager's truck parked in the postmaster's driveway. It was often there in the mornings, so at first Flanders didn't give it a second thought. Whatever was going on between the store manager—or his wife—and the postmaster wasn't his business. His business was ousting the OP.

He had a good feeling about today.

Amanda Brown took her second cup of coffee out to the terrace. Although Protruding Navel had whined about the intense cold, Amanda found it bracing. Of course, she was wearing a sweater over her blouse and had on shoes and socks. The housekeeper had none of those, a situation Amanda would rectify—even though she was planning to let him go.

But it could have been minus forty degrees instead of forty above, and Amanda would still have wanted to take her coffee outside. It was absurd. Back in South Carolina, she couldn't have imagined spending a chilly morning in the Congo sipping coffee beside a waterfall, but being outside here was pure magic.

She settled her cup on the retaining wall and leaned over as far as she dared. This was Amanda's favorite spot to view the falls. Her parents had recently purchased their first television set, but even it wasn't as interesting as this.

Once she'd seen an uprooted tree sweep over the edge, only to disappear in the roiling water. Yesterday she'd thought she'd seen a crocodile on the other side of the basin—yes, there it still was, propped against a jumble of boulders, to the left of a sandy beach.

But wait, what was that? Something was moving directly beneath her on the wet rocks. It was black, and looked small from here, but it was so far down to the water that the distance was deceiving. Perhaps it was an otter. She'd read there were giant otters in some African rivers. Maybe this one was stranded on her side of the pool, afraid to go back into the water because of the crocodile. Well, whatever it was, it was gone now.

Ah, but something was happening across the gorge at Branca's house. A sleek sedan had apparently just pulled into the drive, and two men—it looked like they were white men—were moving at a fast clip to the front door. Was there an emergency? Could the Nunez family be in some sort of trouble?

There was something very odd about the Nunez couple. The senhora seemed to spend most of her time sitting on the terrace, writing something. Maybe her journal? Letters? Senhor Nunez, on the other hand, was almost never home. The grocery store closed promptly at six every evening, six nights a week. But the senhor was seldom home before ten. That was not the kind of marriage Amanda hoped to build someday—unless the Lord required it of her.

That was the most difficult part of being a missionary; doing what the Lord wanted, while you wanted to do something entirely different. Something like—well, anything but run a missionary guesthouse. Still, it was infinitely better than being in prison. There was much for which to be thankful.

Their Death had heard descriptions of the white man's house—their servants were highly regarded gossipers—but he'd never actually been in one. Like the post office, the walls were made of concrete block and the roof of corrugated galvanized iron. The window openings were filled with sheets of glass, and not only was the floor paved, but colorful mats had been strewn about to enhance its beauty.

There was a room just for eating, if you can imagine that, which contained a large table and chairs. In the main room there were soft chairs of such great size that Their Death entertained the thought that they'd been created specifically for giants. On one wall hung a rectangle of bright colors, which Their Death supposed was meant to be decorative, although it was certainly not like any of the paintings he'd read about in novels.

But the most remarkable feature of the house was that it had a room devoted entirely to the body and its natural functions. It was just as Cripple had said. Their Death listened with great interest as Monsieur Dupree explained that the long white trough was used for bathing (imagine sitting in one's dirty bathwater), the large bowl with the lid was for waste (one actually sat where others had sat before), while the third water feature was for washing hands and scrubbing teeth.

There was even a room just for cooking. Instead of an open fire, one cooked on a large metal box that was attached to heat-producing wires. Uneaten food could be stored in another box, this one cooled by wires that looked to be very much the same as the heat-producing ones. When asked for details about the wires, Monsieur Dupree merely shrugged, as if such magic was to be taken for granted.

Their Death was perplexed. Why did the Europeans need so many servants if there were machines available to do the work for them? Someday they might even invent a machine that could cut grass and whitewash trees. If that day ever came—and it was beginning to look like it might—what would Their Death do about a job?

But speaking of servants, the three in the kitchen appeared not to believe their eyes. An African as a guest? And a primitive witch doctor at that! Would he eat off the same dishes as the white man? *What* would he eat? The youngest, still very much a boy, actually laughed when M. Dupree told them to serve the African the same dishes they'd planned to serve their employer. Just wait until Cripple heard about this. Even *she* did not get to eat at the same table as the American woman.

The postmaster took him back to the living room and pointed to a chair. "Sit—if you please."

"*Merci, monsieur.*" Their Death had never sat on anything nearly this comfortable. If the white man could build something this comfortable, what might they do with their beds?

"We shall eat shortly, Their Death. In the meantime, how about something to drink?"

Their Death popped to his feet. "*Oui, monsieur*, I will get you some water."

"Sit down again. Please. I'm asking if *you* would like something to drink. Maybe whiskey—or gin? Water?"

"*S'il vous plait, monsieur*, but I am unfamiliar with these words." French was a lot more difficult than any of the African languages Their Death spoke—which was five, although his Kipende was only so-so.

"Whiskey and gin are types of alcohol. Like your palm wine—only stronger, I believe."

In that case, Their Death longed to try one of the alcoholic drinks offered. He was, of course, curious, but he was also in need of relaxation. Palm wine always relaxed him—not that he drank it on a regular basis. Men who habitually drank palm wine or smoked hemp tended to lose their jobs and didn't make very good husbands or fathers.

But now was not the time to indulge himself in a foreign pleasure. More than ever, Their Death needed his wits about him. Monsieur Dupree was up to something devious, that much he knew for sure.

"*No, merci*," he said, trying not to inject a bit of wistful regret into the words.

"In that case, I hope you don't mind if I *do* indulge. I've been thinking, Monsieur Their Death. Thinking very hard." Mr. Dupree paused, the drama of which was not lost on Their Death. Neither did his use of the formal "monsieur" go unnoticed. "You see, I believe it is a crime the way that we Belgians do nothing but take, take, take, and take some more from your beautiful country, and put very little back. Where were you educated, Monsieur Their Death?"

"At the Catholic mission school."

"Exactly. A mission school. Do you realize that all the schools in this country—excuse me, this colony—are run by missionaries? Catholic, Protestant, what have you. But not by the government. In other countries the government pays for the schools and so they are everywhere. *Everywhere.* Other countries supply buses—uh, like very long cars but with many seats—to transport the children. Sometimes they can be at school within minutes, even if they live some miles away. Monsieur Their Death, how long does it take for your children to walk to school?"

Husband didn't own a watch—only the alarm clock he used to wake himself—but he'd timed the trip so as to be aware of his children's whereabouts, like any good father. Now he was ashamed to speak."

"Two hours," he said softly.

"Excuse me? I didn't hear that."

"Two hours."

"But that's terrible!" The postmaster shook his head. "Do you have electricity, Monsieur Their Death?"

"*Mais, non!*" Now that was a silly question. Of course he didn't have electricity. Even the village chief didn't have electricity.

"Ah, but in Belgium even the poorest family has electricity. At night the parents can read many newspapers and books, and the children can study. I tell you, Monsieur Their Death, that is why I am sitting here today, having this conversation. Because of electricity. Every nation that colonizes has electricity, whereas every nation that *is* colonized, does not have electricity. Or at least it did not have electricity when it was colonized. I'm telling you, Monsieur Their Death, that the man who invented electricity was a genius."

"*Oui*, but monsieur, I hear it is very expensive. That is why even the chief cannot afford it."

"Too true! But, if you agree to my plan, you will not only have electricity, you will own a shiny new automobile, a house with many rooms, and even shoes for all your children."

Their Death leaned forward, every cell in his body yearning for a better life. "What is your plan, monsieur?"

CHAPTER TWENTY-SEVEN

The Giant pangolin (*Smutsia gigantea*), is a bizarre mammal that is covered in large thick scales instead of fur. The scales, which give the animal a reptilian appearance, serve as armor. Pangolins give birth to one highly developed offspring at a time. The baby is born with soft scales that harden quickly. Pangolins eat termites, ants, and other insects, and can grow as large as seventy pounds. Unfortunately, pangolin meat is very tasty to humans; this animal's survival is not assured.

Luluaburg seemed as large as Lisbon—compared to Bell Vue, that is. It always impressed Cezar. That such a metropolis should exist in the heart of the Congo was something to be marveled at. Leopoldville was, of course, much more cosmopolitan, and Elizabethville enjoyed a better climate, but Luluaburg had everything a man really needed, *if* he knew where to look.

Cezar Nunez knew exactly where to look for most things. He'd been to Luluaburg a number of times on business, and like many other red-blooded businessmen, had assuaged his after-hours boredom by seeking out the pleasures to be had in the seamier part of the city. On one of these forays into Babylon, Cezar had made the acquaintance of a man whom he knew only as "the Syrian." Whatever items could not be supplied legitimately in Luluaburg—a quick loan, an abortion, agreeable substances, women prostitutes, even men—all could be had, as long as enough money eventually passed hands. And if the Syrian couldn't provide the service himself, he knew someone who could.

An old customer by now, Cezar didn't waste any time telephoning when he reached the city outskirts. A block from the Syrian's office he left the truck in the care of some street urchins (it was better to pay for their protection than have them trash the vehicle). And anyway, the Syrian refused to conduct business with anyone who parked in front of his shop.

His shop! Each time Cezar entered the Syrian's shop, he was both horrified and amused. Ostensibly it was like a hundred other little shops in the Congo that catered exclusively to Africans. The wares included bolts of brightly colored cloth, half-meter-long bars of blue and white soap, pans filled with glass beads, pans filled with pocket-size mirrors bearing the king's portrait on the back, crates filled with bottles of a sugary red drink called *bakamoosa*, sacks of dried yellow-and-black-striped caterpillars, stacks of small tins of sweetened condensed milk, bottles of rank perfume, plastic sandals, and a large wooden box with the salted remnants of a fish called *makayabo*. The difference between the Syrian's store and any other of its kind was that everything in this shop was covered with a thick layer of dust—including the fish.

Even the stupidest Fleming authority could not mistake this as a viable business, but then the stupidest Flemings were never assigned a beat that included Rue de Vole. Just as long as appearances were maintained and the Syrian paid well for the privileges extended to him, who cared if the store's inventory remained untouched?

Cezar knew better than to knock. The protocol was to step behind the counter, push aside the sagging curtain, and see if the Syrian was occupied. If he was, he let you know in no uncertain terms. In fact, that seemed to be his chief pleasure: yelling at the imbeciles who dare disturb his opium-induced reverie. This particular morning the Syrian was alone, hunched over an elaborately carved rosewood table eating a plate of rice and beans.

"Pardon, monsieur," Cezar said quickly, "I did not expect to interrupt your lunch."

"My lunch? Does this look like lunch? This is my breakfast, you idiot. I just woke up."

Silly Cezar. Of course. A man whose business catered to creatures of the night would not rise at the same time as a grocery-store manager.

"Pardon," he said again.

The Syrian pushed aside his food and stared at Cezar. "Do I know you?"

"*Oui, monsieur.* I've been here many times."

"Then tell me," the Syrian said, tapping his cheek, "how did I come by this scar?"

Scar was almost an understatement. The livid red streak ran from his left temple, across his forehead and right cheek, and ended just in front of his right ear. It reminded Cezar of a Venetian mask, the ones that are half black and half white.

"Monsieur, the scar was inflicted on you by a drunken Corsican in Marseilles. He mistakenly thought you'd insulted his wife. But the man was a pig, and so was his wife, so how could one insult either of them?"

"*Bien,*" the Syrian grunted. "Now tell me why you're here."

Cezar withdrew the packet from his trouser pocket and immediately handed it to the man. The Syrian didn't play games.

"It's a diamond," Cezar said. "A diamond of exceptional size and beauty, as you will see. I need to sell it as fast as possible."

The Syrian's hands seemed to move with deliberate slowness. Cezar found himself holding his breath while the stone was uncovered and then held to the light of a wall lamp. The Syrian turned it all directions and just as deliberately placed it on the table.

Cezar gasped for oxygen. "Well?"

The Syrian picked up an enamel coffee mug and brought it sharply down the gem, shattering it into a million little pieces.

"*Madre de dios*," Cezar cried, his French momentarily forsaking him. "What have you done to my diamond?"

The Syrian ground the mug into the shards, turning them into powder. "You ignorant fool! Wasting my time with a piece of glass."

Glass?

"Monsieur, you are mistaken. I have it on the best authority—a former diamond cutter—that this"—Cezar gestured helplessly at the pile of dust—"was one of the best diamonds he had ever seen."

"*Merde!* You imbecile! Get out of my office."

Unable to fathom what had just happened, Cezar stepped forward and brushed the powder into his hand.

"My plan is to make us both very, very, rich. Beyond your wildest dreams. You and your family will soon be able to live in a house like this, with electricity, and servants. Your wives will no longer have to toil in the manioc fields and your children will have the finest shoes—made from leather, not canvas like the ones you are wearing now. And all your children, even the girls, can ride to school in your own automobile, which you will drive, because you will no longer need to work for me. Or even at all, for that matter."

Dupree smiled to himself as he watched the expression on Their Death's face change from one of skepticism to one of intense longing. He'd obviously kicked a goal. Call it altruism, or even being a loving father, but it was still greed. That's what really ran the world, wasn't it? Greed for money, greed for power, greed for the most converts. Hitler, Rockefeller, missionaries—the one thing they all had in common was numbers. The more countries you conquered, the larger your bank account, the more souls you saved, the greater your reward in heaven. More, more, more. That's all anybody really wanted.

"But Monsieur Dupree—"

"Please! Call me Julian."

The fellow stared openmouthed. No doubt this was the first time a white had made such an offer of intimacy. A shame, that. But if one wanted to establish the type of rapport needed to pull this off, it was absolutely necessary. And of course the bonding had to go both ways.

"So if you please, Monsieur Their Death, may I have the honor of calling you by your Christian name?"

The poor man looked like a caged animal. "I have no Christian name."

"*Ce n'est pas possible!* You went to a Catholic school. Surely the fathers turned you into a proper Christian."

"No. But yes, I went to their school. What I mean to say is that I am not a Christian; I am a witch doctor, monsieur."

"This is a joke?"

"No, monsieur."

"But you can't be a witch doctor! You're my yardman."

"*Oui*, but I am a witch doctor as well. It is something I got from my father."

"Like an inheritance?"

"Exactly. But you see, I am not very good at it and my people, the Baluba, no longer have much need of one. Therefore I must work cutting grass and whitewashing tree trunks."

"How interesting. Well, in that case, is Their Death your personal name, or your family name?"

"My personal name. We have no family names such as you have, but are known by our clans."

"Fascinating. I would love to hear more." Just not today, when there was a priceless diamond to chase down. "Their Death, do you know how diamonds are made?"

"They are not made, monsieur; they come from the earth—ah, it is you who jokes now, yes?"

"Not at all. You see, Their Death, diamonds are indeed made; they are made by time. They begin as carbon—do you know the word?"

"No."

"Then never mind. It is enough to know that diamonds are never found alone. Where there is one, there is bound to be another. Possibly even many. There may even be other stones similar to the one you described to me yesterday." Dupree locked eyes with Their Death. "I propose that you and I find as many diamonds as we can—secretly, of course—and remove them far from the clutches of the greedy Consortium."

"*Monsieur?*"

"Don't look so scared. Once the diamonds are out of the Congo, I will personally cut and mount them into jewelry, and once that is done, we can sell them directly to customers. There will be no middle man, and no way to trace the stones back here, because"—Dupree forced a conspiratorial laugh—"no stones this large have ever been found in the Belle Vue mine."

"But they have!"

"So there are *more*?"

"No, I mean that one such stone was found and—"

"And now it is gone, so there is no proof. You don't honestly think Senhor Nunez will report the origin of his stolen gem, do you?"

"No, monsieur. But isn't what you propose also stealing?"

Dupree couldn't help but laugh. "*Stealing?* From whom? All the diamonds in the Congo rightfully belong to the Congolese, not to Belgians, who forced the chiefs to cede their lands so that we whites could steal from you. Tell me, Their Death, how much money does the Consortium pay you directly for your children's shoes? For manioc, so your wives don't need to risk being bitten by mambas every time they tend the fields? How did you get here this morning? In your own car? And what about that crippled wife of yours? Did she have to walk to work as well?"

Dupree could see that the battle was 90 percent won. Just as long as he remained calm and addressed Their Death's concerns, not his own. He took another much-needed sip of whiskey.

"Monsieur Dupree," Their Death finally said, "I may not be a Christian, but neither am I a thief."

"Excellent point! I always knew you were a man of principles. Unfortunately, however, the Consortium has no principles. They are stealing from your people, and no one is stopping them."

"*Oui, mais—*"

"Do not make excuses for them, Their Death. It is your obligation, as a Congolese, to stop the Belgians from stealing your country's resources. And if you have some resources—that is to say, a great deal of money—not only can you buy an automobile for your crippled wife and clothes for your children, you also can spend some of that money on effecting a political change right here in the Congo."

Their Death glanced widely around the room. Dupree had seen an antelope, trapped by the savanna fires, with the same crazed look in its eyes. It was the fear of entrapment, of horrible consequences, that had put this look in Their Death's eyes. He had to try harder, talk faster, before his employee bolted.

"Yes, go ahead and look around you, Their Death. Is this what your house looks like? I think not. Yet, how is it that I, a greedy Belgian, should be sitting in this luxury while you, a native of this land, must live in the village across the river? Why is it that I am your boss, and not the other way around? The Consortium should, by rights, belong to the Congolese. Of course that will never happen."

"Until we get our independence." Despite this brave assertion, Their Death averted his eyes, as if what he'd said was going too far.

"Ha! Independence! For whom, I ask? Yes, someday the Congo will become independent, but the citizens of Belle Vue village will not be the beneficiaries. The money will stay in the big cities where the politicians live—unless, of course, the average man can find a way to empower himself. And do you know what money is, Their Death? *Really* is? Money is power. Believe me, you will be able to accomplish far more with your life if you take what is already yours. Not only can your family live in comfort, but you can help the others in your village, maybe even help your entire tribe. To say no to this would be stealing their health and happiness. Do you understand now?"

Their Death's long sigh was like the letting of stale air out of a tire. At that moment Dupree knew that he had won.

CHAPTER TWENTY-EIGHT

The bonobo (*Pan paniscus*) is also known as the pygmy chimpanzee. It is our closest relative, and recent studies show that this species is more closely related to humans than it is to the gorilla. One of the many things that set bonobos apart from regular chimpanzees is that bonobos tend to resolve conflicts with sex, rather than aggression. The result of this "make love, not war" approach is that bonobos are highly sexualized, with frequent sexual contact occurring between individuals of all ages and both genders. They are also known to copulate face-to-face, a position rare amongst mammals.

Cezar Nunez pounded the steering wheel of his 1946 Chevy pickup truck and between sobs, cursed God, cursed the Syrian, and cursed himself. What a fool he had been—*again*! He was always screwing up, always making life-altering mistakes, and never really learning anything. Sobbing babies learned every minute that they were awake, but not Cezar.

How many times had he been poised to accomplish something really big, really meaningful, and then sabotaged himself? For instance, he'd known better than to marry the aristocratic Branca. Even back then he'd known enough about himself to realize that he could not function as the husband she wanted and perhaps deserved. And he never should have come to the Congo. What was wrong with living his life, true to himself, in a city as cosmopolitan and full of opportunity as Lisbon?

And what was it that had made him so greedy that he would not only betray his wife, but his lover as well? Dupree was a good man—perhaps a little boring, but kind, and not unattractive. But that was it, wasn't it? Cezar craved something more than average; he wanted it all. And why not? You only live once, and he'd paid his dues supporting a family, helping to raise two children—and he couldn't be even be sure they were his.

Now it was time for Cezar, wasn't it? Yes, some might say that he was going through a midlife crisis, that he was trying to recapture his youth, but they were wrong. Cezar deserved to live well, and if that meant hurting a few people—well, that really wasn't his fault, now was it? It was the so-called victims who were at fault, for allowing themselves to be hurt in the first place. Besides, they would eventually get over it. Then everyone would be happy.

But damn that African who'd convinced Dupree he had a diamond, when it was only glass. And shame on Dupree for being duped like that—of course, Dupree would probably have instantly spotted it as a fake. The man knew his diamonds, Cezar had no doubt about that. Otherwise, he wouldn't be pounding the steering wheel and sobbing like a toddler who'd had a lollipop wrenched from his tight little fist. What did the Americans who visited his grocery call lollipops? Suckers! And that's exactly what he was; a sucker. Well, he'd just have to fix that.

The OP loved birds. The long-tailed ones were his favorite, but he was also very fond of the cattle egrets that stalked the dry lawn, searching intently for grasshoppers. He even loved sparrows. Funny, but sparrows had seemed so common in Belgium. Trash birds. The alley cats of the avian kingdom. Here, just because they were in Africa, they were exotic. And indeed some really were. Recently the OP had seen a pair that bore yellow streaks on their wings. Could they possible be wild canaries? They were definitely opportunistic seed eaters, whichever species they were. He needed to get a good bird book on Central Africa—someday maybe even he'd write one himself.

He'd just parked his car in the reserved space labeled with his name, when, through the windshield, he glimpsed a bit of yellow disappear under the eave. It was just outside his office window. The common sparrows loved to nest under the over-hanging eaves, and although the office staff found the incessant chirping of their chicks annoying, it was music to the OP's ears. How exciting if the yellow-winged birds had taken to nesting there as well.

The OP got out and shut his door quietly and then, as silently as a cattle egret, crept toward the window. He was three meters away, eyes trained on the overhang, looking for a breach in the plywood covering, when his peripheral vision caught something moving *inside* his office. The OP turned, and there, his back to the window, was Flanders. The son of a bitch was rooting through one of his filing cabinets.

The Nigerian could only hope that the white woman hadn't seen him. He'd been stupid to take that risk, but what other choice did he have? At last he'd found an exit from the cave that put him on her side of the river. Although this side of the gorge was just as steep, the cliff showed more erosion, more potential for hand-holds and footholds. But he couldn't climb it at night, not without scouting during the day for a possible route.

Surely if the white woman had seen him, there would soon have been activity along the cliff. That hadn't happened. The woman was there one minute, and then gone—not that he'd stayed in the open to watch her leave. In fact, he'd skinned his leg and twisted his ankle in his haste to drop out of sight. Fortunately nothing was broken and he was still able to walk, albeit painfully. Just before dusk, when the shadows were deep and the bats were emerging from their subterranean home, he'd try again.

It would be a shame if he had to kill the white woman. He didn't particularly enjoy killing women; there was no sport to it. Besides, it seemed disrespectful to the memory of his mother, whom he'd adored, and who'd died when the Nigerian was still a small boy.

But he would kill this woman if he had to. He'd come this far, survived too much in the last few days, to fail in his quest. Perhaps there was something in the white woman's house that he could wear. Maybe she had a husband who was tall. She most certainly had a blanket or some sheets. All he needed was something to cover his nakedness long enough to get him to the village. There he was sure to find something more suitable.

He knew the village—at least he used to know it. He was born in Belle Vue village and had grown up there. His father, a native Nigerian and an educated man, had worked for the Consortium as their first African diamond cutter. He'd been brought in from Nigeria, as a single man, specifically for the job. His mother was a local woman of the Lulua tribe.

It hadn't been easy growing up with a foreign father, especially one with such a high position in the white man's company. Of course it was out of the question for the Ogundes to live on the Belgian side of the river, nor was it seemly for them to live in a village of backward tribesmen. As a solution to the conundrum, the family built a modest—although opulent by local standards— house near the forest, next to a massive baobab tree. There they lived a happy, if lonely, existence until Mrs. Ogunde was bitten by a mamba. At least that is the version of history the Nigerian preferred to remember.

Two years after his mother's tragic death, when the boy was

about ten, his father decided that such an isolated existence was not healthy for the boy's emotional well-being. Mr. Ogunde quit his well-paying job and took his son home with him to Lagos, Nigeria. Neither of them ever returned—until now.

It was shortly before they left when the lad had discovered the large, clear stone with the flashes of brilliant light. When he presented his find to his father, Mr. Ogunde dropped to his knees and emitted a low, haunting cry, like one of the animals they heard every night in the forest.

The child was confused and frightened, but his father refused to explain his reaction. He told the boy only to put the stone back where he'd found it, and made him promise never to speak of it again. Many years later, when Mr. Ogunde was dying of pancreatic cancer, it was he who brought up the topic of the stone.

"It was the finest diamond I had ever seen," he told his son, now a grown man. "But there was nothing I could have done about it. If I'd been caught, I'd have been thrown into prison for life, then what would have become of you? Forgive me, son, if I failed you. After so much time has passed, you couldn't possibly remember where you found that stone."

Now, in his cave behind the waterfall, the Nigerian shivered with anticipation. He knew exactly where he'd found the stone, and where he'd been forced to return it. How could he forget that baobab tree?

When the second wave of nausea hit Cripple, she leaned against the kitchen table and closed her eyes. If she didn't try to fight it, this one would pass as well. No harm done. It was probably just the stress of the morning's events. She couldn't possibly be pregnant. After her miscarriage, the missionary doctor Husband had taken her to see told her in no uncertain terms that she would never be pregnant again.

Besides, this wasn't the same sort of nausea. This nausea was accompanied by dizziness and weakness of the knees. Were it not for the fact that it was almost the end of the dry season, Cripple might have diagnosed herself as having a bout of malaria.

The door to the kitchen swung open and Protruding Navel entered carrying an armful of soiled clothes. Without giving her a second look, he thrust the clothes at her. They all fell to the floor, and when they did, the stench concealed by them was released. Cripple thought she would pass out. Surely there was nothing in the world that smelled quite as bad as the sweat of a white person.

"Here," the arrogant man said. "Take them to the washstand out back and give them a good scrub."

"I am sick."

"Sick of work, is that it?"

"Where is Mamu Ugly Eyes? I must speak with her."

"You can speak to her after you wash the clothes."

Cripple straightened to her fullest possible height, although it was painful to do so. It had always been thus. Not only was one leg shorter, but her spine curved like the letter S. Snake Spine is what the village children sometimes called her, when none of her sister children were around to defend her.

"You are not my boss, Protruding Navel. You cannot tell me what to do. I will not take orders from a—" She stopped abruptly, realizing she'd gone too far.

"From a what? Go ahead and say it."

Cripple shook her head, her eyes still closed. She was no longer in the white *mamu*'s kitchen, but with her own mother on the riverbank. She was a little girl, perhaps five dry seasons in age. Mother and her sister wives and their friends had discovered a new inlet. One created by a recent flood. Here the waters flowed beneath a tumble of boulders that prevented crocodiles from entering the pool. The women had brought laundry to wash, but soon they were stripped to the skin, washing themselves and splashing with glee. Many of the children had never had the pleasure of playing in water, and although they were extremely cautious at first, soon they too joined in the fun.

It took several weeks for the pool to recede, but by then Cripple had learned to swim. That was magical. Buoyed by the water, she was no longer Cripple. Or Snake Spine. For those few, very special, days Cripple was Fish Girl. None of the other children learned as fast, or as competently. For those few days Fish Girl dominated the playing field. She was especially adept at swimming under the muddy red water, where she played "crocodile," terrorizing the same girls who'd tormented her from the moment they could speak.

"Say it!" Protruding Navel shouted, his eyes bulging like palm nuts.

Cripple sighed and opened her eyes reluctantly. "You are correct in your assumption; I was about to say that I will not take orders from a Bena Lulua."

"*Eyo, baba*, that is the truth." Suddenly, Protruding Navel sounded sad, instead of angry. "But you are a woman, and a cripple, and yet you place yourself above me, and simply because you are of the Baluba tribe? I did not choose to be born into my tribe."

"And neither can I help that I am female and deformed."

"Then perhaps we should talk the *mamu* into hiring a Chokwe woman. One with breasts shaped like melons—although since she is Chokwe, they will be no larger than tangerines. Then we can both boss her around." A hint of a smile flickered across Protruding Navel's face. When he wasn't angry, he was almost handsome.

"Let us not forget a Bapende man," Cripple said. "One with lots of mud in his hair and a loincloth that hangs low on the hips."

They stared at each other for a moment, then burst out laughing. Cripple laughed so hard she thought her already painful stomach would burst. Every time she tried to stop, Protruding Navel mentioned the name of yet another tribe, each more loathsome than the one that proceeded it. With two hundred tribes at their disposal, who knew how long they would have kept it up, had not the white *mamu* stepped through the swinging doors.

"What is going on here?"

"We laugh," Cripple said, rubbing her eyes.

"Yes, I see that. What about?"

"Nothing, *mamu*," Protruding Navel said quickly. "Cripple does not feel well."

"That's what's so funny?"

"Oh, no, *mamu*," Cripple said. "I really am sick. Protruding Navel was telling me jokes, in order to distract me."

Ugly Eyes was an American, with quick American ways. She stepped up and put her hand on Cripple's forehead, without even asking permission.

"You don't feel warm," she said.

"No, *mamu*, but—"

"Stay right here." She disappeared through the swinging doors, but was back in a few seconds. "Here, put this under your tongue. Please."

Cripple stared at the object. "*Mamu*, it is a glass stick."

"It is called a thermometer. It will tell me how hot you are."

"I am not hot, *mamu*. It is only my stomach that hurts."

"Open!"

Cripple did what she was told. And to think the missionaries were always putting down the ways of the witch doctor, ways that had been proven over a thousand generations. Herbs and potions, and yes, magic, these were things one could put their trust in, not gods who walked on water and rose from the dead like ghosts. Nor could one put their trust in glass sticks under the tongue.

Mamu Ugly Eyes made Cripple stand with the tube in her

mouth for many lifetimes, and it would have been unbearable except for one thing. When the white *mamu* saw that Protruding Navel was staring at her with a smirk on his face, she ordered him to pick up the fallen laundry and take it outside.

"But *mamu*, why must I be the one who does all the work? Besides, laundry is women's work."

"Hush, Protruding Navel."

Cripple marveled at a woman who could tell a man to hush, until it occurred to her that Mamu Ugly Eyes might not be exhibiting such courage if she were talking to someone other than a Congolese. Nonetheless, Protruding Navel took the laundry outside—but not without mumbling under his breath.

At last Mamu Ugly Eyes removed the glass stick and held it up to the window, where she proceeded to squint at it as if it might suddenly change shape before her eyes. Finally she smiled.

"No fever. Perhaps it is just something you ate."

"That is a relief, *mamu*. I was afraid it might be malaria. Still, I ask permission to return to my village."

"Of course. I will send Protruding Navel to get Captain Jardin. He can drive you."

"Oh no, *mamu*. It is not necessary, I assure you. I am not so sick that I cannot walk."

"And I'm not so busy that I can't walk with you."

Cripple's heart raced. It was hard enough not to draw attention to oneself when one was the size of child and waddled like a duck, but to be accompanied by a white woman—well, one may as well dance naked on the roof of the men's palaver shed.

"No, *mamu*. I will walk by myself."

"Nonsense. What if you collapse along the way? In my country we have a saying; don't look a beast of burden accompanied by gifts in the mouth."

"Forgive me, Mamu Ugly Eyes, but that saying is nonsense."

"Hmm. Yes, perhaps it didn't translate well. The point is, when someone offers you something, just accept it."

"And if they offer you a snake?"

"Cripple, stalling will do you no good. I intend to walk you home, and there will be no more discussion about this."

Unfortunately there was very little discussion of any kind on the walk up the hill. If she had to be seen with the woman, Cripple had hoped that at least they could converse about many things that she'd been wanting very much to know. For instance, what did foreign women do when they had their monthly bleeding? Did they also have a communal woman's hut with a dirt floor, where they kept themselves secluded until their time was over? If not, what did they do about the blood?

And why was it they bound their breasts? Cripple had seen one of the devices used to hold the breasts in place; it had looked very uncomfortable. Did their men find this attractive? And why did they wear a garment like pants—but much shorter—under their dresses? An ignorant person might conclude that unless white women wrapped themselves tightly, they were in danger of breaking apart, like peeled bananas.

Cripple had many more such questions, but no sooner had they joined the main road than they were mobbed by village children. Dozens of them, and none of them afraid.

"Look! It is Mamu Ugly Eyes," they shouted, and repeatedly, as if it were an anthem.

"*Mamu!*" Cripple was annoyed that she too must shout, or not be heard. "I will walk alone from here."

"No, I forbid it."

"You cannot forbid me, *mamu.*"

Cripple edged through the crowd of children, many of whom were taller than she. Wisely, the *mamu* did not try to follow. It was the first time Cripple could remember that she was not taunted.

In fact, no one paid her any attention, so focused were they on the exotic creature from America. What freedom there was in nonexistence. What joy!

But as she rounded the hill and could see the top, Cripple felt the happiness drain out of her, like the water from the *mamu*'s bathing tank.

CHAPTER TWENTY-NINE

Although the cattle egret (*Bubulcus ibis*) is native to Africa, in the 20th century it spread across the world. It first appeared in Brazil in the late 1800s, having either flown over from Africa or stowed away on a freighter. From there it worked its way north, across the Caribbean, and then throughout much of the United States. It followed a similar pattern with Europe and Asia. Cattle birds are egalitarian, with the male helping the female build the nest by bringing her materials. Both birds incubate the eggs and feed the chicks when they hatch.

Flanders had to hurry. Fortunately the OP was stupid enough to keep the key to his filing cabinet in his desk's middle drawer. But you wouldn't believe how jam-packed the filing cabinet drawers were; every time you opened one, files would spill out.

Fortune, however, had not deserted him. When he opened the third drawer, a familiar file literally landed on his feet. It was the same one that had been lying on the OP's desk when the postmaster dropped by yesterday.

Flanders knew the file well—after all, he'd been the one to type the pages and pages from squiggly handwritten notes, ones that may as well have been written in Chinese, maybe even by a Chinese doctor. He'd had to bother his boss a million times to help him figure out words, but even the OP had been unable to decipher some of the scribbles.

The gist of the report concerned a newly discovered deposit of gem-bearing gravel in a canyon about twenty kilometers away. As far as Flanders knew, no copies of the report had yet been sent to Brussels. This was an odd state of affairs, given that the home office had made it clear to Flanders that they were unhappy with profits. And yesterday they had made that clear to the OP with their aerogramme. Why didn't the old fool send back a report detailing his new discovery? What was he waiting on?

If he was waiting on the new deposit to turn a profit, he was hanging himself. That certainly wasn't going to happen in time to save his neck. First, he had to build a road. Then he had to build barracks for at least one hundred workers, and then—*mon Dieu!* It wasn't that at all; the OP's delayed response had nothing to do with the potential to increase production.

The OP was waiting to see the monstrous diamond that the Walloon postmaster had babbled about yesterday. Flanders had heard only snatches of the conversation, but it sounded like the wishful thinking of an ex-pat—and probably a drunk one—in a dead-end job.

He'd been warned about this type of man by the CEO. Congo Dreamers, they were called. They came in all stripes: some searched relentlessly for the fabled elephant graveyard that was supposedly littered with thousands of valuable tusks; others prospected for gold, some for uranium; and even a few were more concerned with fame than with fortune, and as such set their sights on locating the mythical Congo dinosaur. The last quest was really not as far-fetched as it sounded: there were still thousands of square miles of unexplored rain forest, and as late as 1901 the first European laid eyes on the okapi, a large mammal that looks like a cross between a zebra and a giraffe.

Flanders flipped open the file he now held on his hands.

Across the top of the report, the clueless OP had scrawled, "Possible major find—Dupree." Just four words, but enough to prove that the man was both an idiot and a dreamer. How had such a slow-witted man made it this far in the corporate world? Perhaps he had something on the CEO. That would certainly explain why the CEO was taking his sweet time in giving the OP the ax. And, if indeed there was something to this theory, Flanders might rise to the top faster than he'd thought possible.

But not too fast. Africa was fascinating; there was still so much more to see, so much to learn, so much to love. The other whites at Belle Vue were cretins who didn't give two francs about the local culture. They were like white pustules on the face of Africa.

Last night Flanders had lain awake for hours, listening to the village drums. They were obviously talking drums, given the varied rhythms coming from various parts of the village. He'd asked Monique what they meant, but she claimed not to know. These drums were different from the ones she'd grown up with— she said. In the morning he'd asked his houseboy, an *évolué* named Julian, what the drums were saying. Julian, however, had refused to tell him anything illuminating until he was given a ten-franc note.

"Muambi Ask Questions"—that was Flanders's African name—"the drums speak of the day when this land will again be ours. They tell of the riches that will be ours at this time."

"How will you get the riches?"

"We will kill you and take them," Julian said, and despite his initial reluctance, he didn't even bat an eyelash.

No doubt the other whites would have been horrified by Julian's declaration, possibly even incensed, but not Flanders. If only he had more time. This evening he would ask Julian a slew of questions. Did they plan to kill all the whites? What about the mulattoes? Even the women and children? By what means?

Would there be the opportunity to negotiate first? And if so, before he had to leave, could he possibly visit the village—not as a white Belgian, but just as an interested man? So many questions that even Monique couldn't answer.

Flanders froze as he felt the hot breath on his neck, even before he heard the voice. "Flanders!" the OP roared.

What was Their Death to do once they reached the village? Baby Boy couldn't talk, so he couldn't very well tell Monsieur Dupree where he'd found the stone. After all, you can't get pineapple juice out of a manioc tuber, no matter how hard you squeezed. As for Second Wife, she was a good mother and a hard worker, but she had never been one for details.

Most probably the stone had come from the manioc field, and it was possible that the older children, in whose care Baby Boy had been entrusted, might remember where they were when he first put the stone in his mouth. One of them might even have found it and given to the baby. Their Death had not questioned the children, because children cannot be trusted with secrets. In no time at all, word would have spread through the village like a savanna fire, and people would have dug up their family compounds with *lukasu*, the short-handled weeding hoes.

But neither can most adults keep a secret. If M. Dupree had been able to keep a secret, Their Death would not be seated beside him in an automobile, wondering what to do next. On one hand, it was a relief to have a partner, especially a white man who was knowledgeable in the ways of the world. Yet, as much as Their Death liked his employer—who was now his partner in the diamond business—he knew that ultimately it all boiled down to race.

If they were caught and accused of stealing, M. Dupree could point the finger at Their Death and say that it was all his fault.

There was nothing Their Death could say to exonerate himself. No one in authority would believe a black man over a white. Absolutely no one.

That meant Their Death had to be as clever as a jackal, which, although it can hunt small animals on its own, prefers to sneak food away from other, larger, predators.

Heilewid felt strangely rejuvenated by the morning chill. For the first time since her twin sister's tragic death she enjoyed the act of waking up, drowsing off, and waking up again. But it was a guilty pleasure, one that she would stop when she was awake enough to attend to her morning needs.

Geete would also have reveled in a day like today. She would have seized it with both hands and not let go until she was spent with joyous exhaustion. And had things somehow been reversed, Geete would have grieved as hard as anyone, although at the earliest opportunity, she would have weaned herself from the addiction of anguish and gotten on with her life. But that was Geete. That was part of who she was. That wasn't Heilewid.

Heilewid, as everyone in Belle Vue knew all too well, was weak. Heilewid didn't have the strength of character to recover from grief. Heilewid had folded up, as some blossoms do at night, and refused to open again in the morning. Heilewid was a drunk who ignored her husband and lay comatose beside a swimming pool that she lacked the energy to enter.

Today was different; today she had energy. The cold had brought life back into her. But it was only a pilot light that had been rekindled; there would be no full-blown flames—God, how awful the pain must have been! The terror.

Heilewid splashed water on her face. Again. And again, as if to douse the images in her mind. It was constantly like this. Ordinary thoughts turned into memories of tragedy. Pain. Flames.

Screams. Pain. It was never going to end. Not unless—well, the thoughts of it had been with her all along, but she'd not had the strength. Not until today.

Today. Heilewid smiled at her dripping face in the bathroom mirror. It was Geete's smile too. So was the long blond hair that framed her face. And that's how she would remember Geete, this, her last day on earth. She turned away from the mirror and dressed quickly before other thoughts eroded her resolve.

CHAPTER THIRTY

Basenjis are a breed of hunting dog that originated in the Congo. In the Tshiluba language the word *basenji* (*basenshi*) means "uncivilized" or "barbarian," with connotations of heathenism. Basenji dogs stand about sixteen inches high at the shoulder, have upright ears, and tightly curled tails. They do not bark, but are capable of vocalizing in other ways. (Barking is not natural to the dog family, and is a quality that was bred into them by early man to warn of approaching danger.) Because basenjis are silent, their owners attach rattles around their bellies before taking them out to hunt, so that they can keep track of them.

But Muambi, the village is across the river."

The postmaster inhaled through clenched teeth. "Yes, but Senhor Nunez lives down this road. Perhaps his wife knows something—she's got to know something. Be in on it somehow."

"Yes, certainly," Their Death said.

In truth, women always knew what their men were doing, although often they pretended not to. It was the old women in the tribe who one went to for knowledge, not the men. Women saw everything, and they thought about everything. The result was wisdom. For men, this was a frightening state of affairs, which is why they insisted on holding on to power.

But there was among the Bajembe tribe a woman chief. A queen. She was said to be very powerful, and the men listened to her. This was, of course, the exception. But if the Baluba were ever to have a queen, Cripple would make an excellent candidate. She would rule with a firm hand, dispense mercy when appropriate, and always be just. If only Cripple . . .

"Their Death, you haven't heard a word I said!"

"*Oui, monsieur.* For that I apologize."

"Don't apologize. Just come in with me."

"Into the *house*?"

"Of course the house, you imbecile."

"*Oui*, monsieur, but I—I—"

"Are an African? Come to think of it, I have noticed that before."

Their Death laughed nervously. Contrary to what most people thought, the white man did possess a sense of humor. It was just difficult to recognize. This, however, was clearly an example.

"Monsieur Dupree, perhaps Madame Nunez will object to my presence."

The postmaster knocked loudly on the front door. "Let her object. What can she do about it? Now that her husband is a thief, and on the run, she will be shipped back to Portugal on the next plane. You have my word on that. And by the way, when speaking to her, you should refer to her as senhora, not madame. Otherwise that Latin temperament—on second thought, never mind. Her objections no longer matter."

The door was opened by an *évolué* in a starched white uniform. "*Bonjour, monsieur.*"

"*Bonjour*, Francois Joseph. We have come to see Senhora Nunez. Is she in?"

"Just a minute, sir."

For Their Death the minutes stretched into eternity. While they waited he studied the details of the stone porch: the heavy wooden rafters, the corrugated roofing, the cracked mortar that held the stone floor together, the scarlet bougainvillea that spilled from a trellis and engulfed the railing on one side. It was odd that the French language contained numerous words for red. In Tshiluba there was just *kunze*, which sufficed for yellow, brown, red, even purple.

Looking slightly deflated, the *évolué* returned. "She says to come in."

Their Death felt the postmaster gently push him. "*Après vous.*"

The servant's eyes widened. "No, no. *You* may come in, sir, but not the other."

"The *other*?"

"*Oui*, the tribesman."

"And which tribe would that be?"

"Monsieur, judging by his primitive features, I would guess that he is a Mupende."

"I am a Muluba," Their Death said, his pulse racing in anger. "And so are you."

"Perhaps. But I am civilized, as you can see."

Speaking in their mother tongue, Their Death responded immediately. "Yes, I can see that you have become the white man's monkey. When our day of independence arrives, where will you go then? To Belgium with your masters? Oh, forgive me, I have forgotten. In your case it would be Portugal."

The muscles in Francois Joseph's jaw twitched. "You will be sorry, Their Death. And you will not need to wait until Independence Day to get what you deserve. Now come with me."

Today the colors were brighter. The edges of leaves were crisp, so well defined that Heilewid could have counted every emerald leaf on every mango tree, and every pea-green leaf on every jacaranda tree, and every flower on every sprawling mass of purple bougainvillea—except that bougainvillea flowers weren't flowers at all, but modified leaf bracts. Nevertheless, she could have counted them as well—*if* she'd had the time.

Today odors were especially intense. From somewhere nearby, or perhaps even far away, came the overpowering scent of a gardenia bush in bloom. Even the dust had an odor today; like chalk powder with a hint of your grandmother's bath salts. Not too unpleasant, really. And what was that strange smell? Perhaps carrion? Belgian men were fond of running down jackals at night (when the jackals stared dumbly into headlights) and leaving them to rot in the elephant grass at the side of the road. Sometimes they left the carcasses right in the road.

Belle Vue must be the only town in the world that had a sign that read, JACKAL CARCASSES MAY NOT BE DEPOSITED CLOSER THAN THREE METERS FROM THE ROADWAY. FAILURE TO COMPLY WITH THIS RULE COULD RESULT IN A STIFF FINE. How stiff? As stiff as a tumbler of Irish whiskey—straight up. The OP was far too genial, so that a round of drinks at the club had been known to soften just about every stiff fine.

Oh, the sounds! Birdsong had never been so sweet. And the noises of the village across the river; the happy shouts of children at play, the odd timing of a rooster, the chatter of women at their chores. How was it possible to hear these sounds above the roar of the falls? Well, today Heilewid could. That's all that mattered.

Today Heilewid cut through yards and gardens, rather than follow the roundabout boulevard. Boulevard! Ha! Only an egomaniac like the OP would built a dirt road in the Congo and declare it a boulevard. That was like christening your bathwater, then calling it Lake Heilewid. Never mind, that was his foolishness.

But the Kasai River was genuinely a river, and the Belle Vue Falls were certainly a falls. Of course the OP had no part in naming them. The amount of water that surged over the rock lip of the precipice was staggering when you heard the numbers, but then was quickly forgotten, because who remembers numbers anyway?

The important thing, the compelling thing, to remember is that the Kasai River poured into the Congo River, which, in turn, emptied into the Atlantic Ocean. Eventually it mixed with the salty blue waters of the South Atlantic, and they mixed with the North Atlantic, and they lapped against the coast of Belgium, where Heilewid and Geete had spent their summers with their grandparents in a rented chalet. So in a sense, if you stuck your big toe into the Kasai River, you were also touching Belgium—and the past.

Were both Africans and whites staring at Heilewid as she walked across the bridge? Did they stare as, halfway up the hill, she veered from the main road? Did they watch as she followed a gravel lane to the entrance of the white cemetery? Did they observe her pass between the tallest pair of whitewashed pillars, the ones that were topped with crudely molded plaster cherubs?

So what? Let them stare. What harm could stares do? Perhaps plenty, if you were a young German soldier, and the Dutch stared at your crotch, which is what the Dutch did to unnerve their Nazi occupiers. But you had to be alive in order to be affected by people staring at you. At least alive enough to care.

Heilewid knelt on the carpet of fallen leaves that blanketed Geete's grave. There was supposed to be a caretaker, one whose primary task was to sweep clean the concrete slabs that kept the European dead from being exhumed and robbed by needy villagers. The caretaker, however, was afraid to step foot in the cemetery ever since he'd been accosted by the ghost of a Belgian old-timer, who—to hear the groundskeeper tell it—had beaten him about the head and shoulders with a length of hippo hide. He had the scars to prove it.

In the end it didn't matter if the cemetery was tidy or not. Or even overgrown. The dead had moved on—well, most of them. Geete was most certainly not here. Maybe never even had been. An African had been killed in the fire as well, but the charred lump buried beneath the concrete slab might just as well have been the remains of an antelope. Having a marker, a place to focus one's thoughts, that's what was important.

"This time I'm not going to say good-bye," Heilewid said in Flemish, her mother tongue. "This time it's more like hello."

She stood, brushed the leaves from her skirt, and glanced around. Over there, by the ostentatious monument erected by a grief-stricken government official whose wife and two children had all died from malaria, was a path that led through some bushes before joining the road to Luluaburg, The intersection was above the village, on the crest of the hill, and from it one could see in all directions. To the east was savanna, to the north forest, to south scrubland, and to west, across the mighty Kasai River, was the town of Belle Vue, nestled in its mango and jacaranda trees. From up there, Heilewid knew from past experience, she could even pick out her own house.

The path was a shortcut between the village, where the caretaker lived, and the cemetery. Now that the current *mulami* was afraid to do his job, elephant grass was reclaiming the trail with a vengeance. For Heilewid the sharp blades that whipped her arms and the exposed parts of her legs were more fascinating than aggravating. See how the shallow cuts on her arms drew fine streaks of blood, too fine to form droplets, so that the blood dried in threadlike lines? And the flies! How quickly they found her blood.

Geete's blood too. When they were nine or ten—yes, it was their tenth birthday—they'd received a breeding pair of Flemish giants as a gift. Of course these were a breed of rabbits, not exceptionally large humans. Soon after this the twins sneaked into the garden of an abandoned house on their street to look for wild greens for their new pets. The children had been told many times by their parents to stay away from the property, but Heilewid could talk Geete into doing anything. Before they could gather even one small apronful of mustard leaves, Geete tripped on a stone, gashing her forehead open on a brick. The wound was not serious—requiring just two clamps to close—but it bled profusely. The flies appeared almost instantaneously then as well.

When asked for her version of the story, Geete immediately took full responsibility, claiming it had been her idea, and that she'd been acting silly. She'd deserved to fall. That's the way Geete was: quick of mind, and expansive of heart. Despite having just come from the doctor's office with metal in her head, Geete was sent to bed without any supper, and was made to wash dishes by herself for a week. But Geete was always like that, always willing to take the fall for her twin.

So what would Geete think of Heilewid's plans, were she still alive? No doubt she'd disapprove. She might even try to stop her. But ultimately she would understand. She always did.

"And now the path has joined up with the road," Heilewid said aloud, still in Flemish. "You might recognize the place where we are now; you spent almost an entire roll of film trying to capture this view. To the right is the savanna where you—uh—" She couldn't utter the words needed to finish her thought. "To the left is—oh, my God! I can't believe what I'm seeing. Thank you, Geete, for answering my prayer."

CHAPTER THIRTY-ONE

Wild dogs are a genus of Canidae found exclusively in Africa south of the Sahara, where they are extremely endangered. Their Latin name, *Lycaon pictus*, means "painted wolf." Their calico coats are randomly blotched. They live in packs, but only one pair—an alpha pair—breeds at a time. The other pack members assist in raising the pups by regurgitating food for them and babysitting. Wild dogs hunt animals that are up to twice their size, pulling them apart when they catch them. This has earned them the reputation of being vicious killers.

If Branca was even the least bit upset by a black man's presence in her living room, she most certainly did not show it. Either she was every bit as noble as she claimed, or else she held very progressive social views. Dupree almost wished he'd taken the time to get to know her better, under more congenial circumstances. Perhaps even they could have been friends—no, only the Danes were that open-minded.

"Well," she said, "would you gentlemen prefer your morning coffee out on the terrace, or in here? The terrace has an incomparable view." She smiled at the African. "It is said that it is the finest view in all of Kasai Province. Perhaps even in the Congo."

"Senhora," Dupree said, "while we appreciate your offer, we did not come for coffee."

"Yes, I am aware of that." She rolled her eyes slightly. "But you see, monsieur, these walls have been known to possess ears."

"The terrace would be very nice," Dupree agreed quickly.

"Certainly." She called out instructions in Portuguese before leading them to the terrace.

Dupree had sat there only once before, when Branca was in Portugal visiting her children, and the staff had been dismissed for the day. Sitting there again tore scabs off the wounds that had barely begun to heal.

"Now," she said, and flashed her husband's lover a smile. "What does the slimy little bastard have to say for himself?"

The postmaster could see the horrified expression on Their Death's otherwise handsome face. Too bad. He was a nice enough fellow, but if he didn't know by now that whites could behave this way, then he should be thankful for his luck thus far.

"This slimy little bastard," Dupree said, enunciating each word clearly, "has a business proposition for you."

"Save your breath, Monsieur Dupree, I'm not interested."

"I see. Not only is your family titled, but it must be enormously wealthy."

"Monsieur Dupree, my finances are no concern of yours. Whatever Cezar promised you, the deal is off. But I must say, your audacity is exceeded only by your bad looks."

Dupree touched his hair. "What's wrong with my looks?"

"A pig would refuse to sleep with you. Whatever it is Cezar saw in you, it was nothing physical. I can assure you of that."

"Hmm. Were I not such a generous man, I would wax eloquent about your personality, which surely has driven many other men screaming from your boudoir."

"Why you—you—" Inexplicably, Branca Nunez burst into laughter.

Dupree watched, transfixed for a moment, then felt compelled to laugh as well. Meanwhile Their Death regarded both of them suspiciously. Who could blame the man? Certainly not Dupree. No wonder many Africans thought the white man was crazy and unpredictable.

But it was Branca who came to her senses first. "So what is your proposition?"

"Let us assume," Dupree said, taking his own sweet time, "that you don't know where your husband is—"

"Which I don't!"

"Then one might also assume that you feel betrayed—"

"No need to assume, you idiot. Of course I feel betrayed."

"In that case, you might be interested in helping me set a trap."

"Go on."

"Cezar's mother was born and raised in Angola. That side of his family has been in Africa for six generations, and he still has cousins in Nova Lisboa, right?"

"Why don't you tell me. You seem to know as much about him as I do."

Dupree smiled to himself. As angry as he was at Cezar for stabbing him in the back, it felt good to have his wife acknowledge their relationship, even in a roundabout way. If only Cezar hadn't been so greedy, life could have been perfect.

"Yes," he said, "he still has family in Angola. My point is that since he is a man on the run, he might well contact them. Or he might try to contact friends he's made in other parts of the Congo. So my plan is this: you contact all these people as well. Tell them to tell Cezar that you need to see him."

"That's a silly plan. He ran out on me. Why would he risk seeing me?"

"Tell him that one of your children is deathly ill—"

"Shut up, you horrid little man. How dare you drag my children into your affair with my husband?"

"This isn't about our affair; this is about diamonds."

She laughed shrilly, a like screeching parrot. "Yes, I know all about this fabulous diamond—one that you almost had, but then got snatched away from you."

"Tell Cezar that there are more diamonds where that came from. Lots more."

"What?"

"Are you deaf, as well as stupid?"

"I heard you. Go on."

"Tell him that you have learned the exact location where the diamond was found. Tell him that there are literally hundreds more like it. Some even much larger."

"How am I to convince him that I know this information? Theoretically, you're my enemy. Why would you have shared this information with me?"

"Oh, I didn't. This gentleman here did. When he learned that you were the wife of the man who had robbed him, he came to you for compensation. Of course you refused, but then you got to talking, and it came out in the conversation that there are more gems and—well, to make a long story short, you saw the source with your own eyes. You and Monsieur Their Death have come to an understanding, and all you need now is someone in Angola to help you smuggle the stones across the border."

"That sounds so far-fetched that it's laughable."

"That may be, but greed is blind."

"So you're serious about doing business with that little rat?"

"Absolutely not. All we want is a chance to steal the diamond back from him."

"But why, when you have hundreds more at your disposal?"

"*Mon Dieu!* Cezar was right; you really *are* as thick as a post. That part is a ruse as well. Branca, perhaps you should know that Monsieur Their Death and I are prepared to split the money three ways. Evenly, of course."

Branca took her sweet time to respond, staring off into the distance, almost as if she were catatonic. Suddenly she sat ramrod straight.

"*O meu Deus*," she said softly. "I can't believe what I'm seeing."

Cripple knew that the truck belonged to Senhor Nunez. There was no doubt. It was the only truck she'd ever seen that was green. Funny, she'd told herself when she first saw it, that Tshiluba had no word for green. French did; in fact it had many words, describing different shades. But in both France and Belgium, the landscape was gray and brown, or sometimes white with snow. She'd learned this from her brother's teachers, who often marveled at their good fortune for not having to live through yet another Brussels winter. But here in the Congo, where everything was green for most of the year, the only way to describe the color was to say *mai wa matamba*. Literally it translated as "water of manioc leaves," and referred to the green water that was the result of cooking tender manioc leaves.

And now the truck, the very one that had been aimed at Husband, and which had almost mowed down a dozen people, was sitting beside the entrance to the path that led to her family compound. There was no one in the truck—at least that Cripple could see. This was very bad news indeed.

Cripple's first impulse was to rush home and protect her family, but before she could hobble three steps, the words of an ancient proverb came to mind: let the jackal fight the jackal, and the hyena fight the hyena. Of what use would she be defending her family against a white man? None. And although the *mamu* was not a man, she was white, and knew the ways of white men. At the very least she might know what to do.

Never had Cripple moved so fast. It is possible even that she flew, although later she would have no memory of that. But luck was not with her, nor were the spirits obliging, for when she rounded the bend again, there was no sign of Mamu Ugly Eyes and her entourage.

Kah! The *mamu* was going to be sorry she'd gone off with the village children: they were going to pester her beyond endurance. And what did this say of her concern for Cripple? More importantly, what did this say *about* Cripple?

Stupid, stupid Cripple. How foolish she'd been for entertaining the idea that she and the young American woman might someday be friends. Husband was right; there can be no friendship between master and servant, predator and prey, white people and Africans. One may as well expect a lion and an antelope to be friends. Yet if the situation were reversed . . .

The sound of the approaching green truck tore through her reverie just in time. Without even turning to look, Cripple threw herself out of its way, landing in a cloud of dust. When it cleared, her heart was still pounding.

The Nigerian thought he was hallucinating. He'd smoked hemp on many occasions, and snorted cocaine, but only to be sociable. Drugs didn't seem to do anything to him. Friends told him that was because his mind was too powerful, too unwilling to relinquish control of his body. "Just let it happen," they said. "You're among friends." But he couldn't. Or wouldn't.

Now, trapped in a cave behind a waterfall, with nothing to rely on except for his mind, it suddenly decided to take a detour from reality. How else could he explain a green truck passing right before his eyes? It was gone in a second, buried by tons of foaming water—no, there it was again, bobbing up to the surface of the catchment pool, beneath the overhanging mouth of the cave.

The water in this relatively quiet spot still boiled with energy, but a few random things—some logs, a raft of water hyacinths, a drowned hippopotamus calf—were briefly resurrected before disappearing forever. The long-dead calf had surfaced six times, as if unable to accept its fate.

It was only when the truck broke the surface of the catchment pool a second time that the Nigerian allowed himself to believe in its existence. With this new awareness came the realization that there was a person inside the cab of the truck. Although the face was covered with blood, he could tell by the long blond hair that it was a white woman.

The Nigerian didn't have to think what to do next; he would not let a woman drown. Even a white one. But as he dove into the pool, the truck began to sink. He lunged at the door and managed to grab the handle. It would not open.

The woman pressed against the glass, her lips somehow moving. She was like a bloody siren beckoning him ever downward. Again and again he tried to wrench open the door. To smash the window. He would not let go, would not give up. It was not in his nature.

Then the two of them, separated only by glass at the moment of their death, were caught forever in the undertow.

CHAPTER THIRTY-TWO

The sitatunga (*Tragelaphus spekei*) is a bovine (as are buffalo and cattle) that lives in swamps and along waterways in much of the Congo, and seems to have originated there. Its long legs and splayed hooves are adaptations to its watery environment, and make it awkward on dry land. When danger threatens, sitatungas often submerge themselves in water so that only their nostrils and the tops of their heads are visible. Gestation lasts more than seven months. The calves are born on platforms of trampled reeds.

As fast as flies alight on a carcass, the people of Belle Vue, both black and white, converged on the bridge that spanned the falls. Tragedy knows no skin color, and for perhaps the very first time, the races mingled freely. Or so it seemed to Branca Nunez.

One minute there was a green truck—her husband's truck—hurtling down the steep hill on the native side of the river, crashing through the barrier on the downriver side. The next minute the bridge was crawling with blacks and whites, like house ants and termites exposed to the sun. Meanwhile Branca sat rooted to her chair, as did the postmaster and his native employee. It was as if the three of them were spectators at a play, watching a live drama unfold. Who knows how long they watched, before the postmaster was on his feet

"Did you see that? My God, I can't believe it. Cezar—oh, my God!" Dupree ran to his car and drove off without another word.

Branca stood slowly, gripping the edge of the round terrace table for support. "Monsieur Their Death, how well did you know my husband's truck?"

"Well enough, senhora."

"Then he is dead, yes?"

"*Oui. Il est mort.* No one has ever survived the waterfall. Even the heavy dugout canoes that go over are broken like twigs."

"Yes, but this was a truck made of metal. Surely that is stronger than a canoe."

"Let us see," said the African. He moved quickly along the edge of the terrace, although it was clear by the way he gripped the railing that the height scared him.

Branca was right behind him, scanning the frothing surface for the glint of a shiny bumper, the black of a tire. Anything, any part of the truck. She dared not allow herself to imagine Cezar being thrown from the vehicle. Had this been the case, survival was impossible.

Even if he managed to survive having tons of water dumped on him, and was lucky enough to avoid being bashed against hundreds of rocks, Cezar stood no chance with the Nile crocodiles that waited hungrily where the river resumed its normal activity. The giant reptiles waited eagerly to grab whatever bounty the falls delivered: a monkey that had slipped from its perch, an antelope that had misjudged the current's strength, a human, even large fish that hadn't turned back soon enough. And, *if* by some miracle, Cezar survived both the falls and the crocs, he could not possibly survive an attack from the territorial hippos that claimed the more placid waters further downriver.

But there was nothing to see. The green pickup that had swept over the edge like a bit of flotsam had completely disappeared. No one knew how deep the catchment basin was; no one had ever needed to know. Perhaps the pickup was well on its way to China, or perhaps it was under a few feet of water, forever pinned down by the thundering torrent.

Even though Branca felt as if her heart had been ripped—still beating—from her chest, she felt a need to get closer. She needed to stand on the bridge, by the broken railing, as close to the space last occupied by the man with whom she'd spent all of her adult life. The man who'd fathered her children.

"I'm going down to the bridge," she announced, more to herself than to Their Death.

"I will come with you," the African said.

Branca scarcely heard him.

No one paid attention to Cripple as she tried to push her way through the crowd for a better view. No one cared that she finally gave up trying to fight a sea of elbows and shifting feet. No once noticed a small crippled woman, barely larger than a child, who climbed a frangipani tree to see something—anything—that confirmed what she'd been told: that the Portuguese man who'd stolen the diamond from Husband was now at the bottom of the Kasai River.

Cripple wondered how long the crowd would mill about on the bridge, held back from the gaping space in the railing by Belle Vue's two policemen, one white, the other an African of the Bakongo tribe. She supposed that some would wait even until dark, not wanting to miss the possibility that the waterfall would regurgitate the man, once it had tasted his bitter flesh. Well, let them wait. It was enough to know that the man was dead.

Having climbed down safely from her perch (Why was it always harder going down than up?) Cripple walked slowly back up the hill to the village. The excitement of the crash had temporarily eased the discomfort in her belly. Now it returned, even more intense than before.

Although there were still many hours of light remaining, all Cripple wanted to do was lie on a sleeping mat in the darkness of her hut. Perhaps she would even fall asleep, something she rarely did during the day. Sleep was the enemy of illness, and often brought with it the promise of healing. Many a night the children had fallen asleep with fevers, only to wake the next day as healthy and vigorous as young baboons.

The children—aiyee! They could not be counted on to let her sleep in peace while the sun yet shone. Sister Wife was a good mother but lacked the ability to control her offspring. "Do not disturb your sister mother," she'd call out, as the children ran screaming, in and out of the hut, but she would do nothing to stop this inconsiderate behavior.

Cripple supposed that this lax attitude toward child-rearing stemmed from the fact that Second Wife came from a family of prolific breeders. She claimed to have eleven living brothers and sisters, even though her mother had no sister wife, and the infant mortality rate in her birth village was one in four. This ability to spit out healthy babies every year was precisely why Husband had chosen her to be his second wife, and had been willing to pay such a ridiculous bride price. Who ever heard of a woman that was worth eighteen goats, seven sheep, three pigs, and twenty-nine chickens? And yes, three bolts of cotton cloth in the most beautiful patterns and colors imaginable. Clearly, some things were overvalued.

When she reached the family compound, Cripple was slightly annoyed to find that no one was there. Not a soul. What a waste of valuable emotion it was to prepare oneself for an unpleasant encounter, and then be unable to vent. No doubt Second Wife had gathered up her brood and rushed them down the hill to gawk at the bridge. Cripple hadn't seen them in the crowd, because she hadn't been looking for them.

But you couldn't blame Second Wife. She lived a dull life, one made interesting only by calamities and illness, and only rarely did she have a reason to celebrate. She had never been in a European's home. Curtains at the windows, rugs on the floors, sheets on beds so soft that if you lay down, you'd never want to get up—these were all beyond her ken. She had never seen a fork, much less used one.

At first Second Wife hadn't believed Cripple's story about a chair upon which one sat to do one's most personal business, dismissing it as so absurd that it wasn't worth laughing at. But when Husband corroborated Cripple's outlandish tale, it was all Second Wife could talk about for days. As cruel as they were to Africans, there was no denying that the whites—of any tribe—were an endless source of entertainment.

So yes, it was fitting that Second Wife should gather her young ones in her arms and run down the hill to see if the white man had been killed when his truck plunged off the bridge. What she saw and heard that afternoon would help relieve the tedium of pounding corn and manioc in the mortar, and of working in the fields. Whether found dead or alive, or never found at all, the Portuguese store owner was helping to make Second Wife's life more tolerable. Good for her.

With no one to complain to, Cripple picked up a corncob and tossed it at a rooster. The stupid bird stood his ground and cocked his head, as if to say, "Watch out, you little woman. I'm almost as big as you are. There's no one here to save you, so I might just decide to peck you to death and eat you for *my* supper."

Cripple stepped into the cool, quiet darkness of the hut, hoping to fall into a deep, healing sleep. It did not happen.

CHAPTER THIRTY-THREE

The rain forest that covers the Congo Basin is so vast and impenetrable that large areas of it remain unexplored by outsiders. Legends persist of dinosaurs inhabiting the swamps, and ape-men living in the dim light beneath the forest canopy. Far-fetched for sure, but until 1900 one elusive, and rather large, resident of this forest—the okapi—was unknown to science. Standing approximately five feet high at the shoulder, the okapi is a five-hundred-pound relative of the giraffe. It has black-and-white-striped legs like a zebra, a reddish-brown body, and a long, prehensile tongue. The males have horns.

Amanda Brown had just stepped through the back door of the kitchen when she heard a loud boom and felt the house shake. Her first thought was that dynamite had been used in the mines, although she couldn't recall ever reading about explosives being used to extract diamonds from gravel deposits. Then she thought of an earthquake. Her Aunt Doris and Uncle Jimmy had moved to California, and then back to South Carolina just three months later, because Aunt Doris's nerves couldn't stand the strain of waiting for the next tremor. But Belle Vue wasn't in a quake zone. That left option number three: a chunk of the cliff had broken off and fallen into the river far below.

Although they were undoubtedly very nice people, the Singletons had been stupid to build a house on the very edge of a precipice. A view, no matter how fabulous, was not worth the risk to human lives. And what about the children of guests? How was one to safeguard them—lock them in their room? She visualized the youngest tyke falling over the edge, and then the second eldest, who was trying to help her sibling, and so forth, until the entire family plunged over the edge. Finally even Amanda, who'd been lying on her stomach grasping the father's hand, was pulled kicking and screaming into the watery abyss.

Squashing the thoughts of impending doom, Amanda rushed outside to see what was really going on. From the left she could see hundreds of Africans streaming down the steep hillside, the bright clothes of the women giving the impression of a flock of butterflies. On the right, running toward the bridge—although a few were on bicycles—were more Europeans than Amanda had met so far in Belle Vue. In the middle, where the two groups would converge, was the bridge. A gaping hole in the railing filled in the rest of the story.

A shiver of recognition ran up Amanda's spine.

Flanders was sitting in his driveway, still in his car, nursing a cup of tepid coffee when he heard the crash. The coffee was in his left hand. With his right he was scribbling furiously on a yellow notepad with a No. 2 pencil.

All but five pages of the tablet were full of scribbles, even the margins. Almost every page bore its own headline. This one read, "The Bastard Tries To Sack Me."

Tries. That was the key word. When the OP discovered Flanders rummaging through his private files, he'd let loose with a string of invectives that only a man who'd served in the military would know. He'd even raised a clenched fist to eye level, threatening to punch Flanders all the way back to Belgium if he didn't promptly confess what he was doing with the OP's papers.

Who was it who said, "Silence is the best weapon"? Probably a mime. Flanders wanted to punch a few mimes himself from time to time. There really was nothing quite as ire-producing as someone who refuses to speak, especially in a heated situation. Bearing that in mind, Flanders had smirked while the OP had sputtered with rage.

Unable to get Flanders to answer, the OP had finally shoved him to the door and shouted: "Damn you, you Flemish imbecile! You're fired!"

Fired? Ha! It was the OP whose job was at stake. Just as soon as Flanders completed his notes, he was driving to Luluaburg. There, with any luck, he'd be able to make a phone connection to Brussels. If that didn't work out, he'd fire off the world's longest telegram. The OP and the idiot postmaster were up to something nefarious.

Possibly a major find, the OP had written. If that was really the case, why hadn't he informed the Consortium? That answer to that was obvious. The egocentric OP and the half-witted postmaster—his name had been on the document as well—were planning to reap the benefits of this find by themselves. They couldn't legally mine the diamonds, of course, but they could smuggle them. And what better vehicle than to use the OP's comatose wife?

No one in customs would even suspect that the operations manager would stoop to smuggling. After all, if he really wanted diamonds, he could acquire them legally—or so they'd think. Surely he was in cahoots with the big boys back in Belgium. And of course the same thing could be said of his wife. They'd wave the pair of them through the line with smiles and good wishes, while hoping that word of what polite, efficient fellows they were would get back to their bosses.

But if the customs people really knew how the system worked, in this dog-eat-dog world, they'd know that the OP was nothing more than a Chihuahua. They'd put nothing past this twerp at the bottom of the corporate food chain. They'd run their fingers along the hems of every article of his clothing, feeling for lumps. They'd squeeze out his toothpaste and smear it around. They'd shine a flashlight—to search the OP, they'd need the long-handled variety—where the sun never shines.

Flanders smiled. In just a matter of hours that smug, racist son of a bitch was going to get his comeuppance. The OP was about to be yanked back to Brussels so fast that his head would still be spinning when he arrived. How Flanders wished he could see the OP's face when his plans came crashing down around him.

Imbecile! He scribbled the word on his yellow pad.

And then he heard the crash.

The OP stared out the window at the dry, crackling lawn. The long-tailed birds seemed to have fled the premises along with Flanders. The OP shook his head. He still could not believe he'd found that young man rooting through his filing cabinet. As if that weren't bad enough, when the OP was giving him a piece of his mind, Flanders had turned around and walked from the room like a rebellious teenager. Well, guess what? The kid was fired. There was a plane due in on the morrow, and if that boy's skinny ass wasn't on it, then the OP would see that he was arrested. What's more, he'd better have cleared his things out of company housing. If not, his belongings would be distributed among the natives.

What the hell was up with headquarters anyway, sending out a punk kid with a chip on his shoulder bigger than Luxemburg? He'd asked for a family man, someone stable. Too bad he knew the answer to that question: Flanders was a spy. That's just what the OP had thought all along.

The men in suits who ran the Consortium hadn't a clue about geology, or what it took to oversee a successful long-term operation in the Congo. All they cared about was immediate profits. In a way that was understandable, given the political situation and probable outcome of the independence movement. At the same time, if they could wait just one more year, they would get their damn profits. They would probably even be shocked by how much money the Belle Vue mine was making.

Too bad. They'd had their chance. Screw them now. The OP would continue to run the Belle Vue mine until they forced him out, which would be sooner, rather than later. In the meantime he would arrange a couple of solitary "hunting" trips to the box canyon he'd discovered. Of course he'd bring back a monkey or two, or maybe an antelope, for the houseboys to eat, but he'd also return with his retirement stashed out of sight in his rucksack.

Getting the diamonds out of the country would be the easy part. He'd send Heilewid back home on a visit, with the lining of her suitcase stuffed with a fortune in uncut stones. The beauty of this plan is that Heilewid wouldn't know, and therefore wouldn't act suspicious. If he sent her back before he was dismissed, while the customs officials still believed that he was in charge, her bags would not be searched.

The hard part was going to be fencing the diamonds, but it was not insurmountable. He just needed to proceed slowly. Heilewid had a cousin in Antwerp who specialized in shady business deals. The man couldn't be trusted not to sell his own grandmother as a sex slave, and he was willing to do anything for money. *Anything.* That was going to make him very useful.

A long-tailed bird flitted into view, and the OP smiled. And then he heard the crash.

CHAPTER THIRTY-FOUR

Potto (*Perodicticus potto*) is the name given to a species of small, wooly tree-dwelling mammal that is a forerunner of the monkey. Pottos are about fourteen inches long with stubby tails. They forage for fruit and insects at night, spending the daylight hours lying utterly still atop branches. They have developed a specialized vascular system that permits adequate blood circulation during these long periods of immobility. Superficially, pottos resemble South American sloths, but there is no close relationship.

The whites of Belle Vue met at the club that evening to commemorate the passing of Senhor Cezar Nunez. It was a spontaneous gathering, but included virtually everyone except the deceased's widow and the American. Families brought their children with them to play in the pool, where they splashed solemnly. Women packed sandwiches and cakes—even though the club sold food—and stood or sat in tight clumps, as if seeking safety in numbers. For the most part, the men lined the bar, standing three deep, lost in their thoughts. No one spoke above a whisper.

The blacks of Belle Vue Village congregated around their family hearths, where the story of Senhor Nunez's suicide—for surely that's what it was—was told over and over again. There were manioc mush and cassava greens for the women and children, meat and palm wine for the men. There was even laughter, for death was a frequent visitor who needed to be entertained. Better to divert death's attention with stories and reenactment than let his gaze wander and settle upon his next victim.

When darkness had fallen completely, extinguishing the last pink streak on the horizon, the village drums began to talk. On their side of the river, the whites heard them too. Old-timers were consulted, but they were unable to decipher the message. Then the Muluba bartender was asked to interpret, which he did, but not without hesitation.

"The drums say that a witch doctor placed a spell on this white man, causing him to drive into the river." He paused a long time, and shook his head before resuming the translation. "They also say that many witch doctors will work together to put spells on all the white people, not in only Belle Vue, but in all the Congo. If the Belgians do not leave the country by the time the rains come, they too will take their own lives."

The old-timers muttered words like "nonsense" and "scare tactics," but the furrows on their foreheads spoke of fear. Young men drained their drinks and asked for more. Mothers pulled their children from the pool and hugged them, oblivious to wet skirts and sodden shoes.

In the hills to the west, the dominant female hyena bared her teeth and flattened her ears. She had just allowed the dominant male to mount her one last time; now she was done with him. He was substantially smaller than she was. If he didn't take the hint next time he attempted to mate her, he would be painfully rebuffed.

In about four months she would give birth to one or two cubs in the safety of an abandoned aardvark's burrow. Until then she would gorge at every opportunity, but first she had to kill.

* * *

Heilewid was not to be found. After searching their home, the OP had inquired at the homes of neighbors and the few friends Heilewid still had, but no one could remember seeing her. Because no plane was scheduled that day, he could only hope that she'd somehow managed to catch an automobile ride to Luluaburg.

Yes, that had to be it. On average there were two or three housewives a day making that trip with their chauffeurs, and perhaps another half dozen cars belonging to merchants or missionaries passing through town on their way to the big city. Any one of them would have given a ride to a white woman walking along the road. That had to be it, because the alternative was too awful: Heilewid getting too close to the edge of the gorge and losing her balance.

Under normal circumstances—but when were they ever normal?—the OP would have contacted the police captain, and together the two of them would have organized a search party. Maybe they would have found her, soused, sleeping off her drunk under a mango tree, or passed out in a tool shed. The captain was a good man, a friend, and he wouldn't have written an official report on their little adventure. As for the OP's white underlings—well, in normal times they would have been too afraid for their jobs to say anything directly to his Consortium superiors. That wouldn't have stopped them from gossiping to their relatives back home in Belgium, but by then it would be idle third-party gossip, something the board members eschewed.

Of course, these weren't normal times. The Africans were restless, needlessly energized by independence fever, and the bigwigs in Brussels were putting the pressure on all their companies to squeeze every last drop of profit out of the Congo before they had to turn the power over to the indigenous people. As if that weren't enough, the pimple-faced spy from Flanders was out to get the OP. That had been the case from day one, but was especially so now that the kid had been fired.

Given that the world was as mean and ugly a place as it ever had been, was it really so awful if Heilewid had slipped and fallen into the churning waters of the gorge? Wouldn't death by nature be preferable to death by bottle? If it put her out of her misery, her unbearable pain, then one was forced to view it as a blessing. There were far worse ways to die in Africa, and Belgium, with its murders and automobile traffic, was hardly better. Besides, if she fell into the gorge, death would come instantly, and by the time the crocs fed on her, she would be just a corpse. This would not be the case if she lay drunk, in her own vomit under a hedge somewhere, and the hyenas got to her.

The OP made an appearance at the club, said some general words of comfort to the assembled throng, and then made his exit as soon as possible. The mood at the club was depressing as hell. The somber colonialists, faced with the death of a white man, reminded the OP of a movie he'd seen set in America's frontier West. The whites in the film had been butchering Indians for years, and now they were on the defensive, huddled behind a wooden stockade waiting for dawn to come. For most, it came too late.

The OP returned to a darkened house—the servants had long been dismissed—and set about polishing off a full bottle of Irish whiskey. Even out on the patio, the OP could barely see his outstretched hand, which he'd extended in a toast.

"To my Heilewid," he said. "May the angels ease your fall, even as they take your soul to be with your beloved Geete."

With his headlights illuminating her, Flanders immediately recognized the woman by her walk. Roads in the bush were not paved, just two dirt tracks with a strip of elephant grass growing down the middle. The woman was in the left track, but staying as close to the center of the road as possible. This was wise at night, when predators were about, but during the day it was better to keep one's distance from the median, because that's where snakes preferred to lie in wait of their prey.

When she heard Flanders's car, she automatically stepped over to the bush to let him pass. The woman only turned to look when Flanders stopped the car adjacent to her.

"Where are you going?" he asked in French.

"Luluaburg."

"Why didn't you tell me? I would have given you a ride."

"I don't mind walking."

"But at night! Isn't it dangerous?"

"At night I have only animals to worry about, not people."

"Touché. But not from this one." He leaned over and opened the passenger door. "Get in."

They rode in silence for several kilometers. Once a nightjar, blinded by the headlights, seemingly flung itself at the car, its wings brushing Flanders's arm through the open window. Finally he spoke.

"How long were you going for?"

"I don't know. The talk in the village scares me; I no longer feel safe there."

"*Oui, je comprends.* But why did you leave without saying good-bye? Don't I mean anything to you?"

"I was going to write you once I got settled."

"But do I *mean* anything? Don't you care about me at all?"

"*Non,*" she said quietly.

He waited for a few minutes before glancing her way. Even in the dark he could see the tears streaming down her face.

"You lied back there; I do mean something to you. Monique, I love you, and I know that you love me too. I want us to be together—to be a couple. Maybe even get married someday."

"That can never be."

"Why not?"

"You will suffer for it."

"Fine, then I'll suffer. That's what I want."

"How can you be sure?"

"Because I know that without you, I will suffer anyway. Without you I will always be weak."

He felt her hand touch his shoulder, alighting there for just a second. He turned to see her smiling through her tears.

"Then we will be strong together," she said.

Flanders knew that the culture she'd been raised in didn't subscribe to the concept of romantic love. Marriages were arranged, alliances were formed, and children brought into the world. Love was sometimes a by-product, but never the instigator of the union between two people. Yet what he had just heard was, in its own way, an unequivocal declaration of love.

It was time to change the subject, before she could take it back. "Did you hear about the truck going over the bridge?"

"I saw it. It was terrible."

"Strange how that happened, if you ask me. You would think that even if the brakes failed, he'd still be able to steer the truck, and then once he got to the other side, there's another bit of hill that would have slowed way him down, maybe even stopped him. Then again, it is impossible to really understand those Portuguese—unless you are one. Which I'm not, I'm glad to say." He laughed, feeling surprisingly happy. "And neither are you—Portuguese, I mean."

She smiled.

CHAPTER THIRTY-FIVE

The giant hog (*Hylochoerus meinertzhageni*) was long thought to be just a legend. Today it is found in scattered locations across a wide stretch of central Africa. It is the largest species of wild pig; the males can weigh as much as 600 lbs. Giant hogs prefer to live in shady habitat, such as thick brush at the edge of forests. Unlike many other pigs, these animals are grazers, and not rooters. The males engage in head-to-head combat, sometimes cracking their skulls in the process. Giant hogs will stand their ground to defend their young and their territories, and thus are easy prey for hunters. They are becoming rare, and some subspecies are endangered.

They were obviously hunters, judging by the pack of basenji dogs at their heels. There were four of them, two in one lane, two in the other. When they got closer, Flanders could see that the men on the right were carrying a dead antelope, which was hanging from a pole slung over their shoulders. By rights they should have been scared out of their wits by the automobile and its headlights, but they didn't seem the least bit afraid—unlike Monique, who was crouching beneath the dashboard.

To the contrary, the hunters had turned and were facing the car head-on. The two men not burdened had drawn back their bows. They were the largest bows Flanders had ever seen, possibly even six feet in length, the approximate height of the hunters.

Out of courtesy, Flanders cut the headlights. "What tribe are they?" he asked.

"Bashilele."

"Then why are you hiding? Isn't that your tribe?"

"My mother's tribe, not mine. This is their territory. No one stops here. Not at night."

Flanders had heard that the Bashilele were territorial, and had been known to kill interlopers. In fact, a boy was required to kill someone of another tribe as a rite of passage. From then on, as a sign of status, the newly minted man had the privilege of wearing one of his victim's ears on the rope that held up his loincloth. Rumor also had it that the Bashilele men used the skulls of the men they'd killed as drinking cups.

He'd asked Monique about these customs, but she'd refused to confirm or deny anything. Now she was trembling so hard, he could feel the vibrations through the seat.

"But you were going to walk through here," he said. "I don't understand."

"I was going to walk through here *alone*," she whispered. "Please, back up."

But it was too late. Two more hunters had joined them from behind. They also carried a pole slung between their shoulders. From it hung the largest baboon Flanders had ever seen.

"I can't back up," he said. "They're behind us as well. They must have come out of the tall grass."

"If they see us together, they will kill us. Can you not drive around them?"

"I can try."

It was a waste of breath to say that. On either side of the road were dirt embankments a meter high. The low-riding American car he'd leased couldn't begin to scale them. Even a jeep would tip over.

The only thing to do was to convince the men that you were friendly, that your intention was only to pass through their territory. Probably the quickest way to do that was through gifting. Didn't everybody appreciate gifts? Of course Flanders wasn't exactly prepared for that, but there might be a few expendable things in the trunk of the car.

The important things to remember were to move slowly and to smile a lot. Don't panic under any circumstance. Quietly invoking the name of God and that of his mother, Flanders inched open his door.

"What are you doing?" Monique whispered hysterically.

Flanders didn't answer; he was smiling. And so far so good. See? There could be peaceful interaction between disparate peoples. All it took was . . .

The arrow traveled so fast, Flanders couldn't see it coming. It packed so much force that his Adam's apple was shoved through the back of his neck, severing his spinal chord. His head toppled backwards, connected to his body only by a pencil-thick cord of muscle tissue. His lifeless trunk, however, remained defiantly erect for a moment, spraying blood like a geyser.

Early the next morning a pair of brothers driving a truck, ivory merchants from Northern Rhodesia, happened upon the abandoned car. The keys were still in the ignition. Assuming that the driver was somewhere in the elephant grass relieving himself, the brothers waited patiently for half an hour. This was merely bush courtesy. Besides, anyone obsessed with keeping track of time had no business coming to the Congo.

Two hours was another matter. By then the brothers had shouted themselves hoarse and honked both horns—theirs, and the car's—so many times, they feared losing their hearing. Heck, whoever owned that snazzy American-made car didn't deserve the privilege. It's not like he—or she—had run out of gas and struck out on foot. There was still plenty of gas. And there was no sign of foul play, either. Okay, so maybe those brown spots on the inside of the driver's-side door may have been blood, and the dirt in that general area had been disturbed, but what did those two things really prove? Nothing concrete.

One thing was for sure: the car had to be moved in order for them to pass by with their panel truck. And as long as they had to move the car, why not continue to drive it for a while? After all, whoever owned the beautiful machine no longer had a use for it. That was as plain to see as the English noses on their faces.

Cripple was late to work. It might not be so aggravating, except that Amanda had given her an alarm clock—green, with bells on top—and shown her how to use it. She was supposed to show up at six thirty, prepare the coffee, and watch as Protruding Navel made hotcakes and set the table. But here it was almost seven thirty, and still no sign of her.

They hadn't waited on her, of course. The whole purpose of this week without guests was to serve as a dress rehearsal, and a play has to start on time. So Protruding Navel had made the hot-cakes by himself, grumbling as usual. Fortunately his bad mood did not affect his cooking.

"Protruding Navel," Amanda said, trying her best to sound pleasant, "these are the best hotcakes I've ever eaten."

"Does that mean you want more, *mamu*?"

"Oh no, this is quite enough."

"Then you do not like them."

"But I do!"

"If you like them, *mamu*, you will eat until your stomach hurts, and then still you will continue to eat."

"Is this how you eat, Protruding Navel? Until your stomach hurts?"

"Does the *mamu* mock me?"

"What? I mean, of course not."

"*Mamu*, tell me, have you seen many fat Africans?"

"No, I guess not."

"That is because we do not eat until our stomachs hurt."

"That's very sensible."

"No, *mamu*. It is not a choice we make; we do not have the food to waste. If I were rich, I would like to become very fat—like an American."

Like an American! Well, she, for one, wasn't fat, although she knew what Protruding Navel meant. It seemed like more and more Americans were living to eat, rather than the other way around. At church potlucks people joked about how much food they had piled on their plates. She'd even heard of a dessert called "girdle-buster pie."

"Do you ever go hungry?" she asked softly.

"No, Mamu Ugly Eyes. Because of this job I am able feed myself and my family."

Suddenly Amanda felt ashamed. How could she fire him after that? Just because he was annoying—make that extremely aggravating—didn't mean that his family had to suffer. It was frightening to think of how close she'd come to making them suffer, just because she had thin skin—although there were the rumors that he was a wife beater. But what proof did she have of that? Just stories from someone with a very active imagination.

Starting now she would not listen to the gossip about him, although she would make an effort to visit his wife. Starting now she would let his cutting remarks roll off her back. She would let his grumbling go in one ear and out the other. She would try very hard not to respond in any manner to his goading; she would not purse her lips, roll her eyes, or shake her head. Starting now she would respect the man who dreamed, not of owning a television, or even an electric washing machine, but of one day being fat.

The longer the day wore on, the cheekier Protruding Navel became. Still there was no sign of Cripple. Amanda began to feel as if Protruding Navel was hell-bent on destroying her newfound equanimity. At one point she caught him hobbling about in the kitchen like a cripple.

Unable to take any more, Amanda fled to her room to read her Bible and pray, activities that always seemed to have a calming affect on her. "A peace that surpasses all understanding," as Amanda had heard others describe this feeling. But her solitude lasted only minutes. Somebody was pounding on the door.

"Protruding Navel!" she called, and then realizing it was a lost cause, went to answer the door herself.

What an agreeable surprise to find Captain Jardin standing there. "*Bonjour*, Amanda," he said politely. Too politely.

"Please come in," she said.

He stepped briskly past her. When she invited him to sit, he did so at once, barely waiting for her to do likewise.

"Would you care for some coffee?" she asked graciously, although it felt like she'd tried to swallow a stone, which was now caught in her throat.

"*Non, merci.* I am afraid I am here on police business."

The stone—actually more like a large rock—dislodged and landed in her stomach. "Is it my parents? Is something wrong back home?"

"No, Amanda. I am sorry to say this, but one of your employees has been arrested for murder."

Amanda's blood ran cold. "How can that be," she whispered, "when he's here now? He's supposed to be making dinner, but I wouldn't be surprised to learn that he has his ear pressed to the kitchen door."

CHAPTER THIRTY-SIX

The common hippopotamus (*Hippopotamus amphibius*) was once found from the Nile delta to the cape of South Africa. Their range is much reduced now. They are large animals, and can weigh as much as 6,000 lbs. Although hippos can be extremely dangerous when threatened, and their incisors can grow to be six inches long, these animals are strict vegetarians. Hippos live in water during the day and graze on riverbanks at night. They breathe air, like any other mammal, but are capable of staying submerged for as long as 15 minutes at a time. Hippo calves nurse while underwater, returning to the surface for air every few seconds.

The handsome Belgian appeared puzzled by her question, but only for a second. "Ah, but not *that* employee! This is a woman who gives her name as Cripple."

Amanda jumped to her feet. "Cripple? Arrested for murder? I can't believe it! There has to be a mistake. A short woman, maybe in her late thirties? And she's uh—uh—"

"Crippled?"

"Yes. But it's not her, right?"

"It is, I'm afraid."

Amanda sat again as her legs refused to support her. "I don't believe this. Who is she accused of killing?"

"Here, in the Congo, we call it murder—especially when it concerns a white person. This may not sound fair to you, but I am just telling you how it is."

"I understand. But what you're saying is impossible. Cripple didn't murder anyone. She's not capable of that—I mean spiritually. Although she's most probably physically incapable of it as well."

He chewed on his lower lip. Amanda found that—well, seductive. She would have slapped herself, had she been alone. Except that then there would be no reason to do so. Why on earth, when Cripple had just been accused of a heinous crime, was her mind steering her on that course? What was wrong with her?

Thank heavens Captain Jardin was unaware of her shameful thoughts. "Amanda," he said gently, "how long have you known the woman?"

"Okay, so I haven't know her very long, but I'm an excellent judge of character."

"Is that so?"

"Yes, that's so!"

"Ah, but just a minute ago you jumped to the conclusion that it was Monsieur Protruding Navel whom I'd arrested for murder. Am I not correct?"

When proven wrong, change the subject. It was a tactic Amanda had learned from her mother, who'd learned it from her mother before her. Even the most charming Southern lady could get only so far by arguing.

"Captain Jardin, I hate to be rude, but I simply must ask you about Cripple. Whom did she kill? And why? And where? This is all so hard to take in."

"*Oui*, but of course. Let us begin with whom. I am sorry to say that she killed your neighbor across the river, Senhor Nunez."

"But that's ridiculous—I mean impossible. Senhor Nunez was killed in the bridge accident yesterday. Or maybe it was suicide. But I assure you, Cripple had nothing to do with it. She was in her village when it happened."

"You sound very sure of this."

"I am, because I accompanied her there myself. Just before the accident. She wasn't feeling well."

"And then what?"

"And then I returned, of course. Or tried to. You see, by then Senhor Nunez's truck had gone over the falls and the entire village had come out to see what was going on. It took me longer to get down the hill, than it did up."

"*Oui, oui.* Tell me, mademoiselle, how well did you know Senhor Nunez?"

"Oh, I never met him. But just yesterday his wife was here for tea. She wants us to be friends."

Captain Jardin removed a small spiral-bound notebook from the pocket of his khaki shirt and began to scribble furiously in it. Handsome or not, he was taking an inordinate amount of time to answer her questions.

"I repeat myself, Captain Jardin," she said, adopting a formal tone. "Where did this alleged murder take place?"

He pointed to the window. "On the bridge, of course."

"*How* did she kill him? She is, as you've noted, a tiny handicapped woman."

"She disconnected the brake cable on his truck, as well as compromised the steering. As the truck came down the hill it gained speed, and without the ability to steer, the curve at the bottom of the hill sent him straight through the railing, and then over the falls. We expect his body to appear quite a bit downstream—if the crocodiles don't get to him first. If it's the crocs, we may never know. Then again, last year a hunter shot a crocodile several kilometers down river. The beast had eleven copper bracelets in its stomach. Most probably the victims were women washing clothes along the riverbank."

Amanda shuddered. "That's awful."

"*Oui*. It was a terrible fate for Senhor Nunez, and it remains a terrible loss for his wife, as well as for his children back in Portugal."

"I couldn't agree more, Pierre. But I still say that to blame this on Cripple is ludicrous. How would a simple village woman, one who has never even been to school—not officially at least—know how to disable a car?" But before her last word was uttered, she recalled something Cripple had told her the day before, as they walked up the hill, but before they'd been mobbed by the kids.

The inspector seemed to have read her mind. "Her father was a mechanic's assistant, and she claims to have spent much of her childhood watching him repair cars and trucks. When one knows how to repair, then one also knows how to destroy, yes?"

"Perhaps. But what would be her motive? Every murder has to have a motive, right? Otherwise, it's called an accident."

"*Touché*. But you see, the woman has already confessed to disabling the truck, with the intention of sending Senhor Nunez through the railing and over the falls. However, she will not give a reason. I am hoping that you will be able to help in this matter."

"Where is she?"

"She is in prison. I will take you to her if you wish."

"Yes, of course. Does Branca—Senhor Nunez's wife—know you are conducting a murder investigation?"

"*Oui*. I was just there. She is understandably very—how shall I put it—"

"Upset? Distraught?"

"*Oui*. She asks that you visit her."

Amanda's head reeled. Barely more than a week into what should have been a cushy assignment, and suddenly she was involved with an alleged murderess *and* the murder victim's wife. Was this any better than living back home in South Carolina? Had she jumped from the frying pan into the fire? If so, this was so unfair. All she'd asked for was a chance to make up for one horrible mistake. And now this!

"I can't take it."

"*Pardonez mois?*"

"What I mean is—well, it's too much to take in all at once." Despite the fact that she was fighting back the tears as hard as she could, they came anyway.

"Amanda," the captain said, his voice soft and gentle, "it is, indeed, a lot to take in, as you say. Perhaps I should come back this afternoon, after you have had more time to process this information."

"No! I want to see Cripple. Take me to Cripple. Please."

"*Oui.* And then perhaps you will speak words of comfort to Senhora Nunez?"

Amanda promised.

Cripple was surprised to hear Amanda's voice outside her tiny cement-block cell, and somehow even more surprised when the heavy wooden door was pulled open, and she saw her employer standing there in the flesh. She wasn't dreaming after all. But why had the white *mamu* come? To berate her for being a disappointment? To remind her of the chance she'd taken by hiring a cripple, a woman her existing housekeeper loathed?

Cripple didn't know how to interpret the smile on Mamu Ugly Eyes' face, so she laughed. Immediately she regretted this. Husband was forever telling stories about cross-cultural misunderstandings that arose from different body languages. Europeans, he often reminded her, laugh only when they perceive they have heard a joke. Sadly, their jokes are seldom funny.

"*Mamu,*" she sputtered. "I did not expect to see you."

"Well, I must say, I didn't expect to ever see you like this—in jail. Tell me, Cripple, what happened."

Cripple glanced at the man who had arrested her and thrown her in jail. He hadn't used force, as she'd expected him to. He hadn't even seemed angry upon hearing her confession. Still, she did not wish to have him present at the moment.

"Very well," he said, as if reading her mind. "I will be in the office, completing her paperwork. Call out, if you need me." He began to walk away.

"*Bula matadi*," Cripple called after him. Literally the words meant "rock breaker." They too were the legacy of King Leopold II's cruel reign, when Belgian officials had presided over gangs of forced labor, as they toiled breaking rocks with which to build houses for their masters.

The police captain turned. "Yes, madame?"

"Do not act so surprised, you baboon's bare ass," Cripple said in rapid-fire Tshiluba.

"What?"

"You told me to call you if I needed to. I want to know why you haven't bothered to lock the door. Aren't you afraid that I'll run away?"

"You seem to me to be a woman of honor," the captain said, answering her in flawless Tshiluba. "And *baba*, there really is no need for insults."

Cripple was shocked. Not only did the man speak her mother tongue, but he had respectfully addressed her as "mother."

"*Baba*, are you surprised that I speak Tshiluba?"

"*Eyo*. Forgive me, but I thought you were a Belgian."

"I am. But I was born here in Kasai Province. Tshiluba is the language I learned first. From my caretaker."

"This is surely a wonder."

"It is nothing. There are wonders far greater than that in Belle Vue."

Cripple looked away. "Truly?"

"Truly, truly," the white man said, then walked away.

Second Wife breathed a sigh of relief as she watched the little gourd disappear down the toilet hole. What had she been thinking? What had come over her? Clearly she had not been in her right mind to even contemplate killing another human being—even one as selfish and unlikable as Cripple.

Murder was a serious sin, one which would surely have sent her to hell. Even if there was no such place as the Christian hell, as Cripple claimed, there were serious consequences for taking another life. Just to wish another person dead was to diminish one's own humanity. This was something Second Wife could feel in the middle of her heart, something no missionary had to tell her, for her to know it was true.

Perhaps she'd been under someone's spell; that would explain it. Perhaps she had inadvertently offended another woman while working in the manioc plots, and that woman too had searched out a witch doctor. Whatever the reason for her poor judgment, Second Wife was better now.

Cripple was immensely relieved that the missionary had not heard her call the captain a baboon's bare ass. The only reason that Mamu Ugly Eyes hadn't heard was because the white woman possessed a sense of curiosity equal to that of Baby Boy. At the moment she was peering into Cripple's empty cell.

"There is nothing to see," Cripple said. "Only a blanket and a bucket. Not even a bed platform. Of course, there are many flies."

"It's awful."

"Not so bad, I think, for the killer of a white man."

"Stop that nonsense, Cripple. You didn't kill anyone."

"But I did, *mamu*. I fixed it so that Senhor Nunez could not stop his truck, nor could he control the direction in which it moved, and thus he plunged to his death in the falls."

"Why did you do that? It doesn't make any sense."

"*Mamu*, you have been very kind to me. Forgive me then, when I say that I will not speak further on this matter."

"But you must! I need to understand this. I need to understand why you're lying."

"Very well, *mamu*. If you wish to call me a liar, that is your prerogative."

"But I don't! Yet you are lying. I *know* it."

Tears welled in the white woman's eyes, which really were not all that ugly. Absurdly pale, yes, but not hideous. Too bad that a name given in haste, cannot easily be taken away. For it is not we who own our names, it is they that own us.

There followed a lengthy silence, which Cripple was determined not to break. She pretended to be absorbed by the antics of a "backwards bug." When disturbed, the tiny beetles burrowed backward into the sand, leaving cone-shaped depressions. It was a children's game to try and catch them before they disappeared altogether.

"Cripple, I will speak to the captain about giving you a better cell. At the very least, he should provide you with a sleeping platform and some fresh water."

"Thank you, *mamu*. But please, do not make trouble for yourself."

"It won't be any trouble. Cripple, can I do anything else for you? Maybe take a message to your family?"

"My family? No, *mamu*. The Bula Matadi has already seen to that."

"Very well. Just so you know, even though you call yourself a heathen, I will still pray for you."

"As you wish, *mamu*." Cripple turned so that the young white woman could not see the tears in her own eyes.

CHAPTER THIRTY-SEVEN

The cheetah (*Acinonyx jubatus*) is one of the smaller "big cats," with adult males seldom weighing more than 125 lbs. Because they are long-legged, with enlarged hearts and nostrils, they are able to run faster than any other animal. A cheetah can reach speeds as high 65 miles per hour in a matter of seconds, although they cannot sustain these speeds for very long. When a cheetah catches up to its prey, it knocks the prey off balance and then pounces on it. Death is by strangulation. Proportionally, cheetahs have smaller mouths than other big cats, and their claws, which are used for traction, are duller. As a consequence, cheetahs are unable to defend their kills against leopards and hyenas, so they gulp their food down immediately.

Amanda was astounded how easily Captain Jardin gave in to her demands. In fact, he seemed almost eager to comply. To be absolutely honest, it was downright embarrassing.

"Anything else?" he asked, his fountain pen poised above the yellow pad of paper.

"What about food? What will you be feeding her?"

He shrugged.

"Does that mean you don't know?"

"It means that I will have to confer with the cook."

"Who does the cooking for the prisoners?"

"Well, you see, that's the problem. There is no official prison cook, so the cooking will have to be done by me—or someone I hire."

"Who feeds the prisoners now?"

He surprised Amanda by laughing. "At the moment Cripple is our only prisoner. You see, in small matters—petty theft, fights, marital disputes—we turn the matter over to the tribal chief. In larger, more important matters—such as murder—I drive the accused over to Luluaburg, our provincial capital. The cells you saw are essentially just places to hold the prisoner until I can top off the petrol in my truck. Cripple is the first female arrest I have ever made. And I doubt if there has ever been a previous case, here in Belle Vue, of an African accused of killing a white."

"Oh. What will become of her? Will you be sending her off to Luluaburg as well?"

"I plan to keep her here for the time being. For her safekeeping, more than anything. Very few African women commit crimes against the crown, and the few women prisoners I have seen in Luluaburg were either hardened prostitutes with histories of soliciting Europeans, or else—how do you say—not right in the head."

"Mentally ill, I believe, is the term used today. Pierre, I appreciate the fact that you obviously have Cripple's best interest in mind, but what will happen to her if she stays here? How will the other Europeans react? As I understand it, Senhor Nunez was employed by the Consortium, which is a very powerful force here in the Congo. Cripple, on the other hand—well, she is just one woman."

"React? Amanda, here I am the law. I was appointed by the Home Office of His Majesty's government. I do not work for the Consortium—if that is what you mean."

That was exactly Amanda's point. Back home a black woman

who killed a white person would need a lot more than a wooden door to keep her safe.

"So then what happens next?"

He rubbed his chin, as if searching for stubble missed during his morning shave. More likely, he hadn't had time to shave at all.

"After I have made a thorough investigation, and if I decide that there is sufficient evidence to back up her confession, I will recommend the case to a magistrate in Luluaburg. He will then arrange for a trial to be conducted."

"I'm afraid I don't understand. So a confession isn't enough?"

"Not in this case. I'm sorry, Amanda, but I am not at liberty to say more."

Amanda knew he was throwing her a bone, a tidbit of revealing information, but she couldn't for the life of her figure out what that might be. Word games had never been her forte.

Words have astonishing power to both heal and wound, that much Amanda knew from experience. She also knew that there is no sequence of words good enough to say to a grieving person who has lost a spouse. On the contrary, there are many inappropriate things that can tumble out of one's mouth during moments of stress.

Amanda had been nine when her grandfather died. At his funeral a woman of good intentions had tried to comfort Amanda's grandmother by saying, "He's better off where he is now." No doubt the would-be comforter was unaware that Granddaddy Brown was an unrepentant sinner who'd often stated that Heaven sounded like a boring place to him. Amanda vowed not to make a similar mistake.

Not only did the Nunez house boast the best views in all of Belle Vue, it also laid claim to the most beautiful garden. Tropical foliage with dark leaves that tapered to drip points served as a background for white gardenias, hibiscus in a variety of gem tones, and clumps of bird of paradise. Stone paths meandered through thickets of flowering plants, repeatedly crossing a slow-moving stream that gave birth to pools clogged with water lilies and lavender hyacinths. There were even stone grottoes clothed in emerald-green moss and trimmed with ferns. It was as magical a place as Amanda had ever been, and quite frankly, seemed very much out of place in a small African town on the edge of nowhere.

"It is a bit overdone, don't you think?"

Amanda jumped. The senhora, clothed head to toe in deepest black, had appeared out of nowhere.

"I did not mean to scare you."

"The police captain said—well, I heard about your husband. I'm here to say how sorry I am."

"*Sorry?* What did you do?" Her diction was crisp, and her tone was cold, so that the words tumbled out of her mouth like ice cubes.

"No, I mean that I feel bad for you. About your husband's death. It must be so awful."

"You have no idea. But thank you. Please, come with me to the patio. We can take our refreshments there."

Amanda followed Branca through the lush greenery to a stone patio that had a stunning view of the falls. Whereas from her side of the river Amanda could only see one rainbow at this hour of the morning, from this vantage point, between clouds of mist, she caught glimpses of three rainbows.

"Oh my gosh! I have never seen anything as beautiful as this."

"Nor I." The senhora rang a little bell that could barely be heard over the roar of the falls. "Would you care for tea, or coffee?"

"Tea, please."

The senhora gave her instructions to a tall African, dressed in a white uniform and white gloves although his feet were bare. Branca must have had eyes in the back of her head, because nothing escaped her.

"He prefers it that way. He says that wearing shoes make—how do you say—they will dull his senses. Yes?"

Amanda shrugged. She honestly didn't know what the senhora meant.

"In his feets."

His *feets*? Well, it was no surprise that an educated woman like the senhora would still be having trouble with the plurals of English words. In that regard, English was one of the most difficult languages to master. Far more difficult than Tshiluba, which at least followed rules.

"You see," the senhora continued, "with bare feets he can feel the temperatures of the stones—if they are warm or cold—and can also feel the vibrations of other feets. In other words, with the bare feets he knows when I am coming, so that he can act busy."

How stereotypical, Amanda thought, then immediately tried to expunge the judgment from her mind. "How are you doing?" she asked.

Branca Nunez offered up a soft sigh, one that was immediately absorbed by the background sound. "I loved my husband very much. My heart is broken. *This* is how I am doing."

"Is there anything I can do to help?" she asked, knowing full well her offer would be refused.

"Yes. There is something I need very much; I need a friend."

Their Death did not believe in bad luck, even though he was experiencing a series of most unfortunate events. Either someone had placed a curse on his family, or the spirits were upset with him for failing to be a good witch doctor. It was most probably the latter. Their Death had inherited a wealth of sacred information, secrets that could benefit many people, but what had he done with this knowledge? Very little. Truly, he had been too concerned with emulating the ways of the white man, of wanting to appear progressive. And now Cripple was in prison and it was all his fault.

But wait, there was yet another possible reason for the terrible misfortune that had struck his family. What if it was because Their Death had publicly turned his back on being a Christian? All the boys who attended the Catholic school were required to convert and be baptized, and Their Death had been no exception. Even now Their Death's sons were baptized Christians, although privately they were quite happy to be little heathens.

It was a pity how the Church made you pick sides. How very limiting. Why couldn't one respect the various spirits, which were found in everything, and still worship the Christian god? Because the Christian god was the jealous type, that's why. Yehowa made it very clear in his book, the Holy Bible, that he did not like to share. In fact, that was his third commandment.

Yes, Cripple's imprisonment had to be the doings of Yehowa, the only father of Jesus. No doubt he was angry about Their Death's backsliding, and the fact that Cripple had never even been baptized. As a good Christian, Their Death should have insisted that she be baptized. So you see? This too was Their Death's fault.

After Their Death removed the stone from Baby Boy's mouth, he should have dropped it down the hole in the toilet hut. Then he should have returned to the church and made a confession of sin. Ah, but that would not have worked. The priest would not have given him absolution as long as he was married to Cripple. One man, one wife, that's what the Church insisted on, even if both wives were Christian.

Yet Jesus had many wives—thousands of them, in fact. Did not the nuns consider themselves to be the brides of Christ? When challenged on that point, the priest had waffled, saying that the nuns were only spiritual brides. Finally, after much discussion, the priest admitted that it did indeed all boil down to sex; Jesus could have many wives, but only because he didn't sleep with any of them.

If giving up sex with Cripple was going to appease Yehowa, then this is what Their Death was prepared to do. If need be, he would even give up his inherited position as a witch doctor—although Their Death did not see how his profession could possibly be incompatible with Christianity. After all, the Bible made it very clear that Jesus was a Jewish witch doctor; he healed the sick with incantations, cured the blind with potions made from mud and spit, and performed feats of magic, such as walking on water.

Cripple did not belong in jail. Despite her confession, she had not tampered with the senhor's brakes, or made it impossible for him to steer. Someone else had done that. Someone else was threatening to do bodily harm to her, or her family, if she didn't volunteer that she was guilty. That was the only explanation Their Death could accept.

Who was making such threats? Well, it did not really matter, did it? Not as long as Yehowa was in charge, pulling the strings on the citizenry of Belle Vue, much like in a puppet show Their Death had once seen performed in Luluaburg. The only solution was for Their Death to go to the priest with the honest intention of giving up Cripple as his wife. Then perhaps a miracle might happen, and whoever was threatening Cripple would turn his attention away from her, or maybe even disappear altogether.

But giving up Cripple was not Their Death's decision alone; there was Second Wife to consider. Although Their Death was certain Second Wife would be pleased, and would readily agree to such a move, it was necessary that he should go through the formality of asking.

He looked over to where she was pounding dry manioc tubers

into flour. The pestle was heavy, and it was a job made easier when two pounded in sync, chanting a work song. From the very first day he'd brought Second Wife home, Cripple had refused to pound any longer. She claimed that the jarring hurt her back. Second Wife had been livid, but by now she was used to working alone. Still, she deserved a say in the matter.

Their Death walked over to the pestle and stood quietly until Second Wife looked up. She brought the pestle down one more time.

CHAPTER THIRTY-EIGHT

The mandrill (*Mandrillus sphinx*) is a baboon, a type of large terrestrial monkey. Their coats are a drab olive brown, but the males have brightly colored faces and buttocks, sport orange beards, and have blue muzzles, accented with scarlet and white. Their buttocks are blue shading to mauve, and they have scarlet penises. A single dominant male leads a harem consisting of a couple dozen females and juveniles. Mandrills are omnivores with a preference for fruit, although they eat meat when available, and have even been known to kill and devour baby antelopes.

Second Wife," he said, "how are you today?"

Her eyes widened. "I feel well, husband. And you?"

"Also well. And the children? How are they?"

Using her chin, she gestured from side to side, as if to say, "Look around you. Here they are. See for yourself."

"Yes, I can see that the children are fine," he said. He stared momentarily at a hen with seven chicks that were just a day old. The hen had led them as close to the mortar as she dared, in hopes that someone would toss them a sprinkling of manioc flour. Chicks that small relied on human intervention, especially in the dry season, when there were so few seeds and insects available.

And sure enough, Second Wife, herself the mother of seven off-spring, threw the chickens a large handful of what had taken her a great deal of energy to produce.

"You are a kind woman, Second Wife," he said, moved by her generosity.

"Aiyee," she said, sucking air through her teeth.

Clearly she was not comfortable with praise. And whose fault was that? Their Death's, of course. It was he who had continuously heaped praise upon Cripple, all but ignoring Second Wife.

Dishing out praise was done at a husband's discretion; it was not obligatory by any means. Their Death could not remember his father praising anyone, except for his sons. Neither First Mother nor any of her sister wives had ever complained on that score. For them to have expected compliments would have been as silly as a Muluba boy believing he could fall asleep at night and then awaken the next morning with a white skin. And of what use were insincere compliments?

Their Death cleared his throat, uncertain how to proceed. "Second Wife, I have made a decision that will affect you. So now listen, if you wish to know what it is."

Second Wife gripped the pestle with both hands. "I am listening, Husband."

"Are you aware that early this morning Cripple confessed to causing the death of the European?"

"Husband, I am not clever like Cripple, but neither am I stupid. I have both heard and understood this news."

"And so I assumed. Second Wife, it has been brought to the attention of my heart that this confession—whether or not it is true—is ultimately my fault."

"*This* I do not understand."

"I have neglected the practices of my forefathers, and I have sinned against Yehowa. These are both grave matters, but it is Yehowa who wishes to punish me."

Second Wife opened her mouth to respond, but then must have had second thoughts. That was to be expected. She had been raised as a Protestant, and was thus not equipped to argue theology. At least not with someone who had attended a Catholic school. Unlike Cripple, however, Second Wife was not an avowed heathen; she was merely one by attrition, there not being a Protestant church within walking distance.

Their Death squared his shoulders. "Second Wife, it is with a heavy heart that I say this, so please do not make light of it in any way."

"Husband, please do not divorce me." Her voice quavered, cutting Their Death to the core. "I beg you on behalf of my children. Please do not divorce me."

Their Death smiled sadly. "No, it is the opposite. I have decided to divorce Cripple."

She stared at him, not comprehending at first, and then her eyes filled with tears. "No, you cannot!"

"*What?*"

"You must not divorce Cripple."

"I do not understand. I thought this would make you happy."

"But who will take care of her?"

"Her father yet lives."

"Yes, but he is old. Soon she will be old as well, unable even to work for a white *mamu*. Do you think the sons and daughters of her siblings will care for her as we do? Do you think the children of that village will refrain from mocking her? Here, the children have become accustomed to her presence. 'Life to you, Cripple,' they say, and, 'Are you well today?' There they will call her names and say, 'Oh, look at the woman whose body is as twisted as a ball of *lukodi* vine.' Then they will laugh and run away, for such is the behavior of children when they encounter something that is not as it should be."

Their Death stared in disbelief. Never had he heard so many

words tumble from the lips of Second Wife. Even when she was angry at one of the children, or complaining about Cripple, she used words as sparingly as she used salt, that most expensive and rare of all cooking ingredients. When Second Wife spoke, one listened carefully.

The younger children—the older boys were at school—had stopped their play and were clustered in a tight group. She Generates Happiness, a girl of four years, stepped forward as their spokesperson.

"*Tatu*, is it true that you wish to send Second Mother away?"

How was he to answer a question like that? "No," he said softly, "it is not my wish. But perhaps it is the wish of Yehowa."

"Why would he want to do that, *Tatu*?"

"Because he is angry with me."

"Why? What have you done?"

He swallowed hard. "I have loved Cripple as much as one would love a normal wife. Perhaps even more than that."

She Generates Happiness crossed her arms defiantly and stamped a foot. "Then I think that Yehowa must be a very mean man."

"Child!" Second Wife had dropped the pestle and was reaching out to grab the little girl, but Their Death stepped between them.

"Our daughter is right," he said. "If Yehowa does not approve of Cripple, then indeed he must be a very mean man."

Second Wife smiled. "Husband, you are crazy. And reckless to say such blasphemous words in this place. Are you not afraid that the children and I will be struck by lightning?"

"No," he said, and he was entirely serious. "You and the children are innocent. But I—I have been wrong to show favoritism to Cripple. That is my greatest sin."

She Generates Happiness was at the age when everything must be explained. "*Tatu*, what does 'favoritism' mean?"

Their Death reached into the pocket of his work shorts and extracted a one-franc piece. "Here," he said. "This is the beginning of great wealth. Now go and resume your play."

She Generates Happiness squealed with delight, although she had no knowledge of money and could not have distinguished a one-franc piece from a million-franc coin, had such a thing existed. That it was from her beloved *tatu*, and that it was shiny, and above all, a novelty—these were the things by which she judged this addition to her fortunes. For she was by nature a happy child, and thus already in possession of immeasurable wealth.

But her squeals of delight attracted the other children, and so Their Death gave each of them a coin, except for Baby Boy, who was too young and might have swallowed it and choked. Instead Their Death picked up the child and gave him a finger to suck on, which pleased them both. And certainly there was little danger of the child swallowing that.

With the children thus occupied, Their Death turned his full attention back to Second Wife. "Can you forgive me?" he asked bluntly.

"Do not be so silly, Husband. There is nothing to forgive."

"There is much to forgive."

"Nonsense."

"Forgive me anyway!" Was this behavior not typical of a woman? They complain and complain, and finally you give them what they want, yet it is not what they really want. To understand a woman, a man had to peel away layer after layer of words, much as one must peel away an onion skin to get at the desired part.

Second Wife picked up the dropped pestle. "If that is your wish, then I forgive you. But only on one condition."

"Yes?"

"Do not divorce Cripple. She is a good woman, with a kind heart, and even though she is lazier than—than—"

"A village full of teenage boys?"

Second Wife laughed, then quickly clamped here free hand over her mouth. Still laughing, she nodded vigorously.

"Truly, truly," she said when she could speak, "but still, you must not divorce her."

"Do you really mean this? In the middle of your heart?"

"*Eyo*. But maybe you can instruct her to help more with the children—when she is not working for the white *mamu*, of course."

"Of course." He paused to choose his words carefully. "Tell me, Second Wife, does it not bother you that I share myself with another woman? You know—at night."

He had been prepared to face a hard truth, perhaps even to compromise, but instead of taking him seriously, Second Wife dissolved into gales of embarrassed giggles. This time she covered her face entirely with her hands.

"Stop it," he said. "I want an answer.

It took her far too long to gain control, and when she did, it was with the sound of mirth still in her voice. "Look around, Husband. Do you not see four children? And there are three more at school. This means one child for every year we have been married. Believe me, Husband, when I tell you that you have shared much with me already." She was no longer able to contain her laughter.

Their Death smiled.

CHAPTER THIRTY-NINE

There are four species of otter native to Africa. The largest is the African clawless otter (*Aonyx capensis*). Males can weigh more than 60 lbs., and occasionally there are reports of specimens much bigger than that. The fingers and toes of African clawless otters lack webs, and the nails are rudimentary. They eat crabs, fish, mollusks, and even small animals. They are notorious for raiding fish farms. Because of this, and their beautiful fur, they are hunted unmercifully.

Prisoners in the Belle Vue jail were responsible for securing their own food. Between Amanda Brown and Cripple's family, Belle Vue's only prisoner was well cared for. Even Protruding Navel brought a handful of overripe bananas and a not quite ripe pineapple.

On Cripple's third day in jail, Captain Jardin brought her a plate of chicken cooked in palm-oil gravy, dense manioc mush—known as *bidia*—and tender manioc leaves flavored with tiny green chili peppers. He had with him an identical plate for himself, and protruding from the pockets of his baggy khaki shorts were the glass necks of two beer bottles. He set the comestibles on the stump of a large tree trunk while he fetched a pair of canvas folding chairs.

"*Baba*, it is time to eat," he called in his unaccented Tshiluba.

Cripple, who'd been watching him, pretended to blink as she appeared in the doorway of her miniscule cell. "I have no money for this food."

"No money is needed. His Majesty, King Baudouin of Belgium, is paying for it."

"The king?"

"In a matter of speaking. Now sit. And here is a beer."

Cripple had never seen beer in a bottle. A fair amount of palm wine was consumed by the village men, but they drank it warm from battered enamel cups, or from small hollow gourds. Certainly she had never seen anyone drink from a bottle.

"I do not know if I can drink this beer," she said.

"Why is that?"

"There is such a small hole on the bottle, and I have a large mouth."

The Captain smiled. "Here, watch." He put the bottle to his lips and tilted his head slightly. Cripple could see his Adam's apple bobbing as he swallowed.

Cripple picked up her bottle and reluctantly put it to her lips. The liquid was bitter and reminiscent of urine. Still, it was purported to make men happy, so Cripple was determined to have the experience.

Getting liquid from the small hole was not the challenge; the challenge was preventing the beer from escaping around the sides of one's mouth. But after a half dozen sips, some of which dribbled down her chin, she caught on, and by then the taste seemed to have improved.

"Now let us eat," the Captain said, "before the flies get it all." He tore off a chunk of *bidia* and using his thumb and forefinger shaped it into a scoop, which he then filled with a bit of chicken, greens, and the palm-oil gravy.

Cripple watched in amazement. She'd always believed that white people ate only with knives and forks, and sometimes spoons. She, however, had never owned a fork, much less used one. As for spoons, her family owned two, but they were large and used only to stir with while cooking.

"Where did you learn to eat our way?" she demanded.

"From my *baba*, and others who worked in the house. Do you disapprove?"

Cripple laughed. "Why would I disapprove? How you eat interests me, but only that. It is not up to me to judge."

"What a nicer place this world would be, if there were more people like you."

"Ha! I am a very wicked woman."

"If you say so."

"But I am! Did I not kill a man?"

"I am not so sure."

"Truly, I did. There were a thousand witnesses."

"*Baba*, unfortunately that is the case. I am afraid I have some very bad news."

Cripple's heart raced. "Eh?"

"I was hoping to keep this case at the local level, but because there were so many witnesses—white witnesses, who are demanding answers—and because it is common knowledge that you have confessed, the Provincial Governor is coming from Luluaburg to rule on your case."

Cripple trembled. The rational side of her knew that this had always been a possibility, but still she felt unprepared to receive this news.

"When will he come?"

"Tomorrow."

"Aiyee!"

"*Baba*, there is still one question you refuse to answer. And it is a question the Provincial Governor will ask you. If you don't answer, then you stand no chance of leniency. None at all. The consequences could be very grave."

She didn't hesitate. "How grave?"

The Captain looked away from her face. "Perhaps twenty years in prison. Perhaps even more. And the whip."

The *whip*. That needed no further explanation. Everyone in the Congo knew about the whip, that two-inch-thick strip of hippopotamus hide that could peel the skin off a man's back, just as surely as a knife could peel a ripe mango. But to Cripple's knowledge, the whip was used only on men, never on women.

"Truly?"

"Truly, truly. This Provincial Governor is new, and full of new ideas." He lowered his voice, although there was no one else around. "And not such good ideas either. He believes that those who agitate for an independent Congo can be brutalized into backing down. He has stated openly that in his opinion the former Governor was too lax. He feels that this is his opportunity—God given at that—to teach by example. In this case, the whip. And it is to be used not only on political dissidents, but anyone who breaks the law. Did you not hear about the woman who stole a can of sardines from the Portuguese store outside Brabanta? She did this to feed her children."

"No, I did not hear."

"Probably because she was Bajembe. She was given ten lashes. Unfortunately, she died shortly afterward."

Cripple moaned softly, which was an appropriate thing to do when one heard of death. This moan, however, was for herself. What had she gotten herself into? It had gone on far too long, with far too many logical details, to be a dream. But if it were a dream, at some point, just before she woke up, Husband would tell Second Wife he wanted to divorce her.

"So *baba*, do you now have an answer for me? What was your motive for disabling Senhor Nunez's truck?"

This was a question Cripple had thought about constantly since the morning she'd confessed to killing the Portuguese storekeeper. There had always only been one answer, but it was one that she was ashamed to say. Now things had progressed to the point that shame no longer mattered.

"I killed Senhor Nunez because he was a white man." There, it was out!

The Captain gasped. "*Baba*, this is not a time for jokes."

"I am an evil woman, Captain, but I am not stupid. I would not joke at a time like this."

"But still, you cannot mean this. What did Senhor Nunez ever do to you?"

"Perhaps, as an individual man, the senhor did nothing to harm me. But the whites have brought unspeakable suffering to the Congo. First, there were the Arab slavers, themselves light-skinned, who sold my people to be slaves to the white men of America, then King Leopold—"

"Enough! I know the history of the Congo, and yes, it is ugly. But *baba*, do you want me dead as well? Do I not speak your language? I love this country; this is where I was born."

Cripple could not look into the eyes of the man she'd just condemned. She could no longer eat the meal he'd prepared. If only he would kick her and call her a macaque, a monkey, that perennially favorite word of Belgian racists. One could be strong in the face of brutality, but the face of kindness wore resolve away just as surely as hot coffee poured over a lump of sugar dissolved it.

"I must go in now," she said and stood. "I do not feel well."

"*Baba*, please.*"

Cripple hurried away as fast as her twisted legs could carry her.

* * *

How can just six questions be called a trial? For Captain Jardin, who stood at Cripple's side, the procedure was surreal. The script could have been written by children, the judgment handed down by a punitive eight-year-old.

"Are you the woman referred to as Cripple?"

"*Oui.*"

"Are you responsible for the death of a Monsieur Cezar Nunez, a Portuguese national?"

"No. I am, however, responsible for the death of a Senhor Cezar Nunez."

The Provincial Governor reared back like a startled horse. "*What?* Is this a laughing matter to you?"

"No, monsieur."

"You are charged with tampering with the brakes and disengaging the steering column of his truck. Did you do this?"

"*Oui.*"

"Why?"

"Because I had the opportunity, and because he was white."

The governor's secretary gasped. A stooped African man with thin shoulders that almost touched and horn-rimmed glasses without lenses, he was the only other person in the room. The governor glared first at him, then at Cripple.

"Madame Cripple, are you saying that you wish to kill all white men?"

"*Oui.*"

"I've heard enough. Through the power vested in me, the Provincial Governor, by His Majesty's Colonial Government, I convict this woman, Cripple, of the death of Monsieur Cezar Nunez. She will be punished tomorrow by hanging from the neck until dead. Court is adjourned."

CHAPTER FORTY

Although giraffes (*Girrafa camelopardalis*) can weigh as much as two tons, their long legs allow them to run faster than most predators. However, in order to reach water at ground level, giraffes must splay their legs and lower their front quarters, which makes them vulnerable. Nonetheless, a well-placed kick from a giraffe can be deadly, even for lions. Baby giraffes can stand up within five minutes of their birth, and double their height in one year, but until they have reached their adult size, they are at risk from carnivores. Less than half of giraffes survive their first year.

Branca told Amanda that for the near future she was going to stay with her husband's relatives in Angola. That made sense. As far as Amanda knew, none of the other Europeans in Belle Vue came to call on the widow, to bring her casseroles along with their condolences.

How strange it must be to have a death, but no body. There had been eleven bodies the night Amanda sneaked out of the house and joined her friends on their midnight quest to buy beer in Gaffney. Three of the bodies were in the same car as Amanda. One of them, Beverly Shiker, had been her friend since the first day of kindergarten . . .

"Mamu Ugly Eyes!"

Amanda jumped. She'd been standing in front of the sitting-room window, staring at the falls, but not seeing it. Couldn't Protruding Navel tell that she wasn't in the mood to be bothered?

"What is it?" she snapped.

"It is about Cripple, *mamu*."

"Why can't you leave her alone? She's in prison, for heaven's sake." Alas, the idiom did not translate well into Tshiluba. The words for "heaven" and "nose" could only be distinguished from each other by one very tricky diphthong. Amanda could never remember which was which.

She must have gotten it right, because Protruding Navel didn't even smirk. "*Mamu*, she is to die tomorrow."

"What a horrid thing to say!"

"But it is true, *mamu*. Do you not hear the drums?"

"Drums?"

"Come, *mamu*." Protruding Navel reached as if to grab her arm, but then just as quickly dropped his hand to his side. "We must go up to the road. You will hear better there."

Amanda felt strangely compelled to follow the irritating little man. As soon as she stepped outdoors she knew that something unusual was going on; the foot traffic in the road had stopped moving, with everyone turned to face the village. Ah yes, now she heard the drums over the roar of the falls.

"What do they say?"

"They say that the Provincial Governor has sentenced Cripple to die tomorrow. She will be hanged."

"But this—this—are you *sure*?"

"Very sure, *mamu*."

Amanda listened for a moment. When she'd first heard drums, she'd found the sound thrilling. It was like living in a

Tarzan movie. But now the sound was ominous. No, more than that. *D-i-e, d-i-e—die, die, die. D-i-e, d-i-e—dead, dead, dead.*

"Protruding Navel, do they say anything else?"

He hesitated, momentarily scanning the ground. "Yes, *mamu*, but it is not something you should hear."

"Nevertheless, tell me!"

"No."

"I order you to!"

"Aiyee, *mamu*, that is something the Belgians say. I thought you Americans were different."

"We are! I assure you. It slipped out because I'm desperate to know more. I am so sorry. I promise it won't happen again."

He grunted, which was as much forgiveness as Amanda expected. "The drums say that workers are needed immediately to build the scaffold."

"The what?" It was a Tshiluba word that Amanda had not been taught in language school.

"It is a small tower from which one is hanged. Do you understand?"

She nodded, her eyes filling with tears. "Where will it be built?"

"The airport. They must have an open place for the many people who will come to see."

"Which people?"

"Everyone, of course."

"But that can't be! This isn't entertainment."

"Ah, Mamu Ugly Eyes, have you never been to a public execution?"

"Of course not!" Amanda was shocked by the question. Americans had moved far beyond such primitive and grotesque pleasures. Even lynchings—her father had witnessed one—were a thing of the past.

The drumming stopped abruptly and the people who had

stood transfixed by the message, as if frozen in place, began to move again. But now the majority of the men were crossing over to the white side of the river.

Protruding Navel seemed to read her mind. "They must hurry if they wish to get work building the scaffold."

"There isn't going to be an execution," Amanda said, and joined the throng headed to the Belgian side of the river.

Their Death had not worked since the beginning of Cripple's incarceration. Although he reported to work every day, the post office was closed, and the tool shed locked. Twice, Their Death had summoned the courage to inquire at M. Dupree's house, but both times the servants had been rude, sending him away with shouted insults. "Village monkey! Killer's husband. See what trouble you make for us, the *évolué*?"

When Their Death was not visiting Cripple, he was in the family compound caring for the children. A man not employed might watch out for his children and still maintain his dignity. But were a man to help with female chores, such as pounding the manioc with a pestle, or pounding the clothes with rocks at the water's edge, such a man was no longer even a man. From time to time such people were born, but they were mocked and ridiculed, and if they persisted in this behavior, they were then forever treated as women. Eventually the ridiculing would subside, but there was no going back. A real man might even have sex with one of these people, just as long as he remembered who played the role of the husband.

So it was that while Second Wife repeatedly lifted the heavy pestle and brought it down with bone-jarring thuds, Their Death pretended to dose in a sling-back raffia-covered chair. He'd built it himself from a sketch; he'd seen the original chair on a European's porch. The children, all of them laughing (except for Baby Boy, who really was asleep on his father's stomach) played at waking their father with turkey feathers.

Then the drums began to talk. At first they spoke in vague terms about an impending disaster. Their Death sat up, pushing all the children away, except for Baby Boy. Second Wife laid her pestle across the top of the mortar. The older children cocked their heads in the direction of the drums, although they had yet to learn how to interpret the sounds.

As the drumming continued, the varied tones, the pauses, it all added up to one horrifying message: *The woman known as Cripple, the First Wife of Their Death, is going to be hung on the morrow. Who wants to help build the scaffold? The pay is fifty francs for a day's work.*

Second Wife was the first to react. She screamed and threw herself on the ground, where she rolled in the dust, as befits a good woman upon hearing of the death of a loved one. Almost immediately the girl children followed suit, their high-pitched shrieks proclaiming their love for their Second Mother. Baby Boy, frightened by the commotion, peed on his father.

"Aiyee, aiyee!" Their Death moaned and pounded on the sides of his head with balled fists. He had failed to see this coming. Captain Jardin had all but assured him that the ridiculous charge of murder would be dropped. Cripple was obviously not herself. How could a crazy woman be punished for a crime she didn't commit?

There were others who shared the family's shock and impending loss. Taking their cue from Second Wife and her daughters, the women of the village joined in the public grieving. Their cries of anguish spread throughout the village like an August fire leaps across the savanna. The basenji dogs, the breed that cannot bark, threw back their heads and howled.

But while the women keened and mourned, the men dropped what they were doing and ran down the hill toward the town. Death was inevitable, but the opportunity to earn fifty francs seldom presented itself.

CHAPTER FORTY-ONE

The African oil palm (*Eleais guineensis*) is a tall tree native to the tropical woodlands of Western and Central Africa. The tree has pinnate (feather-shaped) leaves. The fruits, which are about the size of a small plum, are orange and black, and produce an orange oil that is used for cooking throughout much of the region. Inside each fruit is a kernel, which produces a clear oil. The latter can be used in industry to produce such oil-rich things as margarine and soap. As a result, oil palm plantations have been established in many tropical countries around the world. Because palm oil is highly saturated, usage fell off during the 1970s, but recent research has shown that it has promise as a biodiesel fuel.

In his darkened room, lying in a rumpled bed, Dupree heard the faint thumps of distant drums. Then came a sound so strange, so mournful, it made the hairs on his arms and neck rise. Was it human? Animal? Both? Was it one voice, or a thousand?

Dupree pulled his covers over his heard and tried to block out the sound. Perhaps it was the end of the world, and this was the sound of souls left behind. If that was the case, so be it. He already knew he was destined to hell. Any number of priests could testify to that, a few even from personal experience.

For three days he had lain in bed, unable to eat, barely able to perform bodily functions, while his heart ate itself from the inside out. Cezar had been everything to him, and then Cezar betrayed him—not once, but twice. Wasn't death the ultimate betrayal? To go someplace where a coward cannot follow?

Amanda Brown could not believe what she'd just heard. Captain Jardin, who appeared to be on Cripple's side, had folded like a weekend poker player with a rotten hand. Maybe he could sit this hand out, but not she.

"I thought you were a good man," she said, not bothering to fight back the tears.

"I hope that I still am. But this, mademoiselle, is out of my hands."

"You sound like Pontius Pilot."

He stared at her.

"Look," she said, "if there isn't anything you can do, is there anything that I, as an American citizen can do?"

"Do? Amanda, you Americans act as if you are the policemen of the world and that you have not only the right but the obligation to insert yourselves wherever there is trouble."

"You haven't answered my question."

"Just how serious are you about saving the world this time?"

"Cripple is my friend. I will do what it takes."

He sighed, and there were tears glistening in his eyes as well. "There is something you might try. There is no guarantee. Still, it might delay the execution."

"Tell me!"

Cripple was no longer allowed visitors. She'd been moved from her cell and placed in a windowless room. Outside two African soldiers from Luluaburg stood guard, rifles in their hands.

She was numb with dread. How much would death by hanging hurt? The young Captain who spoke Tshiluba had tried to comfort her. It was over almost instantly, he said. It was the most humane way for one person to kill another. But how did he know this? Not from personal experience! And did the actual parting of soul from body hurt? He could not answer that, he said. Did she want to have a priest there? For what? Could the *priest* speak from experience? Hardly.

Had there been another way? Not really. It had all happened so quickly, there had been no time to think. But she'd made the right decision.

The second that she'd seen the green truck parked in front of the path that led to her compound, she knew what was happening—or at least about to happen. Sure enough, the children were unattended. Baby Boy was crying. Where is your First Mother, she'd demanded. When Eldest Daughter pointed in the direction of the manioc field, Cripple began to run. *Really* run.

The leg she'd always dragged behind her felt as light as cotton, and she was suddenly able to move it just as fast as the other, and place it just as far in front of her. She ran as fast as a boy of sixteen. No, faster. It was as if the spirit of the chicken hawk had joined with hers, and together they skimmed across the ground and then soared above the trees.

Truly, truly, that was what had happened. Cripple's first memory of Cezar Nunez's body had been from above. And how could she, a short lame woman, observe anything from above, were she not airborne? She most certainly did not climb a tree.

"Aiyee," Second Wife had cried upon seeing her. "I did not mean to kill this man."

"He is dead?"

"I hit him with a stone. There. You can see the blood."

And hair. There were long strands of brown adhering to the stone, pasted to it with drying blood. The man's skull was dented. By a single blow you might ask? If you doubt, regard the arms of

Second Wife, she who chops firewood and pounds manioc roots with a heavy wooden pestle. By comparison, the arms of a white woman were like the strings one picks from a peeled banana. Indeed, there is much to admire about an African woman, and her strength is at the top of the list.

"Forgive me, Sister Wife, if the reason is obvious, but why did you hit this man?"

Before answering, Second Wife crumpled to the ground and beat it with her fists, all the while keening. For the death of any man is a tragedy. Is that not so? Even the death of a white man. Or perhaps Second Wife was grieving for herself, for the missing piece of soul that was the price of killing a man. Or perhaps she was afraid of what might become of her.

At last she looked up, her eyes filled with tears. "He came into our compound, Sister Wife. He demanded to know where Baby Boy had found the diamond. *What* diamond? I ask him. I do not know about a diamond, I tell him. But he demands again and again, and then I remember the stone our husband removed from Baby Boy's mouth. But truly, I had not thought it was a diamond."

"It was."

Second Wife flashed Cripple a look of hatred. "Then we must go to the manioc field, I said—for by then the children were frightened. He wanted to take the children with us, but I told him that I was unsure of the exact location. How could I search with so much distraction? I asked. He agreed, but he made me warn the children that if they told anyone where their *baba* was, then he would kill them. And me."

"Aiyee!"

"But what could I show him in the field? I looked here for another such stone, I looked there, I looked everywhere until he became so angry that he grabbed me by the throat and began to choke me. I could not pull his hands away, for they were very strong. But after much struggling, I was able to trip him. Together we fell on the ground, and his hands grew tighter. I had no choice then, Sister Wife, but to feel around for something hard. Something with which to hit him. At last the Protestant God sent me that stone you see lying there."

"I very much doubt that a white God would send you a stone with which to kill a white man. Surely the stone was there all along."

"Oh no, it was definitely the Protestant God, and for that I am eternally grateful. But now I beg you, Sister Wife, tell me what to do."

Cripple resisted the temptation to tell Second Wife that she should ask God for advice, given that God was obviously more powerful than Cripple. Even she could not send a stone.

"I will tell you what to do," Cripple said, "after we bury this man."

"Bury him?"

"No one must know what happened. To kill a white man—that can only mean death."

"But I meant only to make him stop!"

"Why should they believe that? Could it be that you lured him into the field so that you could have sex? Then you changed your mind, but he would not stop?"

Second Wife clamped her hands tightly over her ears. "No, no, no! I would never do that. Cripple, you must believe me. I did not have sex with this man."

"I believe you, Sister Wife. But what will the white man believe? The one whose job it is to pass judgment? If you confess to killing this man, they will hang you. Then who will care for our children?"

So it was that Second Wife, while Cripple stood watch, dug a hole in which to place the body of Senhor Nunez. She dug only with her hands, and it took her a very long time, because the hole had to be deep enough to discourage jackals and hyenas. Before she was done her hands were bloody and her back ached.

At last she stood. "Now what should I do?"

"First, you must promise me that no matter what, you will never reveal to anyone what really happened here today."

"I promise."

"Now promise on the life of Baby Boy."

"Aiyee!"

"Promise!"

The words were whispered hoarsely. "I promise on the life of Baby Boy."

"Now you do nothing. But tomorrow morning I will go the police and say that I killed this white man."

"*You?*"

"Yes. I have a plan. You have not heard, Second Wife, that this afternoon the white man's truck rolled down the hill, gathering speed, and crashed through the railing of the bridge. But I will say that I tampered with his truck, and that he was in it. Now he churns beneath the falls, like a log caught in a vortex. His death is my fault.

"Then everyone's attention will be focused on the river, and no one will ever think to look in a manioc field. No body will ever be found, so that eventually they will have to release me. In the meantime, you will care for our children. Do you not think it is a perfect plan?"

Sister Wife nodded vigorously, tears flying in all directions.

"But right now," Cripple said, "we must hurry back to the compound. I just heard the first hyena."

CHAPTER FORTY-TWO

Cassava (*Manihot esculenta*) is also known as manioc. It is a shrubby plant native to Brazil, but was imported to Africa by the Portuguese centuries ago. Cassava roots are now a staple food in many parts of Central and Western Africa. Unless properly treated, the roots contain cyanide. A common practice in the Congo is to peel the roots and put them in a stream for three days. During that time the cyanide is leached. Subsequently the tubers are sun-dried and pounded into flour. Cassava leaves are edible and contain many nutrients, but they too must be treated. One way is to boil the leaves for some time, thoroughly drain the cooking water, and boil again. The processing of cassava should not be done by an inexperienced person. There is a theory that the first people to successfully consume this plant experimented first on prisoners of war.

It was the perfect day for an execution. The air was both cool and clear, thanks to a steady night breeze that had blown away the mixture of fog and dry-season smoke that rendered most days in sepia tones. Towering white cumulus clouds, tinged in gray, scuttled across the sky, promising rain in a week or two. Perhaps the hanging was a good omen, a signal that new life would return to the savannas and riverine forests of southwestern Congo.

Even before dawn the first spectators began to arrive. Within an hour the main roads and village paths were clogged with people vying to arrive at the airfield in time to secure a spot with a decent view of the scaffold. At one point, so many people crowded the bridge that it began to sway, precipitating a stampede in which three children were seriously injured, and one woman trampled to death.

But like moths to a flame, they kept coming. From every village within a night's walk they came, having been summoned by the drums. Never in the history of the region had so many tribes gathered peacefully in one spot. For some it was merely an exciting spectacle, but for others the beginning of a new era, one in which the execution of a crippled woman, one from the Baluba tribe, would be the turning point. Soon the tables would be turned, and Europeans would be hung for egregious crimes against African people.

Their Death would be among the first to exact revenge. He would send Second Wife and the children back to her village of birth, and then he would devote himself to the cause of justice. He would give up his life if necessary. The Belgians were going to pay.

Feigning indifference to the stares of other whites, the OP took his seat in the VIP section of the grandstand that had been erected behind the gallows. The six-tiered structure had been built the day before and would be torn down minutes after the crippled woman was swinging free at the end of a rope, her neck broken. Built specifically for the European population of Belle Vue, the grandstand was, however, open to anyone white. Or even someone just half white—if his or her skin was light enough. From his vantage point in the center, the OP recognized several missionaries from outlying stations. Even the newly arrived American woman was there.

He knew what they were all thinking. What was he doing,

watching an execution, when he should be out looking for his wife? Why hadn't he even bothered to drive to Luluaburg, to see if she had gotten on a plane there? Well, to hell with them—every single last one of them. He was there because it was his job to be there; the crippled woman had killed one of his employees. The real question was, What were they doing at the execution?

Amanda Brown wanted to vomit. She *needed* to vomit, but her stomach was empty. Not as much as a sip of water had passed her lips, since Cripple's sentencing, that hadn't come back up. It was as if her body was refusing to cooperate with life itself, when that of an innocent woman was about to be extinguished by a vengeful colonialist, one without a molecule of compassion in his heart. And to think that some Europeans had the nerve to call the American South a racist region.

What was the difference between Rock Hill, South Carolina, and Belle Vue, Belgian Congo? Well, for one thing, they no longer held public executions in South Carolina. At least not officially. And even if South Carolina did hold public lynchings, they wouldn't build a grandstand for the public. Still, *if* there were public executions in Rock Hill, and *if* there was a grandstand, you can bet the seats would be for whites only. That much was the same.

But in the United States you almost never heard of a woman getting the death sentence, unless she'd been accused of being a Communist spy. Cripple was most certainly not a spy, nor was she a murderess. She was a brilliant, albeit hardheaded, independent woman. She could be funny at times, but never cruel. She was undeniably selfish, but not the least bit self-centered. Amanda knew she was lucky to have known Cripple, even if just for a few days, and that she was a better person for it.

It was time to give back.

"Not yet," the police inspector said, as if reading her mind again. He squeezed her shoulder.

CHAPTER FORTY-THREE

Some day the author would like to write a book about her own experiences growing up in the Belgian Congo.

Cripple marveled at the height of her gallows. After all, they *were* her gallows, were they not? She would always be the first to have been hanged from them, although probably not the last. Not with more and more people agitating for independence.

At any rate, they were the tallest manmade structure she had ever seen, taller even than the spire atop the Roman Catholic church. Then again, Belle Vue was a city of one-story dwellings. Cripple had learned, while listening to her brother's lessons, that in both Europe and America there were buildings that rose up to meet the clouds. There was even a statue somewhere taller than the gallows, although it was almost impossible to imagine such a thing.

Cripple was suddenly aware that the crowd of thousands had fallen silent, except for the unavoidable coughing from tubercular patients scattered here and there, and the cries of babies and small children. The silence was more unnerving than the babble of excited onlookers, but it was only temporary.

"Can you climb the steps?" a young African in a policeman's

uniform asked. He was sweating profusely, despite the coolness of the morning.

"I can climb."

"Are you sure, *baba*? Others have asked to be carried."

"I am not a sack of corn."

"*Eyo*. Indeed you are not."

Still it was not an easy climb, if only because Cripple had never been so high before. The ground beneath her grew blurry, the people as small as rats. It was so quiet, Cripple could hear sparrows chirping.

She clung to the railing and glanced up. A pair of sparrows, male and female, were perched on the overhead beam, the one from which the rope hung. They cocked their heads when they saw Cripple looking up, but didn't fly away.

It is a sign, Cripple thought. There are two sparrows, not three. Soon they will have a nest together, then chicks, and that is the way it should be. From them will descend an unbroken line of sparrows and that is how the future proceeds—not from days or hours passed, but from one generation replacing another. It is right that our children remain with their mother of birth, and that Husband grows old with the woman from whose womb the next generation had already emerged.

"Step this way," a man barked.

Cripple was startled to see that there were two people on the platform with her: an *évolué* in a policeman's uniform, and a white priest.

For the first time that she could remember, Cripple felt crippled. She was unable to move. Even her good leg would not cooperate.

"Come here now!"

"Give her a minute," the priest said sharply in French. He stepped forward, and after positioning his hands beneath Cripple's armpits, lifted her into the air as easily as if she were a bundle of corn husks. He set her carefully down on what Cripple instinctively knew was the trapdoor.

"Thank you, Father."

"My child, do you wish to make a confession?"

"I am not a Christian."

"A Protestant then? I am prepared to make exceptions at a time like this."

"No."

"Ah, a Muslim."

"Nor that either; I practice the traditional ways."

The priest clucked softly to himself, shaking his head and waving his hands, as if engaged in an argument with a person, or persons, unseen. He took so long, in fact, that an authoritative voice from the stands called out for him to get on with it. Cripple recognized the speaker as the Provincial Governor, the man who had sentenced her to die.

The priest grabbed Cripple's hands and stared earnestly into her eyes. "My superior does not approve of last-minute conversions, but as it just so happens, I have a vial of holy water with me, and I will baptize you, if you're willing to renounce Satan and—"

"I renounce nothing, Father."

He squeezed her hands before letting go. "May God have mercy on your soul."

"And on yours as well."

"*Touché.*"

As the priest backed down the ladder, the Provincial Governor rose from his seat. An aide handed him a bullhorn.

"Ladies, gentleman, and of course, Congolese—especially Congolese—what you are about to witness is Belgian justice in the making. His Majesty's Colonial Government will not tolerate murder in the name of nationalism. We will not allow cold-blooded killers—be they male or female—to go unpunished.

And, as you are about to see, the punishment will fit the crime. Let this be a lesson then, to anyone who contemplates violence against the crown, its representatives here in the colony, and its European residents."

The governor waited while a smattering of applause trickled through the grandstand. Meanwhile the Congolese stared in shocked silence, or so it seemed to Amanda. Even the small babies were quiet for a change.

"Now!" Police Captain Pierre Jardin whispered.

Amanda rose, her legs shaking, her throat suddenly parched. Nonetheless, she was able to call out in a loud, clear voice.

"The accused is innocent!"

The Provincial Governor whirled. "*What?*"

Emboldened by his flashing eyes and haughty demeanor, Amanda cupped her hands to her mouth. "The woman known as Cripple is innocent. She did not kill Senhor Cesar Nunez. It was *I* who killed the Portuguese shopkeeper. I did it because he forced himself on me. But I didn't do it intentionally—that would have been a sin. I tampered with his brakes. I only meant to scare him. At any rate, as I am an American, you cannot hang me without due legal process."

The crowd roared with excitement. The Provincial Governor tried in vain to recapture their attention with the megaphone, but in the end was forced to ask one of his soldiers to fire his rifle into the air. The poor African hesitated, no doubt anticipating that there would be a stampede. Thank God for his hesitation.

One should also be grateful for the fact that the handsome Captain Pierre Jardin was a quick thinker. He snatched the megaphone from the governor and, after several attempts, was finally able to get everyone's attention.

"The American woman lies. *I* am the guilty party. I killed Senhor Nunez because, as you just heard, of what he did to the woman that I plan to marry."

A young Belgian matron sitting behind the police captain jumped to her feet. She too had the element of surprise and was able to grab the bullhorn away from the captain.

"Governor, I beg you not to listen to either of these imbeciles. They are both liars. It is I, and I alone, who am responsible for the death of Senhor Nunez. The man was a swindler. A robber. He sold us garbage and charged us a fortune for it, all the while pocketing the profits, instead of handing them over to the Consortium. I got tired of his price gouging, so I poisoned him by serving him his own tainted food—"

The megaphone was ripped from her hands. "Your Excellency," panted a stout man in a pith helmet, "these people are all to be despised for the mockery they make of our noble legal system. They claim to be guilty of a crime they have not committed, and to what end? To put on a show? I beg you, sir, charge them all with obstructing justice, for they are nothing but liars and miscreants. It is I, Jean Luc D'Estoilles, who murdered the unfortunate son of the Iberian Peninsula."

Madame Gestang, said to be the oldest white woman in the Congo, thrashed the air with her ivory-tipped cane. "Shut up, you fat moron! I killed the Portuguese swindler."

"No, I did," someone else yelled.

"Not so. It was I!"

"No, I!"

Amanda listened, dumfounded, as the admissions of guilt seemed to ricochet around the grandstand, growing louder with each new voice. Then, like a lightning bolt seeking a new target, the plot to save Cripple leaped from the grandstand and into the vast crowd of Africans. The first native voice was tentative, but it was immediately succeeded by a stronger cry, and then another, and then another, until within seconds, thousands of people, in dozens of tongues, shouted their bogus confessions. Their voices combined to form an entity with a life of its own, a beast whose cry of anguish grew louder and louder, until it was eventually heard in the halls of Parliament, back in Brussels.

The Provincial Governor reddened, and then grew pale. But it was only after the people began to stamp their feet in unison that he leaned close to his aide. After a brief consultation, the aide beckoned the priest to approach. A longer conversation ensued. When it was over, the Governor departed hastily, followed closely by his aide and a half dozen Belgians, none of whom had helped to save Cripple.

When the priest began to climb the scaffold a second time, a hush fell across the multitude. Amanda watched, hardly able to breathe, as the priest walked in slow motion across the platform to confer with the executioner. It was a brief conversation that lasted a lifetime. Cripple, meanwhile, stood erect and motionless, the loose end of her wraparound skirt rippling in the breeze, like a partially unfurled banner. From that great a distance Amanda was unable to see the expression on her face, but she imagined it to be one of controlled relief. Finally the executioner addressed the remaining Belgians.

"The charges against this woman have been dropped," he said. He turned to the African audience, cupping his hands to his mouth. "She is free!"

At once a mighty cheer went up, and a thousand hands were raised in the victory sign made famous by Sir Winston Churchill. Then somewhere, someone started chanting. Amanda heard it first as a murmur, and then as a single voice that grew louder and louder until it was a roar.

"Independence, independence, independence!"

Amanda, self-confessed political novice that she was, thought she would burst with joy. And pride. Captain Jardin had promised her it would work, and it had! But not only that, the very capable Cripple had gone from death's door—literally—to suddenly becoming an icon of freedom.

"Isn't it wonderful," she shouted into her handsome companion's ear.

He pressed his head against hers. "Not really."

"*What?*"

"It means your days here are—how do I say this in English—finite?"

"Numbered?"

"Exactly. When independence comes, we'll all get booted out. Even you American missionaries."

"Is that really so bad? I mean, there are many Congolese quite capable of spreading God's word—"

"This is my home. What will become of people like me?"

At a loss for an answer, Amanda again did what any well brought up lady would do; she changed the subject. "Just so you know, I'm not going to hold you to your promise."

"What promise?"

His answer had to wait. The executioner had slung Cripple over his shoulder, as if she were as light as a sack of dried caterpillars, and was climbing down the ladder. The multitude held its collective breath for this, but when the pair was safely down, the natives rushed forward, breaking through the bamboo barrier that had been constructed to keep them back. Their Death was in front of the mob, and he lovingly hoisted Cripple up to his shoulders.

The chanting resumed immediately, and some people began to clap. Soon everyone was clapping. Their Death began to dance, and the crowd danced too. Then, like a modern Moses, Their Death began to lead the vast throng out of the airport, down along the main road that bisected Belle Vue, and across the mighty Kasai River.

Amanda watched, fascinated, as the thousands of people assembled, representing a dozen or so disparate tribes, danced in perfect unison. It was like watching a Conga line fifty people wide and a mile long. Nothing she'd ever seen back home compared with this, not even when Rock Hill High School won the state football championship for the second year in a row.

Whether or not the other whites were equally as mesmerized, they remained seated in the grandstand until the procession was well enough on its way that the dust began to settle. Even then they took their time, conversing in small clumps, their urgent tones betraying just how nervous they'd suddenly become.

Amanda tried to tune the others out. "Of marriage."

"*Excusez mois?*"

"You said I was the woman you planned to marry. I know you were just saying that to make a point, in order to save Cripple's life." She felt herself flush with embarrassment. How stupid of her to have even brought it up.

"You are correct, Mademoiselle Brown; I was making a point. I cannot marry a woman I hardly know"—he smiled—"*but* I would very much like to get to know this woman. The sooner, the better."

"Mamu Ugly Eyes, there are people here to see you."

"Who?"

"A village urchin accompanied by its mother. People of no consequence. Shall I send them away?"

"Listen to me, Protruding Navel. There is no such thing as a person of no consequence. Now let these people in."

"Into the house? *Mamu*, this is simply not done. Only an *évolué* may enter a white man's house."

"Yes, but I am a white *woman*. Now show them in."

But when she saw how frightened the African woman was, Amanda immediately regretted her hasty decision to fly in the face of colonial etiquette. The child, however, was as curious as a kitten; his large dark eyes seemed to be taking in everything.

"*Muoyo, baba,*" Amanda said, and followed the greeting with what was meant to be a reassuring smile.

"*Muoyo, mamu.*"

"*Muoyo, muana,*" Amanda said to the boy, although he was obviously too young to talk.

The African woman stared at her feet. "*Mamu*, I am the second wife of Their Death, the great witch doctor of the Baluba people. I am also the sister wife of Cripple."

"Yes, of course! Welcome. Is Cripple all right?"

"*Mamu*, there is no need to concern yourself with Cripple. She is fine. Already she has begun to resume her old ways. 'Sister Wife,' she says, 'I am thirsty. Bring me some water.' Never mind that the water gourd is but an arm's reach from where she sits. 'Sister Wife, you need to put more chilies in the meat pot. Sister Wife, next time you wash clothes, do a better job of removing the stains on my new wraparound. *Mamu* will beat me if she were to see me wearing this.'"

"I would *not* beat her!"

"Eh, I did not think so. But there you see; Cripple is fine."

"Then what I can I do for you?"

"It is not for me, *mamu*. It is for the child."

"The little one here?"

"Yes, *mamu*. I would like your permission to name him Amanda."

"Him? Amanda?"

"*Eyo, mamu.* Never have I seen such a brave woman as you—except for one. And since the boy is not crippled, *mamu*, I wish to honor him with your name."

"It is I who am honored," said Amanda, because she did not see herself as brave; she'd only been desperate to save a friend.

In a country where names had meanings and were tied to everyday events, people were given names such as Their Death, Protruding Navel, and Cripple. What then did it matter that Amanda was a girl's name? Not one iota.

EPILOGUE

The dominant female danced along the edge of the manioc field, impatiently awaiting the arrival of her pack. Her sudden appearance had scared away the jackals whose yips had filled the air since sunset. Although her jaws could crush the bones of a buffalo, she dared not attack an adult human by herself. Something in her primitive brain told her that a human, although unarmed by fangs or claws, was a beast to be feared. A tasty beast, nonetheless.

In only a day or two the female would give birth to her second litter. Already she'd co-opted the burrow of an aardvark in which to have her cubs. But for now, despite her distended belly and swollen teats, she was ravenous. If her pack did not arrive soon, she would have no choice but to move on, in search of some less dangerous prey.

Cripple was aware of the hyena's presence; the disappearance of the jackals had been the clue. At first she'd thought a leopard was responsible for the silence. But then the hyena, apparently unable to restrain her excitement, burst into the hideous laughter that characterized her species.

Cripple dug faster, strong fingers raking the damp soil. A leopard might have been scared off by a show of strength—false bravado in this case—but a pack of spotted hyenas would tear a person limb from limb, and then laugh about it afterward. Cripple knew that the pack would announce itself by whooping, from perhaps a kilometer away, and when it did, a life-or-death decision must be made.

But just as the first faint sound of the advancing pack reached Cripple's ears, her digging fingers touched something cool and hard. A moment later the priceless object glinted in the light of the rising moon.

It had been six months since she'd replaced the stone that Their Death had hidden in the banana grove with a piece of glass she'd recovered from the crashed plane. It had been just over six months since she'd buried the diamond next to the body of the Portuguese store manager. She'd chosen this location because she knew Second Wife would never plant manioc here again.

For six months Cripple had shared her secret with no one, waiting for the day when selling the stone would be worth the risk. The day had finally come when she could wait no longer. Soon there would be another mouth to feed.

Cripple placed a hand under her distended belly to support it as she stood.

Photo by Penny Young

Tamar Myers

TAMAR MYERS was born and raised in the Belgian Congo (now just the Congo). Her parents were missionaries to a tribe which, at that time, were known as head-hunters and used human skulls for drinking cups. Hers was the first white family ever to peacefully coexist with the tribe.

Tamar grew up eating elephant, hippopotamus, and even monkey. She attended a boarding school that was two days away by truck, and sometimes it was necessary to wade through crocodile-infested waters to reach it. Other dangers she encountered as a child were cobras, deadly green mambas, and the voracious armies of driver ants that ate every animal (and human) that didn't get out of their way.

Today Tamar lives in the Carolinas with her American-born husband. She is the author of thirty-six novels (most of which are mysteries), a number of published short stories, and hundreds of articles on gardening.